Reviewers Love N

"Melissa Brayden has become one of the most popular novelists of the genre, writing hit after hit of funny, relatable, and very sexy stories for women who love women."—*Afterellen.com*

The Last Lavender Sister

"It's also a slow burn, with some gorgeous writing. I've had to take some breaks while reading to delight in a turn of phrase here and there, and that's the best feeling."—*Jude in the Stars*

"I have loved many of Melissa Brayden's characters over the years, but I think Aster Lavender may be my favorite of all of them."—*Sapphic Book Review*

"*The Last Lavender Sister* is not only a romance but also a family saga and a journey of transformation for both characters."—LezReview Books

Exclusive

"Melissa Brayden's books have always been a source of comfort, like seeing a friend you've lost touch with but can pick right up where you left off. They have always made my heart happy, and this one does the same."—*Sapphic Book Review*

Marry Me

"A bride-to-be falls for her wedding planner in this smoking hot, emotionally mature romance from Brayden…Brayden is remarkably generous to her characters, allowing them space for self-exploration and growth."—*Publishers Weekly*

To the Moon and Back

"*To the Moon and Back* is all about Brayden's love of theatre, onstage and backstage, and she does a delightful job of sharing that love… Brayden set the scene so well I knew what was coming, not because it's unimaginative but because she made it obvious it was the only way things could go. She leads the reader exactly where she wants to take them, with brilliant writing as usual. Also, not everyone can make office supplies sound sexy."—*Jude in the Stars*

"Melissa Brayden does what she does best, she delivers amazing characters, witty banter, all while being fun and relatable."—*Romantic Reader Blog*

Back to September

"You can't go wrong with a Melissa Brayden romance. Seriously, you can't. Buy all of her books. Brayden sure has a way of creating an emotional type of compatibility between her leads, making you root for them against all odds. Great settings, cute interactions, and realistic dialogue."—*Bookvark*

What a Tangled Web

"[T]he happiest ending to the most amazing trilogy. Melissa Brayden pulled all of the elements together, wrapped them up in a bow, and presented the reader with Happily Ever After to the max!"—*Kitty Kat's Book Review Blog*

Beautiful Dreamer

"I love this book. I want to kiss it on its face…I'm going to stick *Beautiful Dreamer* on my to-reread-when-everything-sucks pile, because it's sure to make me happy again and again."—*Smart Bitches Trashy Books*

"*Beautiful Dreamer* is a sweet and sexy romance, with the bonus of interesting secondary characters and a cute small-town setting."—*Amanda Chapman, Librarian (Davisville Free Library, RI)*

Two to Tangle

"Melissa Brayden does it again with a sweet and sexy romance that leaves you feeling content and full of happiness. As always, the book is full of smiles, fabulous dialogue, and characters you wish were your best friends."—*The Romantic Reader*

"I loved it. I wasn't sure Brayden could beat Joey and Becca and their story, but when I started to see reviews mentioning that this was even better, I had high hopes and Brayden definitely lived up to them."—*LGBTQreader.com*

Entangled

"Ms. Brayden has a definite winner with this first book of the new series, and I can't wait to read the next one. If you love a great enemies-to-lovers, feel-good romance, then this is the book for you."—*Rainbow Reflections*

"*Entangled* is a simmering slow burn romance, but I also fully believe it would be appealing for lovers of women's fiction. The friendships between Joey, Maddie, and Gabriella are well developed and engaging as well as incredibly entertaining…All that topped off with a deeply fulfilling happily ever after that gives all the happy sighs long after you flip the final page."—*Lily Michaels: Sassy Characters, Sizzling Romance, Sweet Endings*

Love Like This

"Brayden upped her game. The characters are remarkably distinct from one another. The secondary characters are rich and wonderfully integrated into the story. The dialogue is crisp and witty."—*Frivolous Reviews*

Sparks Like Ours

"Brayden sets up a flirtatious tit-for-tat that's honest, relatable, and passionate. The women's fears are real, but the loving support from the supporting cast helps them find their way to a happy future. This enjoyable romance is sure to interest readers in the other stories from Seven Shores."—*Publishers Weekly*

Hearts Like Hers

"Once again Melissa Brayden stands at the top. She unequivocally is the queen of romance."—*Front Porch Romance*

Eyes Like Those

"Brayden's story of blossoming love behind the Hollywood scenes provides the right amount of warmth, camaraderie, and drama."—*RT Book Reviews*

Strawberry Summer

"This small-town second-chance romance is full of tenderness and heart. The 10 Best Romance Books of 2017."—*Vulture*

"*Strawberry Summer* is a tribute to first love and soulmates and growing into the person you're meant to be. I feel like I say this each time I read a new Melissa Brayden offering, but I loved this book so much that I cannot wait to see what she delivers next."—*Smart Bitches, Trashy Books*

First Position

"Brayden aptly develops the growing relationship between Ana and Natalie, making the emotional payoff that much sweeter. This ably plotted, moving offering will earn its place deep in readers' hearts."—*Publishers Weekly*

By the Author

Romances

Waiting in the Wings

Heart Block

How Sweet It Is

First Position

Strawberry Summer

Beautiful Dreamer

Back to September

To the Moon and Back

Marry Me

Exclusive

The Last Lavender Sister

The Forever Factor

Soho Loft Romances:

Kiss the Girl

Just Three Words

Ready or Not

Seven Shores Romances:

Eyes Like Those

Hearts Like Hers

Sparks Like Ours

Love Like This

Tangle Valley Romances:

Entangled

Two to Tangle

What a Tangled Web

Visit us at www.boldstrokesbooks.com

THE
FOREVER FACTOR

by

Melissa Brayden

2022

THE FOREVER FACTOR

ISBN 13: 978-1-63679-357-3

This Trade Paperback Original Is Published By
Bold Strokes Books, Inc.
P.O. Box 249
Valley Falls, NY 12185

First Edition: November 2022

CREDITS
Editor: Ruth Sternglantz
Production Design: Stacia Seaman
Cover Design by Inkspiral Design

Acknowledgments

I think it's safe to say that everyone remembers their first love. And their first heartbreak. Oftentimes, they're one and the same. Those fresh bursts of emotions, the new discoveries about love and lust, when it feels like nothing else matters but that other person? Yeah, those things can leave quite the impression. Exploring Bethany and Reid's second chance at love took me on a nostalgic roller coaster through my own formative years, and getting to craft their story was a true pleasure. I hope you enjoy their twists and turns.

The thank-you list is long! It includes my editor, Ruth Sternglantz, for friendship, guidance, and insight. Radclyffe, Sandy Lowe, and all of the Bold Strokes associates for making the road to publication a smooth one. Cindy Cresap, Toni Whittaker, and Stacia Seaman for their attention to detail and expertise. Inkspiral Design for the wonderful cover that includes a sweet nod to the past. A big shout-out to the proofreaders, who tirelessly search out my mistakes. To my friends and colleagues in the business who know what writing life is like and certainly make mine lots of fun. To Alan for letting me steal an hour here or there to make sure the story winds up on the page. To my small people for the encouraging hugs and smiles. And to each and every reader for choosing to spend time with my characters. I hope you think it was time well spent. Here's to many more kissing scenes, heart-wrenching interactions, and if all goes well, a happily ever after.

For all those who were lost and found.

PROLOGUE

There were days that didn't seem important until they were. When one breath was so startlingly different than the last that a person didn't know what hit them. One drastic second, and the universe decided that it was time for life to shift onto its head with an ear-shattering thud.

That's exactly what happened to Bethany Cahill on what seemed like a very mundane Thursday afternoon at the clinic just outside of LA. After a lunch that consisted of dictation, a few phone calls, a sliced apple with peanut butter, and a Red Bull—okay, *two*—she was back to seeing patients at the family medical practice she'd opened four years ago with two of her med school classmates, Thea and Veronica. Bethany was the quieter friend in the trio, but happy to share her space with the two people she'd grown most comfortable with over the last few years. Ride or die. That was them. They'd seen each other through the daunting trials of med school and emerged still alive and linked at the arms. It didn't get much thicker than that.

"I'm going to head out early," she told Thea, who was vivacious and fun. The life of their party. Beth exhaled, breathing out the day. "My last appointment canceled ten minutes ago, and I have nary a morsel of food in my refrigerator."

Thea dropped a chart onto her desk as she listened, brown eyes accusatory. "This is unfair. I have two more patients to see and want to go with you. I haven't been to a grocery store since 2003. Or was it four?" She gave her long dark braids an adjustment. They were tied in back, her work ponytail in effect. Bethany rarely encountered it outside of days they saw patients, but Thea knew how to work it from a fashion standpoint. No one accessorized scrubs like she did. She landed on dead sexy when paired with full makeup and heels, scholarly when she popped on her forest-green glasses. Kudos to Thea for the duality. She had it down.

"You're exaggerating as always. Need anything?" Bethany asked. "I can grab you some frozen french toast." It was an allusion to their late-night study sessions and the snack they'd toss into the toaster at two a.m. for a comforting sugar surge when the knowledge wouldn't fit into their brains anymore. Savior food. "You can gnaw on it between patients like a savory little security blanket. You'll be so cute."

"Sold. And I'm not kidding when I say yes. Grab me a box and bring it tomorrow."

"You're getting six."

A voice from the next office over shouted at them. Veronica Tam. "I hear you talking about french toast, and now it's all I can think about. Damn you both. Feed me, too." Their fearless type A. Veronica was the ambition, the visionary, the one who often needed reining in when her ideas overtook the capabilities of their small LA-adjacent medical practice. They had to talk her down when she decided they should most definitely add a barista to their lobby. "Our patient load would double, and my caffeine level would hum pleasantly close to *never have to sleep again*. Picture it." She did happen to have the most awesome, luscious jet-black hair in the stratosphere and knew it, swishing it often to make her point. In school, The Brunette Three were a force of academia.

"Come with me," Bethany called to Veronica. "You know I'm not good with the masses. You'll boss them around. I'll stand there with my arms quietly grabbing for snacks."

"No-go. I'm meeting with the electrician at five," she called back. "The break room overheads continue to blink. The problem plagues me in the middle of the night. I see those lights in my dreams, taunting me."

"She refuses my theory that it's extraterrestrial code," Thea said, far too seriously. "Let's play my favorite: Broken or Sprained? Over here. Now." She turned on the light behind the view box on the wall. Bethany studied the film of a woman's right hand, squinting and inclining her head because it was a difficult read. That was until she caught the faint line of a sneaky fracture on the fifth metacarpal. "I win. Right there. A hairline."

"Eagle Eye Cahill," Thea said, switching off the light. "When in doubt, you're my guy."

"My reward? A stroll through the frozen food section. I'm out."

"We'll miss you," Veronica shouted. "And won't for a second talk smack about you."

"Or your weird shoes from last week," Thea added.

Bethany frowned. Fashion was hard when you had very little free time. "They were comfortable. I'm sorry you don't care for fake fur on footwear."

"Does someone that you know of?" Thea asked, sliding a thin errant braid behind her ear.

"No comment." Bethany blew a kiss to Veronica as she passed her open office door and hit the much needed California sunshine. Ah, the world of the living. She didn't spend enough time in it, and popping on her shades now, in the midst of the warm April afternoon, had her vowing to change that. Embrace her human capabilities to explore the city and connect with other members of the species. Because quite honestly, it felt nice. At thirty years old, she'd spent far too much time with her nose in a textbook or a patient chart. She needed a tan. A mistress. Even a chaste pedicure would do. Something. Her life was egregiously regimented even for her logical brain. A grocery store in the late afternoon was honestly a shift she should embrace more regularly. She parked her gray Range Rover, feeling proud of herself. A shopper out in the daytime. The workaholic version of herself shelved for the day.

"I'll take this one," she told the older woman who seemed to be in charge of cart disbursal.

"Have a good day," the woman said.

Bethany paused. She probably said it to everyone, but today it resonated. "Thank you." She pushed her extra-large cart into the store and surveyed the multitude of food varieties that lined the shelves. Glorious. Speaking of eating, she'd call her dad later and make sure he was taking his cholesterol medicine. His girlfriend who lived with him was an amazing cook, but that didn't bode well for his lab numbers. Oh, strawberry Pop-Tarts. "Don't mind if I do," she murmured.

"Are you a nurse?" a little boy asked, spotting her scrubs. His big brown eyes blinked up at her.

"I'm a doctor," she told him, hoping gender stereotypes eventually worked their way out of the medical field altogether. One child at a time.

"His aunt is a nurse," his mother was quick to explain.

"Not a problem at all. We love nurses. They don't get enough credit."

"Do you like those?" the boy asked.

She eyed the strawberry frosted Pop-Tarts box in her hand. "My favorite. I sometimes eat two. Do you?" He nodded, eyes wide. "Have a good day," she told them both and watched as the mom reluctantly grabbed a box. That kid owed her one.

"Bye," he shouted, smiling gleefully like he'd won a prize at the fair. She sent him a mental high five.

Enjoying her time, she wheeled her cart around the corner to the next aisle, fairly certain that's where she would find that granola cereal she liked, when she nearly careened into a cart coming the other way. "Whoa. My fault. Sorry about that."

"No. Mine. I was on the wrong…" The words died the second the cart-pusher's gaze landed on Bethany's face.

Bethany froze, face-to-face with features she hadn't seen in years. Like a literal record scratch, her casual, lighthearted afternoon came to a halt. It wasn't Reid. It couldn't be. The fluorescent lights over their heads, which had been silent moments before, now buzzed like the chorus of a thousand angry bees. Oppressively loud, which was appropriate, too, because standing cart-to-cart with her was Reid Thatcher. Same light brown curly hair. Same forest-green eyes that could take one look at Bethany and see everything about her. Her heart thumped hard and fast, but there had been a time many years back when it beat solely for Reid, intertwined with hers for what was supposed to be forever. Their forever. Another time in her life entirely.

"Bethany." A pause. "Wow." Reid, this more sophisticated version of her, opened her mouth and closed it. "I don't even know what to say."

"Hi." It was the only word that surfaced on her end. Reid had won the contest. She'd managed more. As ineffective as it sounded, Bethany was trying to both breathe and maneuver her way through this very unexpected conversation. Who turns the corner expecting to find Lucky Charms and Cap'n Crunch and instead collides with their first love from high school? Correction, only love. As in, the girl who shattered her happiness, yet never truly left her thoughts even when Bethany had banished her countless times over. In this moment, her everything stood at attention, on guard and in protect mode. Her senses were overstimulated, too. Sound echoed, her hands felt every inch of the metal from the cart. Her mouth had gone dry. She tried to compensate. No-go. Where was the eject button? Finally, "What brings you to BeLeaf Foods?"

Reid stared at her cart, still not caught up. They were both vamping. "Groceries for a wildly lacking fridge?"

"Fair enough." Bethany smiled. She was doing a good job now of resembling a human running into another human. Not a big deal. Except she still couldn't persuade her chest to feel normal and shifted against its tightness. Her skin stretched, strict and prohibitive. Her right hand shook. She covered it with her left. "Me, too." She pointed behind Reid. "En route to cereal. Super exciting stuff."

"Right. Let me get out of your way." Reid swiveled her cart to Bethany's left so Bethany could go right. She looked so much the same, yet in woman form. The girl was gone. All grown up. She must still use the same plum shampoo because Bethany was right back in Reid's bedroom, staring into her eyes, inhaling that scent that always transported her to wonderful places. It hit her hard now like a door to the face.

"So, are you in town visiting?" Bethany asked as their carts lined up.

"No." A hint of hesitation. "Actually, I moved back to LA last month, but the real estate prices…"

"Are insane so you're out here and driving into the city each day?" This was surreal. Where was the hidden camera? Seriously.

"Exactly that. Yeah."

"Welcome to the club."

The implications of this new development charged toward Bethany like a herd of hungry buffalo. Reid would be back in the LA-adjacent circles. Swarming. Living. Being Reid with her perfect face and addictive smile. Wow. There was potential for future run-ins at grocery stores, restaurants, or social gatherings. Bethany's head swam. Did they have any shared friends anymore? She was pretty positive she'd left them all with Reid eleven years ago. They'd never been hers to begin with, had they. The world felt swirly. The room did.

"It's really good to see you, Bethany." Reid stared at her cart, giving her head a shake. "I honestly wasn't sure if I ever would again."

"Yeah, me neither. Good to see you, too."

But was it? She swallowed, remembering with startling accuracy what it felt like to kiss those lips, now glossy with a more mature shade. They'd tasted sweet like cherries years ago. Did they still? She shook herself away from the thought. Ripped away the image of Reid passing her in full uniform on the cheer mat where they'd worked alongside each other, pushing their bodies toward a shared goal. The secret looks they'd exchanged, what they'd meant to each other, what they'd done the night before. "I should probably get going. Welcome back."

"Wait." Reid turned around, leaving her cart, tracking her. She hadn't been finished. But Bethany sure had to be. It was all too much, and she hadn't quickly figured out how to organize the barrage of old feelings peppering her for attention. She had about 3.8 seconds before her composure evaporated, and she preferred to be far away from Reid when that happened. "This might be entirely inappropriate. But it seems so strange to be standing here in front of each other and not say more. Doesn't it?"

Bethany squeezed the red plastic handle of her cart. "It does. I just am so overrun with work at the moment that I was only dashing in here for a quick Pop-Tarts grab before heading back in. I really needed them. Pop-Tarts emergencies are no joke." A ridiculous thing to say. She checked her watch like a human cliché. "And I'm already late."

Reid deflated. "I understand. It's okay." And then, "Wait!" She riffled through her bag, which Bethany knew would have way too many stray objects floating around. Reid was always chaos and improvisation, a sharp contrast to her own regimented organization. "Take this. In case you ever want to catch up." Her business card. "Um, take care, okay?" It was something people said, but Reid's eyes proved she meant it. She'd always been a nurturing person.

"You, too," she said without looking back. She wasn't proud of that part, the racing away from the scene, incapable of more in the moment. She needed large amounts of air and a chance to breathe it in slowly while alone. Through a straw if possible. She abandoned her semi-full cart, sacrificing the groceries she'd been so excited about, to run out of there like a terrified child from a haunted house. She could have driven home, shelved the whole experience, but given her blaring brain, she knew her chances of success were slim at best. As a pivot, she drove straight back to the clinic in the hopes of burying herself in patient charts and email. Anything that would occupy her thoughts. Given that traffic had been bad in both directions, the clinic was closed and everyone would have gone home for the day.

Well, almost everyone.

Bethany was shaking when she arrived back at her office. She used her key and, once inside, sucked in a big gulp of air, safe now behind the walls she knew so well. What a whirlwind. One minute she was talking pastries with a small child, and the next, the only person she'd ever truly loved was staring at her like a ghost with a shopping cart.

"Why are you back here?" Thea asked as Bethany passed her open office door. The tie was gone and her dark braids fell loose, well past her shoulders.

Bethany doubled back and paused in the doorway. "I just had a traumatic experience and needed to lose myself. I think I'm shaking. Am I? Still unsure."

"In that case, get in here. Let me decide. It's been a boring afternoon and I am a doctor." When Bethany took a seat, Thea sobered immediately. "Oh. I was kidding, but look at your face. You're not. What happened?" Her brows were down and she leaned forward.

"Do you remember how you were always trying to fix me up in med school? You'd meet a lesbian or a bisexual woman and attempt to play matchmaker?"

"I sucked at it. You never liked any of them. Even that smart one with the boobs always on display, who even I had sex dreams about."

"Do you remember why I wasn't into any of them?"

Thea nodded. She never forgot anything, a quality that had her acing every test in school. "Broken heart syndrome."

"She was at the grocery store."

Thea sat right up. "Reid was there? Your first love?"

"You even remember her name? How?"

"You said it enough. Sometimes in your sleep." They'd roomed together at school, but she didn't realize she'd tossed Reid's name around at night. Embarrassing and pathetic.

Bethany scoffed, "I don't think I did that."

"Oh, but you did. I didn't bring it up because you needed space from the topic. Anyone could see that. A cloud came over you every time you brought her up." She studied Bethany. "And honestly, it's happening again." She took a hit from her diet soda. "You look like you've been through it. The tiny lines on your forehead are visible. I'm not acquainted with them. Nor the wild look in your eyes. I don't like it. Neither will your mirror."

Bethany's hand flew to her forehead, covering it. "Stop that. Ignore the lines." She plopped down in the comfy chair catty-corner to Thea's desk. "But you're not wrong. My heart is racing."

"It's okay. Deep breaths." She said it in such a casual tone that Bethany seized hold, attempting to mimic her disposition. It helped. Better. She also took Thea's advice. Slow inhale. Slow exhale. They did it together, holding eye contact, and it started to work.

Once the dust settled, and she had her bearings again, she offered a smile. "Thank you. That was weird."

"I think that's called a mild panic attack, my sweet friend. I do those breathing exercises with my sister, Tasha. She gets them all the time."

"No. Do you think I really had an attack?" Bethany prided herself on her grace-under-fire approach. She moved through intense pressure like a steady, cool cucumber. She could easily diagnose a panic attack in her patients, but from the inside out, it felt entirely different.

Thea widened her eyes and held the expression as if to say *Look at yourself, Dr. Cahill.*

Bethany grappled, at a loss. Even the walls looked weird. "I mean, Reid is Reid. A big part of my past, but I'm comfortable now with where I'm at. Everything that happened had to be for a reason, right? It brought me to this moment, and my life trajectory isn't so awful. So I'm just a little surprised that seeing her would cause this big a reaction."

"Yet it has." Thea handed her a bottle of water from her bottom desk drawer. "You're a human being. Acknowledge it. Shake a little, get all breathy and cry like an angry toddler if you need to. Just let yourself feel what are surely legitimate emotions. I promise you will be okay."

Bethany relented. "I guess so." She gave her shoulders a slow roll and opened the bottle. The water was helpful. She took an extra long drink and let the cool liquid soothe. "Unexpected. All of it. I'm a little embarrassed."

"Don't be. We've been through worse."

She stood, the mostly empty bottle at her side. "I'm gonna do some work, after all. That should help." She had her doubts about how productive she'd actually be, but she had to try. "Thanks for the talk and the water. I think I'm fine now." A rushed diagnosis and she damn well knew it.

"No, you're not. You're not fit for work. Go home. Do not pass Go. Do not collect a lifetime of difficult high school memories. Who needs that? This is your business partner talking and fellow physician. Go eat ice cream and binge *Law and Order*, posthaste."

She balked. "I don't even watch that show."

"Then start." Thea followed up. "I'm not kidding, B. Go."

She shook her head in annoyance. "You're a nag is what you are."

Thea held her arms out. "Call me what you want. I'm right. If there's one thing I know how to do, it's dodge ghosts from the past. My ex? Blocked on all social media on purpose. His ass can wonder about my life." She dropped her arms. "Of course, there's also a restraining order after he threw those oranges at the wall, so that's not the best example."

"You never told me about the oranges."

"For the best, just know that he was *handled*. Does yours need handling?"

"Not for fruit abuse. Some questionable, heartbreaking loyalty-related moves maybe."

"Consider yourself blessed."

Bethany offered a small bow. "You remain the best business partner and friend. Thank you for the talking down. I'll google this *Law and Order* you speak of."

"You're so weird."

"I'm kidding. I've heard of it. Kinda."

"Learn to be a frivolous person. Treat yourself. You've earned it."

Bethany offered a half smile. "I'm not sure there's much fun in that. Tried it once. Didn't go in my favor. 'Night, Thea."

"'Night, B."

Bethany went home to her expansive two-story house with all the fun bells and whistles. She didn't mind gloating about it because she'd worked really hard, and it was her one true splurge. Living in Mission Viejo afforded her more favorable real estate prices, a larger variety of hiking trails, and local culture—with access to Los Angeles clients, who were financially vital to her practice.

She tossed her keys onto the counter in her modern style home, her pride and joy, built only four years ago on the same lot that previously housed a teardown seized upon by a developer. Now, the new build with the huge rooms, gorgeous views, and sound and light automation was all hers. Not that she spent enough time here to truly enjoy those perks. Maybe if she watched more *Law & Order* it would anchor her. A new goal.

Bethany executed a forward roll onto her couch, one of the few remaining moves from her tumbling days, long abandoned now. She set to scrolling mindlessly through her phone. Her email signaled that she had two bites from a dating app she rarely opened. The bites came. She deleted. The bites came. She moved on. Tonight she was intrigued, feeling urgently like she had something to prove. Maybe Reid had kicked her into action, reminding her that she'd once been a romantic. Maybe Thea had. Didn't matter. She opened the app with the logo of two dolphins interlocked at their necks, forming the shape of a heart. An interesting logo choice. She checked her notifications. The women's profiles seemed harmless enough, so she sent a message to the most recent person to nibble.

In the morning, she had a reply. Whoa. This thing worked.

Yes, the biting woman would love to grab a coffee with Bethany and was free that very week. Well, this was exciting. She had an actual date. Bethany took a moment as she packed her lunch to marvel. Things were moving right along. She'd joined the masses. Online dating was actually much easier than she'd thought. She typed back a response, offering up the next afternoon, and sent it. *Bam.* She was a regular single person in the modern dating scene and felt like a badass. And why not leap in? She had a gap in her schedule and could shelve her administrative tasks for one damn day to grab coffee with this woman, Helene, which was a very nice name. Sexy, too. Plus, Thea would not only cover any of her last-minute patient needs but cheer her on. Veronica would likely applaud her effort at finally getting out there.

Even her father would be pleased the next time they chatted on their Thursday night call. The day was off to a great start.

She shrugged into her lightweight black leather jacket with the hood and stuffed her hands into the pockets as she walked to her car. Her fingertips grazed a small square of cardboard that pulled her up short. She glanced down. Reid's card in her hand. Reid's name. Her number. The one she'd left with Bethany should she decide it was okay for them to talk again. The air slowly began to seep out of her inflated balloon. "Reid Thatcher," she mumbled to herself as everything in her sat at attention. "Dammit."

Shrugging it off and trying not to let it kill her buzz, Bethany focused on her job and slowly lost herself as she saw one patient after another. A teenager with a sprained ankle, a sleep-deprived teacher, a consultation with an elderly woman fighting high blood pressure. She tried to limit her new patient appointments, knowing how full her plate already was, but she did pick up a few here and there, including her one o'clock.

In a good groove now, she checked the chart hanging outside the door placed there by Todd, her nurse. "No complaints," Todd said with a shrug as he approached. "Just wants to get established with a new primary care doctor, and you came recommended." He quirked his lips. "She wanted to make sure you were the same Dr. Cahill she'd heard about. Described you and everything."

Bethany smiled. "Well, I like being famous."

"Thought you would enjoy that."

"Why I hired you."

She skimmed the rest of the documentation to get a sense of any critical medical history, nose still in the chart as she breezed into the exam room. "Ms...." Her eyes darted to the top of the form. "Thatcher." She'd missed the detail, groove or not. She raised her gaze and *bam*. It all came together. Reid. Right there in the office. The air felt different for the second time that week. The afternoon had gone sideways.

She stood. Bethany took her in, this time more fully. The changes. The similarities. She was still Reid, but she'd come into herself. This wasn't the eighteen-year-old girl from over a decade ago. She was less gangly, her light brown curls were perfectly styled, her body was what could only be described as more womanly, but everything else was the same. The light green eyes she used to dream about met hers in apology.

"I realize you probably weren't expecting me, again, but I thought you'd have seen my name on the chart before you walked through the door. Doesn't look to be the case. Hi."

"I'll start with the patient's name next time." It didn't sound like the warmest greeting when it departed her lips, but honestly, the fact that she hadn't turned and run from the room was a victory. But she'd had practice this time. Her heart still thudded too hard and her stomach shifted uncomfortably. The two of them in the small room together, alone, fueled an onslaught as the good memories and the bad waged war.

"While I do need a new doctor, I also have to confess that wasn't my exact reason for coming in today."

"Okay," she said carefully. "What is it I can do for you?" She did her best not to broadcast what was happening inside. The rush of emotion all in a swirling cloud, indiscernible. Nostalgia. Anger. Joy. Hurt. Familiarity. She didn't sign up for more of this kind of moment. She didn't want it. "What can I do for you, Reid?"

"First of all, it was really good to see you the other day." She held out her hand. Bethany took it. A mistake. Their contact was like wildfire to her intense feelings. She pulled it back after a brief squeeze from Reid.

"It was nice to see you, too. A blast from the past." She tried to stay light, and not give away her panic, when in fact it was all she could concentrate on.

"I wasn't sure you would take my call, so I'm here on an ambush mission, inspired by our run-in." She paused. "I'm sorry. I just have to pause and gape. I'm in your office right now. You're a doctor, Beth. That's amazing. What you always dreamed of."

Beth. She swallowed that one and chose to move on. No one called her that. Well, no one else. "Yes. A long road to get here, but it's been a fulfilling journey." Reid's lips were still perfectly shaped and full. Like a drawing. She used to stare at them endlessly. Why hadn't the universe been more cruel to Reid, allowed her looks to fade just a little bit. If anything, she'd only grown into her beauty more fully.

"Bold move. But can we grab a drink sometime?" Reid's smile had dimmed. She shifted her weight. She was just as nervous as Bethany and it showed.

"Oh." A pause. "You know, things are really crazy lately." She reached for the chart with her right arm, forgetting herself, and corrected to her left. Reid tracked the action but said nothing.

"I get that. But surely they'll settle down at some point." Hope had entered the chat. How was this real life?

"I have a pretty buttoned-up life, Reid." That sobered things up pretty quick.

"Got it." Her gaze brushed the ground before returning to Bethany. "It's really good to see you, Bethany. I mean that."

"Yeah?" She nodded. "Good to see you, too." She hesitated. "Would you like to talk about patient care? I wouldn't be the right physician for you, but I have two great colleagues. A whole practice behind me."

"You know what? I'm okay." She reached for her bag, her cheeks coloring pink, which Bethany hated. She didn't want to embarrass anybody. Not even Reid.

"Reid." She placed a hand on her forehead, grappling. "It's just a lot. Seeing you."

Reid straightened. "I know. But if I'd called you up? Sent an email? Would you have answered me?"

She knew the answer, but her mind moved a million miles a minute trying and failing to find the right words.

"My point exactly." She tilted her head, looking into Bethany's eyes, which felt more like her soul. Dammit. Reid had a way of doing that, even now. No one else could come close. "I want us to talk. I have no reason to upset your life and no plans to upset you. A glass of wine. That's one thing we never did together."

"They frown on serving minors at most establishments." She offered a smile, trying to project the smallest amount of normalcy over a reunion that was anything but. She'd spent years shoving away thoughts of Reid, burying them, banishing the memories best left alone, and in one unforeseen moment all that work came crashing down. What was there to lose now? She was a grown woman, established and confident. She also had to admit she was curious about Reid and what her life was like. Her card said she worked in academia. Who had she turned out to be? "We can have a drink." Wow.

A smile. Reid's eyes crinkled. "That's all I'm asking."

"My last appointment should be complete by five. There's a restaurant across the street. Hazel's. Do you know it?"

"I'll get to know it. See you at five thirty. I'll buy." She turned back but didn't say anything. Her eyes held Bethany's almost as if she was taking a moment to drink her in after the long separation, and whether or not Bethany allowed it to, the moment left her shook.

"What the hell?" she whispered to the empty exam room once she was alone. She'd heard of the past coming back to haunt you but hadn't taken it quite so literally until this week.

"You okay, Dr. Cahill?" Todd asked. "Need anything? Some water?"

"Hmm?" she asked, touching the wall in the hallway. "Oh. No. I'm fine. I think."

"I'm going to get you that water anyway," he said, eying her with concern.

"Okay. Why not? That might be good."

The thing was, Bethany didn't want to relive those days back in high school. Yet after just five minutes in Reid's presence, that's exactly what she was doing. The intensity of the new feelings, the burst of lust, longing, and the feeling that she was right where she was supposed to be—only to have it all go so horribly wrong. She still lived with the effects of the Reid-and-Bethany implosion to this day, and no kind smile and glass of wine among friends was ever going to change that. What happened, happened. That should be the end of the story. It would be.

CHAPTER ONE

Then

No one liked being dropped into the deep end of the ocean. Seventeen-year-old Bethany Cahill stared at the large multilevel building in front of her, the hundreds of attractive students zipping across the steps along with their different shaped backpacks, soccer balls, reusable lunch bags, and hair bows. Yep. There were a lot of hair bows at United High School. More than one would expect. She instantly realized she didn't own a single bow and wondered where this would leave her, socially. Would this affect her success at this new school? Should she invest in a collection? Because, God, they weren't at all her style.

It was the second day of school of her senior year. She'd missed the first, which only compounded her nerves and had her wishing their arrival in Los Angeles had been sooner. But her father's shoot in Connecticut had gone several days over schedule, and that meant their cross-country drive from the East Coast had been delayed.

"So you'll miss the first day. Nothing exciting ever happens then anyway. Boring central. It's a placeholder on the school calendar for filling out forms," he'd told her a few days earlier over turkey and cheddar sandwiches at a less than glamorous rest stop in Colorado. He always seemed to pick the most rugged, beat-up places to stop because he thought they came with the most memorable character. She couldn't argue because she'd just passed a wall-mounted buffalo wearing a pair of sunglasses and a floral shirt. Culture flared.

"You have cheese in your beard, and missing the first day stresses me out."

"Everything stresses you out. It's what makes you run. It's impressive."

"True, but does this have to? Why add to it?"

He sighed and rubbed his somewhat graying beard, dislodging the sliver of cheese. "I'll see if I can drive faster, but no breaking the law. I'm not putting you in danger for eight hours of filling out forms and learning the names of teenagers you generally won't like. Where's the fun in that?"

"It's all I ask." Relief infused. He was a good dad, trying his very best in his role as single parent. Making some of it up as he went. She didn't fault him. He wasn't the most sentimental of guys. He didn't cry and tell her how proud of her he was, yet he was. He cared about her deeply, and it showed through his quiet grumblings and ruffling of her hair when he felt affectionate. His love language.

But in spite of his driving three miles over the speed limit, they still hadn't made it in time for the first day, so here she stood on the second day of school in a brand-new place, the glitzy and glamorous United High School smack in the middle of all of LA's shiny existence. The kind of place that made Bethany very aware of her own shortcomings both physical and financial. She didn't have the clothes these kids had. She didn't have the makeup or the hairstyles worthy of Instagram tutorials. The swift introduction to this foreign culture had her overcome with the nervous energy of a thousand butterflies and the overwhelming desire to get through the day without embarrassing herself too terribly. A simple goal.

United High School was bigger than the school she'd attended in New Jersey for both her sophomore and junior years, and twice the size of the one in Rhode Island where she'd gone as a freshman. This was her first West Coast academic romp, and though it was more her style to blend whenever possible, collecting As in every class she attended, Bethany wanted this year to be a memorable one. Different. The best yet. She just had to figure out how to make that happen, because it was likely going to take her stepping out of her shell. She smoothed her dark hair into place, gave it a shake to hopefully harness a dose of confidence she didn't actually have, and ascended the exterior stairs into her new, intimidating California life. Fuck.

"Extracurricular fair at three thirty, bitches," a boy with thick dark hair said in a singsong voice as he shoved a flyer into her hand and then into the hands of the three kids standing nearby. "Don't make me come find you and drag you there, Logan Pearson." He held his eyes wide and pressed on, thrusting more flyers, making more sung-through threats, clearly in a hurry to distribute as many as possible before the start of first period.

She looked down at the colorful flyer, her interest somewhat piqued via the threat to Logan's life, whoever he was. She'd normally shy away from events like this one, never having been a big joiner, but new leaves were new leaves. This might be a place to start, find her foothold. She had pretty specific skills. She could play a decent game of chess. Carry a semiworthy tune. And when it came to tumbling, she was right at home, having lived at the gymnastics gym since she was old enough to toddle. She slid the flyer into her bag and muddled her way through the incredibly crowded hallways full of kids who'd likely known each other for years. *Here goes, well, everything.* She attempted to nod and smile at anyone she made eye contact with, but the reality of bold behavior was harsher than in theory. This was going to be tough for her.

The first part of her day went by in a rather unfortunate haze of nothing special. Her classes seemed fine, her teachers wouldn't be a problem, but she'd yet to really connect with anyone other than through those cringeworthy ice-breaker games where she'd had to share with the room that she'd had her appendix out at thirteen.

"Sorry about that whole surgery thing," the good-looking kid in the letter jacket said. He was tall, athletic, and likely beloved by the masses. Wasn't that how it always went? Letter jackets and good hair equaled followers in large numbers. The bell had rung, and they were gathering their things.

"Thanks. I survived."

"Sucks to be you, though. No appendix and all. Name?"

"Bethany."

"Another tough break."

She frowned. "What? Why?"

"No reason. I'm Mateo. Slightly better than yours, but not much. Take it easy." And he was gone, leaving her to question her own name, which had seemed perfectly normal to her until sixty seconds ago. She saw Mateo in the cafeteria later that afternoon, beloved suspicion confirmed when she spotted him sitting with a bunch of other athletic guys that looked so much like him in their matching gear. School royalty, which meant she should go the opposite direction. She marveled at how individuals sought out people that were way too much like themselves and then carved out a space to dedicate to basking in their sameness. It didn't matter the school. Unoriginal and truly unfortunate. The world was so much bigger than these walls, and there was so much to explore. She rolled her shoulders, lunch tray in hand. Her workout from the night before left an acute ache that made her half sorry she'd gone so hard on the pushups and half impressed with herself. She'd need to find a tumbling gym soon to take out some of her extra energy and anxiety. It had been weeks since she'd really let go on the mat.

"Hey, there. Are you new? You look new," a tall brunette with an impressively long dark ponytail asked. Truly not a hair out of place. She was slicked back to perfection, and her predictably pert nose accentuated large brown eyes. She was the leader type. Bethany could tell that after spending twenty seconds in her presence.

"Yeah, I am. Bethany, straight from New Jersey. Hi." She smiled and shifted her weight, somewhat excited to be spoken to, but not sure that her nose was cute enough for this.

"Sunny. That's my name, not the forecast. Nice to meet you." She tossed a gesture behind, making it clear who the alpha was. "This is Jennifer, Ella, and that's Reid."

She surveyed the three really pretty girls, who looked like they were tight. "Hi, guys. Bethany."

The three girls Sunny had introduced paused their overlapping conversation and smiled politely.

"Hey."

"Nice to meet you."

"Hi."

But the chatter stream quickly picked back up as the group floated by, heading for the royal table. Of course they were. She watched them go, only the one named Reid looking back with a final smile and wave. Their gazes held briefly. She was immediately striking. If this had been a movie, she'd be the lead. Very pretty. Longish hair. Looked like green eyes. A tan, signaling their close proximity to summer or maybe that was just LA year-round. She also wore a letter jacket, though Bethany wasn't quite sure for what. Soccer maybe. She looked the part of a trendy athlete and likely homecoming queen. Probably the child of famous actors.

She snapped herself out of it, well aware that she was standing in the middle of the lunchroom without a destination as her sad little chicken burger grew cold in the divot of her blue plastic tray. Right. Well, the table in the corner near the custodial closet would have to do. From there, she ate her lunch and watched the action, captivated by the social dynamics of these LA elite. So much hair, fashion, and about eighteen thousand dimples competing for peak attention. What was she supposed to do with these kids and this place? A sense of hopelessness descended. She took a bite of her flimsy chicken burger, stared at it, and set it right back down, missing the East Coast desperately. This might just be the longest school year of her life.

❖

The day had already gone by for Reid Thatcher in a whirlwind of hugs, laughs, and catching up on gossip. It was a lot to take in after a pretty chill summer of pool time and low-key socializing. She longed for a quiet room and a chance to regather her energy. As luck would have it, Coach Rogan had agreed to let them skip cheer practice in place of hosting duties at the fair, which meant she might even be home before dinner, which was rare. Her parents would be thrilled. Her mom continued to make homemade meals for the family, always covering Reid's plate with tinfoil until she made it home from the gym after seven. They'd been back at practice for a month now, and she missed eating with her parents and her little sister, Alice, who now attended United as a freshman herself.

Before any of that, Reid had a job to do. Represent the squad at the fair and drum up interest in the mascot auditions. Wouldn't be a problem. All she needed was her smile. "Hey, there," Reid said to a boy who'd already collected about fifteen flyers. "We're looking for a new Kenny the fighting badger. Interested?" She held up her own flyer with a question mark on her face and made sure to purse her lips. For some reason, guys always responded to that one.

The gym was bustling and activity swarmed, but the boy was focused square on Reid with a look of awe on his face. It wasn't the first time she'd earned that response today. A senior cheerleader was talking to him in full makeup and uniform. The lowerclassmen were often intimidated by Reid and her friends, a badge she wore with pride. She remembered looking up to the varsity cheerleaders herself when she was a freshman, and now here she was, their cocaptain. "It's a really cool job for the right person. Tryouts are next Monday. Could be you. Just sayin'." She raised one shoulder and gave her nose a tiny wrinkle.

"Monday. Right." He seemed to snap to attention. "I have the dentist that day. Can I come late?"

She knocked him one in the arm, totally casual. Old friends now. She leaned in close. "Talk to Coach Rogan, and I'm sure she can snag you a later time slot that works for your schedule. We want the best, right?"

"Right. Thanks," he said, his gaze lingering an extra few moments. She was pretty sure he was drunk on perfume and attention. Her work here was done.

She pressed on, spotting a familiar face in the crowd and brightening as he approached. "Fighting badger tryouts coming up. Do you think you have what it takes to be the next Kenny?"

Mateo, her boyfriend, looked at her, his dark eyes dubious, his hair coiffed. "Give me the ball any day, but I'm no one's mascot. You're really hot, though. Wanna make out in a dark corner?" His arm went around her waist, a signature move.

She laughed at his raised eyebrow. An excellent smolder. "You're cute, too, I suppose. But I'm on the clock."

He dropped his brow, showing off. "Suave. Debonair. Handsome in a rugged sense. Not cute." He smoldered some more and stole a kiss.

"Mmm. If you say so." She went back down onto flat feet. "Now get out of here, so I can reel 'em in. I have a job to do, and I happen to take it very seriously."

"Text me when you're home."

"If I'm free."

"Send nudes."

"Not a chance."

He flashed a smile. "I see. Hard to get as always. You know I love it." He pointed at her, backed away, and caught up to his boys clad in matching red and white letter jackets.

She shook her head as they clapped each other on the back and then went back to her work. She and Mateo had been together for a little over two years now, a mainstay at United High School. A super couple on campus. She liked Mateo, maybe even loved him. They said the words, but didn't everyone? They hadn't had sex yet, but that didn't mean he hadn't tried. A lot. She'd have to do something about that at some point and join the throngs of sexually active teenagers. Hell, Sunny had lost her V-card at fourteen. She was late. Today, however, was not that day. Instead, she enjoyed what she and Mateo Riojas had. Fame. Attention. And his last name looked good scribbled next to hers in the margins of her physics notes. He was a promising wide receiver on the football team with scouts following him like ducklings behind their mother. She was well known because of her captain status on the varsity cheer squad. They were a pop song in the flesh, living the good life that she didn't for one second take for granted. But as their last year of high school kicked off, she was acutely aware that their world was about to change. College loomed. Mateo had his pick from a handful of colleges and just had to make a decision. He'd mentioned the prospect of them going away to school *together* multiple times now. The option dangled like grapes on the vine. She wasn't quite sure why she hadn't hopped on board that train quite yet, hitched her car to his. Her friends certainly didn't understand, either.

"God, you're lucky, Reid. The way he looks at you. Dead."

"His hair is amazing. When the wind catches it. What? I can't."

"Mateo adores you. I wish my boyfriend held my hand in the halls. I'd pay hard cash."

"You two. Goals. That's all I'm saying."

Things with Mateo were easy and fun. He was kind, if not arrogant, and made her feel important in his life. And she didn't mind the attention they pulled as a duo. The way the other kids in the hall stopped and stared when they walked past, Mateo holding her hand, her head high, her heart full. Not a bad day at the office, as her father would say. She wished those kinds of things didn't matter to her, but they did. The acclaim propped her up when she felt that her life was a little bit of a facade. She wasn't unhappy either, just endlessly restless, reaching for something she couldn't quite see.

"How are we doing?" Reid asked Jennifer, who'd been manning

the table. She had her long blond hair pulled up in a high pony and had gone extra aggressive on the mascara. One year younger, Jennifer looked up to Sunny and came with a side of judgment.

"Most of the mascot time slots are full, and I've handed out quite a few flyers to freshman girls who are interested in trying out for the squad in the spring."

"Awesome. You've represented us adequately, young Padawan."

"Huh?"

"Nothing."

Reid surveyed the gym. The fair was well attended, and eager students zipped from booth to booth trying to figure out their extracurricular trajectory for the year stretched ahead. As for Reid, she loved a good extracurricular activity. Thrived on them. In addition to cheering all four years, she was a member of the art club, as well as student body vice president, which was perfect because the president took all the labor intensive jobs.

"Excuse me. What are the, um, requirements? For this."

Reid blinked. "I'm sorry?" She perked up and found her smile. The blue-eyed brunette looking back at her was familiar. The new girl from the cafeteria. That's right. From back East.

The girl pointed at the stack of flyers in Reid's hands. "Oh, I mean, the flyer. A lot of people are carrying them around. It says there are tryouts for the mascot, which could be cool. I don't know."

"Right." Reid brightened, remembering her part. "The fighting badger. Kenny is his name. Random, I know." She remembered the question and got down to business. "It's the badger's job to get the crowd going before the game and during. Dance experience is a plus. If you could toss in a cartwheel, even better. Sometimes the badger works with us on halftime shows. Stuff like that." She isolated a flyer and held it out. "Are you interested? Say yes."

"I might be." The girl shifted. She was nervous, which made total sense because this was a new school.

"I'm sorry. I'm Reid. We met earlier today, but I wasn't sure if you remembered. You're probably learning a lot of new names or whatever. What was yours again? I promise to remember for the rest of my life this time."

"Bethany. Hi. Cool to meet you. I just—" But whatever Bethany said was drowned out by the arrival of the band playing the fight song and marching straight through the center of the gym, horns hot.

"Sorry," Reid said, shouting on top of the music. "I missed what you said, but welcome to United, Bethany. I hope to see you at the tryouts. Please come."

Bethany nodded, looking a little embarrassed at the failed conversation attempt. "Thank you. I'll just…" She gestured ahead. "Yeah."

Reid watched with interest as she walked away. There was something about that girl that resonated. She got the impression that Bethany wasn't the most confident person in the room, but she also wasn't entirely shy. She decided to seek her out when she could, make sure she was finding her way in this jungle of a place. Though, given her quieter personality, she didn't expect to see her at the Kenny tryouts, and if so, she likely wouldn't rise above Ryan Leonard, the most obnoxious go-getter in school, or his overly talkative sister Tatiana, who'd been very vocal for months about working on her tryout material in front of the full-length mirror in her oversized bedroom.

"Reid! You alive in there?" Sunny snapped her fingers in front of Reid's face. She let the abrasive gesture go. "We're gonna grab dinner at the Pancake Princess after. You in or out? Say in. I'll twirl you around," she said, doing that very thing. The dance move was a signal of their friendship, something they'd done since they were kids.

She blinked her way through the twirl and decided, "Nah, I think I'm just gonna head home. Take advantage of the time off. I have calculus homework, and I'm more than lost in that class."

Sunny scoffed, disappointed and horrified to lose out to calculus. "Look into my eyes." She had big, pretty brown ones. "Ten years from now, you will miss these nights with your friends, and calculus will be a distant speck in your foggy rearview mirror. Fuck calculus. Reevaluate your answer. I'll wait." She said it with a smile, but her cocaptain and friend since kindergarten rarely took no for an answer. Sweet and salty. That was Sunny.

"Gonna still take that pass. I love you, though. I would tackle you in a heartbeat and kiss all over your face."

That seemed to soften her up. "Gonna hold you to that. Also, you can tutor me in calculus when my average falls, for pancake penance."

"See how that all worked out? See you soon, Sun."

"*Bye-eee.*"

Reid, thankfully off the clock, grabbed her backpack and headed to the senior parking lot in front of the school. The sun descended in the sky and her stomach ached with hunger. There, standing in front of the administration building with one arm crossed over her body, was that Bethany girl from earlier, her thick dark hair lofted by the late summer wind like a greeting.

"Hey!" Reid called. Bethany lifted her gaze and raised a half-hearted hand, seemingly unsure if Reid was addressing her or someone else and unwilling to commit just in case. Reid jogged over. "Sorry about the band earlier. Conversation killer."

"Totally okay. Not the first time I've been overtaken by a gang of woodwinds, like yourself."

"Really? Hmmm." Reid tried to follow. "Like me?"

Bethany didn't move a muscle. "Because your name is *Reid.*" She held her ground and left a pause for Reid to catch up. "I was joking. Apparently, not effectively."

"No, no. I get it now."

"Whew." She pretended to wipe her brow.

"So, are you waiting for someone?"

"My dad. I get it. I'm incredibly cool to have my parent pick me up. Don't clamor." She was kidding again. She would keep Reid on her toes. Her deadpans were too good.

"Nothing wrong with catching a ride." A few of her reckless curls flew into her face, and she trapped them on top of her head. Bethany seemed captivated by the move. People without curly hair had no idea the caliber of struggle.

"He's running late on a shoot." Her eyes were still on Reid's hand on her hair.

"Actor?" There were so many around here.

"Lighting guy. Less attractive than the actors but crazy smart."

"I can take you home."

Bethany's eyes went wide. She clearly wasn't expecting the offer and now didn't know what to do with it.

"I'm serious. It'll save him a trip from whatever studio in rush hour traffic. C'mon. If you live in the district, which I think you have to, follow me. Car's over there. Text your dad that I got you."

Reid was walking, positive assumptive, but Bethany still hadn't left the curb, staring at the ground ahead of her like it was covered in lava. Reid paused because it was honestly kind of cute.

"I mean, are you sure?" Bethany asked.

"I don't say things I'm not sure about. You'll learn that soon enough. Come on already."

Bethany took another moment to appear fraught and then jogged behind Reid until she caught up. "Thanks. I'm just a couple of miles that way." She gestured to the left. "I promise."

"That way we go." Reid opened the door to her dark blue Mustang and watched as Bethany nodded at it with honest appreciation.

"Wow. Nice car you have here."

"Birthday present for my sixteenth."

"Are you rich?" She winced. "That's rude. Just flew out."

"Rich? Ha. Not quite. But my parents are comfortable enough to be rich adjacent."

Bethany clicked the seat belt. "I'm far from it, as you're about to see. Small house. Nary a sports car. But nice enough."

"Big family?"

"No. Just the two of us. Me and my dad. He's good people, though." She took a breath. Still on edge. "A little grumpy, which makes for a lot of fun takes."

"Aww." Reid started the car. "I like the guy already."

They drove in silence, listening to a band Reid had discovered that summer and pretty much had on repeat, hanging out at The Corner, the apex of two large lots with food trucks, mismatched outdoor furniture, and a makeshift stage. It had become the unofficial hangout for her friend group and about every other teenager in the vicinity.

"You have good taste in music," Bethany said, nodding to Reid's phone.

She turned up the song about a guy following after a girl who had his heart on a string. Angsty and raw. "They're local. The Skips. I'll let you know the next time I hear of a show. They tend to just pop up."

"That'd be cool." She smiled, and it was a nice one, Reid had to admit.

She stole a glance at Bethany as they drove, now noticing more about her—smooth skin, big eyes with lashes for days. No extensions needed. Damn. Dark and incredibly thick hair that touched her back just past her shoulders. But she didn't go out of her way, keeping it simple. She wore jeans and a solid maroon top paired with white Chuck Taylors. Some mascara at most. Her hair was down. Brushed, but not curled. The look worked for her, even if it did contrast the done-up girls Reid ran with. She liked Bethany's style.

"Oh. Right here. Second on the right."

Reid flipped on her turn signal. "Gotcha."

"Super cool of you to, like, go to the trouble. I'll pay back the favor someday."

"It wasn't any. Plus, I got to know you a little better. See you tomorrow?"

Bethany slid her backpack onto her back and gripped each strap. "I'm mandated to be there, so yeah. Definitely."

It was a good answer. Reid ran her thumb across the leather of the steering wheel as she watched Bethany ascend the three steps that led to the front door of the gray and white stucco house. One story. A few plants in pots out front. The house looked pretty small, but LA was like that unless you were one of the megawealthy. Once the door closed, Reid lingered, ruminating on the last few moments of their exchange. For some reason, it felt like the universe was drawing an arrow sign over this particular moment in her life. Telling her to pay attention, and she was. She just wasn't sure why but took a moment to hover. Bethany felt like an important whoosh of rare air.

She had a smile on her face as she drove herself home, intrigued and somehow refreshed. Bethany Cahill was different, an entire juxtapose to the typical clout-chasing LA kids she was used to. In fact, she thought about Bethany for the entire ride to her house, chalking it up to the fact that she must be really bored with the rest of her life. The new girl was a welcome shiny new penny, who she had quite literally just picked up and driven home. Maybe they'd talk again. Maybe they wouldn't. Either way, Reid had a strong hunch that something in her world was about to shift radically, and she was ready for it.

CHAPTER TWO

It was good to be home at a reasonable hour. Reid burst through the door, dropped her bag, and grinned. "Honey, I'm home." When no one appeared, she dropped her outstretched arms. "Seriously? No one? I'm right here."

"And you're tied for my favorite child. Good second day?" Reid's mom asked, appearing in the two-story open entryway from the opening to the kitchen. She had her curly hair in a ponytail, placed a smacking kiss on Reid's cheek, and slid away in her socks to finish dinner. Her mother was a kitchen slider. Always had been. It was actually kind of fun. She'd been a cheerleader in high school also and had gotten Reid and Alice up and moving when they were very young. Reid could do a forward roll by the time she was two and there was video of her mother doing them right along with her. That's how it had always been with her family. Tight-knit. A group of kidders, who were fiercely protective of each other. She was one of the lucky ones and knew it.

"Yeah. Nothing catastrophic happened, which is, you know, helpful."

"It's nice to have you home for dinner. The empty chair's been a hoot, but you're much more expressive." Her mom slid an escaped strand of curly brown hair behind her ear. Reid had inherited the same light caramel color that carried hints of blond in the sunnier months, which there were a lot of in California. "Your sister already set the table and did a bang-up job, so you're off the hook. You get to show up and eat and regale us with tales from your glorious day."

She grinned, relaxing in the comfort of home and family. Her sister, Alice, was a new freshman at United, excited with her spot on the junior varsity soccer team. Her father was an architect and a partner at his firm, and her mother had slowly cultivated a successful online empire, selling floral arrangements of all kinds on Etsy and beyond. That meant they had an entire room in their home stacked to the brim with any kind of artificial flower one could conjure. Demand for her creative, funky designs had grown over time, and she was now charging quite a bit for each arrangement. Impressively obscene.

"I don't know how you do it," Reid told her mother one night as they arranged a vase of blue and purple flowers with all kinds of wild green stalks and tiny white flowers sticking out between them. Eye-catching in an unpredictable sense. Her mom's specialty.

She surveyed Reid's work and made an adjustment. Too many green stalks. "You have to invent your own path. Every time a door closed in my face, I opened another one."

"You say, from your floral empire."

Her mom sat taller. "Thank you for recognizing my queenship, Sweet Cheeks. You just might be rewarded with an apprenticeship."

"Isn't that already in progress? Look at me, killing myself over flowers."

"No need to state the obvious, royal apprentice."

"How much does an apprentice rake in?" Reid asked, tapping her fingertips together.

"Unending hugs and the affection of her royal mother. Sometimes cake."

"Expected." Reid laughed, grabbed a large purple flower, and handed it over, reflecting on her mother's imparted wisdom. *Open your own doors.* And that was the thing. Reid had been lucky. She hadn't experienced too many closed doors, and that actually made her feel like she had so very much to lose. Life had been easy so far. But would it always be?

Dinner that night was like a warm blanket on an icy day. After weeks of intense cheer practice, sitting with her family, exchanging stories from their days centered Reid and slowed her world. She'd missed it. Since sitting down, she'd learned her mom had spent the day boxing orders, her father had taken a half day off for a charity golf tournament that his team sadly lost, and Alice had, unfortunately, landed Mr. Lopez for algebra, a sentence close to walking barefoot on hot shards of glass. She'd been there.

"Don't turn anything in late," Reid said, remembering her days in his class two years back. She accepted the plate of breaded apple pork chops and helped herself to one. "He will hold it against you later when you ask for help. He will also enjoy it."

Alice blew out a breath, her blond hair falling from her sporty ponytail. "He freaks me out. Talks too fast. Sometimes to himself. Sometimes to us. I can never tell which." Her eyes were large and dialed to medium-sized panic.

"I'm confident you'll pull through this," her father said, giving her wrist a squeeze. "And if not, you'll live off us for the rest of your life like a mooching little parasite. It'll be fun for all." He laughed as he buttered the inside of his bread. She enjoyed his evil streak, knowing he meant no harm. He'd been teasing them both since birth.

"Gasp. Stop it. Dad!" Alice's eyes grew to three times their size. "Don't say that. Why do you hate me?"

He laughed and popped a bite of buttered roll into his mouth. "You make it too easy, kiddo. I don't even have to try with you."

"Lopez is harmless," Reid told her. "Just stick with what I tell you, do your homework, and you'll be fine. He honors effort. Can you pass the corn casserole? I need, like, three helpings."

"You segue like a champ," her mother said, grabbing the square pan with two mismatched potholders and handing it over.

"I learned from the best. Never leave good food on the table."

She and her mother exchanged a fist bump, and Reid dug in, relishing the comfort food after what felt like an extra-long day. In the midst of her spooning the casserole onto her plate, her parents exchanged a look and held it. Were they doing that weird flirting thing again? She'd walked in on them once during sex when she was nine and hadn't yet erased the image from her brain. Her mom reached for her water glass, took a sip, and gave a subtle nod. Her dad seemed to accept it as permission.

"Alert. There's something we need to discuss with you two, and since we finally have you both in the same room, this might be go-time." He looked from Alice to Reid.

He'd pulled an alert before. It usually meant some kind of family project lurked, like, *Next weekend, we're all needed to weed the garden. Cancel your plans.* But the air felt thicker than it had just moments before. Alice stared at their father behind her traditional over-iced glass of Mountain Dew. Reid took a bite of macaroni and moved her chicken to the side, waiting for whatever it was he had to say. The utensils all seemed to go quiet.

"You know that when two people love each other, that never really goes away."

Reid frowned. "Dubious. Did someone die?" She set down her fork, more intrigued than ever. This felt like a key moment. She just wasn't sure for what.

"Your mom and I love each other. Always will."

"Okay," Alice said, drawing the word out. She and Reid exchanged a glance. The same quick check-ins they shot each other when their parents bickered, which was actually pretty rare. They were more the bantering type. She'd never really seen them in a full-fledged fight, even.

"But that love has changed in tone." Her father raised his gaze to their mom, who took over. Had they choreographed this? Met for rehearsals? Because what the hell was happening with that perfectly timed handoff?

Her voice was measured. "We're still the same family that we've always been, but your father will be getting his own place. In fact, he already has one."

"Like, for vacation?" Alice asked, which meant she hadn't quite figured this out yet. It was all too fast.

"No. They're splitting up," Reid said flatly. This made no sense. Her very stable world just took a radical dip, upending like one of those boats from her childhood baths when the power of the drain sucked it down. How had she missed this?

"We're transforming our relationship," their mother corrected. "A family in a brand-new sense."

"That's tree hugging speak for divorce." Reid had completely lost her appetite. She shoved her chair back from the table. She needed answers, but that felt like too much attention to give them in the moment. She was mad and they needed to know it. Air wouldn't be bad, though. She needed more.

"I don't understand. Why would you want to split up?" Alice asked.

Reid sat right back down because there was her sister to think about, and she would need Reid. They would need *each other*. As different as they were, they were also a duo in many ways. The Thatcher kids. Weeding the family garden together.

Her father nodded, as if taking the question super seriously. "Your mother and I are just moving on to a new chapter in life, and that means living apart."

Reid wasn't having it. Anger bubbled and spilled. "Right. But you've said that already. Is there a script we can depart from now to truly understand what's happening in our family?" She looked under the table. "Because I thought I was just sitting down to a regular dinner, and now I hear that we're canceled."

Alice was crying. She didn't cry much these days, and it stabbed Reid deep. She'd take her for a walk, get them both some air and distance. But wait. The table was quiet. Too quiet. Like when the killer was about to jump out in a scary movie.

"He's met someone." Her mom took a delicate sip of iced water.

Ah, there it was. Her father's gaze flicked to her in surprise. Aha. They'd not planned on that part, apparently. She'd gone off script. Rogue.

"It's okay," Reid said. It wasn't. The idea of her father fucking a random woman made her nauseous and sad, but the truth was important. She'd always valued knowing exactly what she was up against. "I'd rather the ugly truth." She met her father's eyes. "Congratulations."

He tossed his napkin on the table and sighed. "Reid. Sweetheart. It's really going to be all right. Feels like crap now, but we'll find our stride."

"It'll be all right for you. I'm not feeling so great about it myself. May I be excused?" Her mother nodded. Her father sighed yet again. Reid turned to Alice. "Let's take a walk, huh?"

To her surprise, Alice shook her head. "You go." Clutching her Mountain Dew, she pushed away from the table and stomped up the stairs, leaving Reid alone with the remnants.

"Okay, then. Just me. I'll be back later." Her parents didn't question her further, which was rare. They must have sensed, just as she had, that she'd grown up exponentially in the past fifteen minutes. Necessity. In total shock, she walked the sidewalk of their small neighborhood, up one hill and down another as night crept in all around her, and she tried to work it all out and imagine what the future would look like. Instead of feeling expansive, the star-filled sky suffocated, leaving Reid in a hypersensitive state, searching for breath while her heartbeat doubled. She heard its rhythm in her ears like a taunt she couldn't escape. With her already sore legs now aching from LA's relentless hills, she found a curb two streets from her house. Not yet ready to face it all quite yet, she took a seat. Deep inhales. Slow exhales. A distraction would help. She slid her phone from her pocket and hit up social, scrolling aimlessly because none of her friends were online. Of course they weren't, because they were all out together. She felt immeasurably alone and desperate to remedy that. On a whim, she searched the new girl's name, Bethany Cahill, smiling when she found her profile almost immediately. The profile photo was a good one, maybe shot by a professional. She stared at it for quite a while. Oranges and pinks of a sunset in the background. Bethany offering a coy smile. It showcased those soulful eyes Reid had noticed right off the bat. Blue. With lashes for weeks. She followed the account and, because this was actually helping, sent a message.

Hey, Bethany. Reid. You around? Be around.

Nothing.

She sighed and dropped her phone. The dread picked back up where it had left off now that she'd unleashed her brain again. Her phone buzzed against her palm. Saved?

Hey, Reid. Bethany. I'm here.

Yes. She smiled at the mimic. A burst of relief landed, and Reid lay back in the grass, absorbing the cold St. Augustine prickles against her shoulder blades. Now what did she say? *You'll never guess what just happened at my house.* Not quite. She improvised. *Cool meeting you.* She chewed her lip, removed a wayward curl from her eye. *Fellow appreciator of The Skips.*

The online reply came quick. *What can I say? Good music=good music. Even west coast.*

Easy now, east coaster.

A notice came on her phone that Bethany had just followed her back. She turned onto her side and then back. They were gonna be friends. She rolled her shoulders and settled in, desperate for distraction and realizing that the new girl was working.

Tell me about back home, she typed.

And they were off. As they talked, riffing in quick, short sentences, Reid found that one muscle group after the other relaxed and let go. She would have a lot to face when she returned to her life as scheduled, but this short break gave her a chance to breathe. The best part was that Bethany barely knew Reid. She had no preconceived notions of her family. There was no reason to be embarrassed. Maybe this was the perfect person to talk to on a night like this one. Reid decided to lean in to the impulse.

❖

Satan stealing groceries on a Monday. What was happening? Bethany couldn't believe she'd been chatting with not only one of the prettiest girls she'd ever seen in her life, but arguably the most popular girl at the new school she was desperately trying to maneuver. A really nice person, too. It was so much easier to talk to someone from behind a keyboard. Bethany had time to think, craft a semidecent response that wouldn't catapult her into the epitome of mortification. When Reid's name had popped up on her screen mid-homework assignment, she'd gone still, unsure how to proceed. Half of her wanted to not answer at all and skip the pressure that would come with chatting. The other side of her couldn't let that happen. Reid made her feel seen, and she couldn't blow this chance for a possible friendship.

She knew one thing for sure. Reid was sought after. Bethany didn't have to attend United for more than a day to understand that. When she walked by, people sat up straight and watched. She'd witnessed it firsthand at the activities fair. Popularity was just the way of the world. Girls that were born looking like Reid and gifted with perfect fashion sense, flawless makeup execution, and confidence for days were in charge of the teenage social regime. So why was Reid with the gorgeous hair and remarkable status taking time for her? Just regular Bethany. Not that she was complaining. They'd been chatting for about ten minutes, and so far Reid showed no signs of intense boredom. That felt like something of a triumph.

She watched the dancing dots until the newest message finally popped on her laptop screen with the crack in the corner. *Have you decided about the mascot tryouts?*

She typed back, *You mean after a whole three hours of deliberating?*

Fair. Lol. Take your time.

Can't hurt to give it a shot. Probs gonna fall on my ass in front of the whole new school. Exile me now.

Will be memorable at least. My afternoon could use that kind of action.

There's that.

A pause. No one sent anything. Bethany went into semipanic, not knowing whether to let the conversation drop or to charge headfirst into a new topic, capitalizing on the moment. It was hard to figure out how to act around new people.

"Just be yourself, you silly rodent," she imagined her dad saying. He'd likely give her head a soft knock, mess up her hair on purpose, then kiss her temple as he walked by, scratching her skin with his beard. Well, the version of herself she knew would try a little more, especially since she enjoyed talking to Reid. And the attention she got from Reid. And remembering the way Reid looked in a cheerleading skirt. She laughed at how basic she was, also too gay for her own good. Even she lusted after the pretty, popular girl. Nothing unique about that.

Having a chill night? she finally typed with a grin.

The dots danced. She kinda thought this would be the moment Reid brushed her off and said good night. Her laptop flickered, and she froze, worried she'd lose connection. It had happened before. She really needed to save up for a new one. Easier said than handled.

It's been an awful night. Parents are splitting up. I just found out. Sucks hard.

Bethany stared at the inept screen, blown away by the gravity of the news displayed and the fact that Reid had shared it with her.

Fuck. U okay? She squinted at the screen and waited.

Yes. No. I dunno. It's just my life now.

Bethany sighed. *Maybe things will be better.* A weak attempt to soothe. She didn't really know Reid's homelife. Hope was all she had to extend.

No idea. They always got along. We were happy. They dropped this like a bomb outta nowhere.

Shit. I'm sorry. She was swearing a lot. The topic seemed to warrant it.

Thanks.

I know it feels awful, but maybe it won't always.

Gonna try and hold on to that.

Good.

She chewed her bottom lip, searching for perfect words.

Reid's message came first. *It was cool chatting. Gonna go. Really sorry I unloaded on you.*

Bethany shook her head as she typed as if Reid could see her. *No reason to apologize. Hit me up whenever.* A pause. She typed again. *I'm serious, Reid. I'm right here. Okay?*

I will. See ya tomorrow.

The edges of Bethany's mouth pulled as she sat back in her desk chair. She was looking forward to tomorrow now. After a day of floating aimlessly without a tether, she felt like she had a foothold. Someone here knew she existed and had been nice to her. Someone who mattered.

She looked around her sparsely decorated room, boxes along the walls, sleeves and hoods hanging haphazardly out of two suitcases in the closet, and knew that it was probably time to make this place feel more like hers. It was time to invest. After all, she was already starting to feel like the year ahead might be a good one. Maybe the best one yet. Who knew?

CHAPTER THREE

Today was the day. The school gym was loud and hot. The mascot tryouts were open to the public, which meant the wooden bleachers along the long wall were full of students and interested parents. In front, a long table with several cheerleaders and their coach sat with pens poised to evaluate each potential Kenny. The coach with short blond hair and way too many layers nodded to the beat of the same Justin Timberlake club mix they used for everyone's slot. Bethany let the counts settle over her. She could work with them.

There was a practice area set up for the tryouts, and in a surprise to no one, it was packed. Bethany exhaled, blowing a small strand of dark hair off her forehead and into the air. She did a few hops to limber up her muscles. Her calves felt tight, and she needed to do something about that. She found a spot off to the side and practiced her run, gaining momentum with each strong step and erupting into a triple back handspring. Landed nicely. After a short breath, she ran again. The little passes felt more natural each time. She tossed in a roundoff. An aerial, which really taxed her legs and woke them up. Her typical warm-up from back in the day. She just needed to dust it off a little and ignore the looks she pulled. Most of the other candidates were working on dance moves. She had a few of those, too. She might be quiet in physics class, but she wasn't shy on the mat. That was for damn sure.

She wasn't exactly clear what they wanted in their Kenny, but getting to show off with her face hidden in that badger head sounded kinda fun. Almost like performing, without people actually seeing you. A win-win. She watched as, one by one, the other potential badgers were pulled into the audition half of the gym, sectioned off by one of those huge hanging curtains. They'd each have a chance to freestyle to the Timberlake mix, showing their personality and what individual traits they'd bring to Kenny. She'd read the flyer over a hundred times, nervous as hell, but using her tumbling history to anchor her nerves.

Bethany's number was next, and that meant game on.

Time to fly. Her favorite.

The edges of the world faded away on command, leaving her alone with her concentration and the air she planned to grab on the way up, up, up. The exhilaration that came from literally soaring in the air under her own power was unique, addictive, and her favorite way to escape. She harnessed it all now.

"Bethany Cahill?" one of the bottle-blond cheerleaders called from the opening in the gym drape. She looked young, probably a freshman put on escort duty for the event.

"Yep. I'm here," she said, jogging over.

"You can put on a costume and wait for the music. Kenny in a football jersey or Rock Star Kenny. Your choice. You got this, girl." She said it with such feeling, Bethany almost believed it. They were cheerleaders, after all, and clearly effective.

"Thanks." It seemed they had a handful of Kenny costumes in rotation. She grabbed Football Kenny and put it on while the person in front of her finished their tryout. If Kenny's purpose was to offer high fives to every person in the stands set to music, they nailed it. Go, Kenny.

When the floor cleared, the cheerleader who'd summoned her offered a nod. Bethany, in Kenny mode, took the open space on the gym floor, faced the serious-looking judges' table, and tried not to focus on how attractive Reid looked in that white shirt against her tan skin. That's when the pressure appeared like a terrifying little gremlin. *Keep it together.* Then she saw it. Reid smiled at her and offered a wink of encouragement. Her eyes were soft. Beautiful. *Focus on her kindness.* She could do that. The music hit, and Bethany used her best knee swaying dance moves to celebrate an imaginary touchdown, then shook her ass all the way to the corner of the mat as the crowd clapped to the beat and the table dwellers studied her carefully. When the beat shifted, she took off into a full run and executed a roundoff double back handspring. She'd have added a full at the end, but the Kenny costume made sticking the landing a dubious prospect. Didn't seem to matter. Half the place lost their shit. The other half slowly took to their feet, making sure they'd just seen Kenny rotate, before erupting into shouts and cheers themselves. She did a victory lap, hammed up some dancing, and ended with another roundoff back handspring that made them go nuts yet again. That was the way she wanted to go out.

Short of breath, feeling a little silly, and on a high, she jogged off the floor to her waiting escort, who accepted the costume as she stepped out of it.

The cheerleader stared at her in awe. "No one's ever tumbled as Kenny before. Who are you again?"

"Bethany. I'm Bethany."

"Everyone's gonna know your name soon enough."

She looked over at the table and saw Coach Rogan chewing the back of her pen with interest. Reid, however, watched her in utter mystification. She gave her head a shake and held out a hand as if to say: *What the hell?* Bethany passed her an easy smile and shrugged, well aware that her tumbling abilities were advanced, and any cheerleader would likely understand the difficulty of what she'd just accomplished while wearing a costume. It felt good to show off what she could do, surprise a few of the unsuspecting, and maybe put herself on their radar. She didn't know if she was Kenny material, but that was for them to decide. She knew she'd given them her best badger and could chill now.

"That wasn't bad," that Sunny girl said with a slight chill as she passed. Where had her cafeteria friendly face gone? Okay, so not everyone was going to be impressed with her. "You can exit right through there, and we'll let you know."

"Okay. Thanks."

Bethany gave her limbs a shake out, found her backpack, and left the gym. The sun was more than half down, and the warmth of the day was escaping with it. Her dad would be by in the next ten minutes, and they'd go out for burgers, tots, and mint chocolate chip milkshakes. He'd promised to regale her with tales from the show he worked on, light design trench stories. Maybe even take her onto the set soon once he was settled in with the crew.

"Bethany, wait the hell up."

She turned, hands in the pockets of her jacket, to see Reid jogging toward her, brown curls bouncing, eyes sparkling. When she landed, she shook her head. "Why didn't you tell me you tumbled?"

"Oh." She lifted a shoulder. "The conversation didn't really, uh, go there on its own. Would have been weird to lead with it."

Reid smiled. "I couldn't have landed those stunts in the Kenny costume, and I'm one of the captains of the varsity squad."

"Well, have you tried? Wasn't that hard."

That pulled a laugh. "I don't have to."

"I was planning to throw a full at the end of the pass, but that costume doesn't give."

"You can land a full?"

"Yeah."

"What is happening right now?" Reid placed her palm flat on her forehead. "This is nuts. Did you cheer at your last school? You had to, right?"

"No, no, no," she said, probably too emphatically. She'd never been drawn to the sport. "More of a practice gym kind of person. I competed when I was little. Now, I just use it to let off steam."

"I can't even believe this. You just keep getting cooler." Reid glanced behind her. "I have to get back to the tryouts, but I'm blown away right now. I want to talk about this more. Can we chat later? Will you be on? You're not off the hook."

"Wouldn't want to be," she murmured, surprising even herself.

"Good." Reid stared at her for an extra long moment. "Guess I should…"

"Yeah."

Bethany watched her run back to the gym, and a shiver hit. She averted her eyes from the toned, tan legs in motion and then, because the universe commanded it, stole another look. Good God with a Popsicle. She didn't often indulge in crushes, but this one was coming on with unusual power. Which of Reid's qualities made Bethany's knees refuse to hold her up properly? Her popularity, her beauty, her vivacious personality? It didn't matter. Bethany was just one of the masses trailing after Reid. Correction. The very *straight* Reid. There was zero doubt about that. She'd seen a million photos online of her with that Mateo kid looking like supermodels. On the beach. At football games. Formal dances. Sitting on cars. That was fine. She could admire Reid from afar like the rest of the school.

She popped her headphones in, turned the volume to loud, and celebrated her day's victory with a tiny smile. She hadn't fallen on her damn face in front of the brand-new school. She'd had them on their feet. They'd been cheering. For *her*.

"You haven't said a word about the tryout thing," her dad asked around his milkshake an hour later. His tone was even, relaxed. Their whole evening was. The throwback diner he'd selected was petite and a fan of the color baby blue. The walls. The menus. The service staff. Sometimes they got lost in the haze. He pressed her further. "Tell me or I'll explode."

"Well, I won't know anything until later this week, but I think it went okay."

"Did you do the loop-de-loops? People love that." Her dad's code for tumbling. He used to take her to gymnastics competitions when she was small, beaming at all she could do but never quite sure what any of it was. It was always a sight, the big burly man in dark clothes standing in a line of perfectly coiffed moms. To his credit, he didn't care. Neither did she.

"I did a few loops. Stayed off my ass. Bonus, right?" She drummed her fingers to the retro music flowing from the speakers. "I might have made a friend. I don't know." She left out the really hot part in Reid's descriptor, thought she'd thought back on that run back to the gym about eight times since it happened. Played it in slow motion.

"Who? Are we keeping her?"

"Just a girl. Reid. She's on the cheer squad and, like, pretty sought after. Preppy. Put together. Not my standard acquaintance, but I don't know. She's nice. I like nice people."

His face lit up. She knew he worried about her quietly. Nothing out loud. "Think she could help you get on the squad, too?"

Bethany scrunched her nose. "What? No. It's like you've never even met me." She surveyed a strangely shaped onion ring. "Plus, they decide those things the year before. But she's been cool to me. Makes being the new kid easier."

His eyes settled into twinkle mode. "Invite her over. I'll make my famous chili and beans. We can watch a *Star Wars* movie."

"I don't think that's the going currency for senior girl friendships, but I'll keep that on the back burner just in case. How's work?"

He nodded vigorously. "Show's not bad. They keep a tight ship and we move along. Makes for shorter days. I like that." *Thicker Than Water* was a highly rated television show several seasons in. The job had been a pretty big score for her dad and would likely open up other offers for him, now that they were local in LA. "Hoping the drama remains in front of the camera. The showrunner and lead actress make bedroom eyes at each other."

That set her on high alert. Because hot damn. The showrunner was female. "That Taylor woman you introduced me to is gay and, I'm sorry, hooking up with the hot brunette who plays the sister?" Her little gay brain was about to explode.

"Yep. Aspen Wakefield. She's awful," her father said around a mouthful of his burger.

Bethany didn't care about that part. She didn't have any lesbian or bisexual friends, so mentions like this one registered big-time. For a moment, it was all she could think about. "Well, well."

"Maybe your friend can come on a tour of the set sometime."

She smiled, coming back to Reid. Wasn't an awful idea. "Yeah. Maybe. I'll feel it out. See if it's her thing."

He offered an exaggerated grimace. "Don't want to look weird or anything. God."

"Dad."

"What? You are so weird." He was enjoying this.

"Dad. Seriously. I can't with you." She shook her head, smiling.

"I can't with you either," he said, impersonating her tone and not doing a bad job. He flung his imaginary hair behind his shoulder. "Now let's get out of here before people see me with you."

"You're so crazy."

"Like a fox." He looked behind them as they exited the diner. "Fries get an A-plus."

"The blue everything gets a B-minus. What's this place called?" She craned her neck to note the sign.

"Blue Moon," he said followed by a cackle.

"I humbly stand down. Next week then?"

They bumped fists. "Done."

That night, Bethany took steps to feel more at home. She put some posters on her wall, a band she liked from back home, a photo of a red rotary telephone, and a quote from Kermit the Frog for the final touch. Next, she lined her bookshelves with a few worn-out paperbacks that served as friends. Juvenile to cling to seventh grade favorites? A little, but she had no remorse. Those books from her youth grounded her, kept her rooted in something good and true. The tattered pages were battle scars, the words her security blanket. She surveyed her work, pleased with the room's new vibe. Little pieces of her had been sewn together in an eclectic utopia.

She fell back onto the bed in satisfaction and grabbed her phone. It was a shock when she found messages already waiting. Well, well indeed. Reid.

What are you doing right now and where did you learn to tumble? God. I'm still shocked and impressed.

Bethany smiled to the empty room and started typing back. Her good night had just topped itself.

Just finished a little deco in my new room. And various gyms back to pre-K.

No cheer at all?

Never.

What? Criminal. Why not? You would have been lethal.

She chewed the side of her lip, trying to figure out how to explain to Reid that all that rah-rah teamwork and cheerleader camaraderie, plus the routines themselves, just weren't for her. She was a goner for the feeling that hit when she soared through the air, completely in control of her own body, turning, twisting, grabbing for height until she landed in a snap on her feet, victorious. That feeling of flying? That's what she was addicted to, and she worked at her tumbling passes until she perfected them. It had nothing to do with the larger sport of cheer, though.

She typed an attempt. *I just wanted to flip is all. Catch air. Work technique.*

You have. Clearly.

Thanks. How are you feeling? About your folks. Bethany knew it was a touchy subject, but something told her that Reid might need checking up on.

My dad hasn't stayed here all week. Each day=more of his stuff gone.

Bethany couldn't imagine her dad up and leaving her, even if there was another parent to hand her off to. Reid must be hurting. How could she not be? *So sorry this is happening.*

Thanks. You're the only person I've told.

Bethany sat up, mouth agape. Why in the world would Reid choose her to confide in? At the same time, she understood the importance of her role and accepted it without hesitation. She could be there for Reid. In fact, she would. Reid had been a friend to her, and she would return that favor. *I'm honored. But...why me?*

Dots.

No dots.

Dots again.

It was taking Reid forever to respond. Maybe she was searching for the answer herself.

They think I'm perfect. Why ruin it?

Interesting. *You don't care if I do?*

I'm a blank page to you. I love that.

Ah. The new girl effect.

Refreshing. You are. I like talking to you.

Her door opened and her dad stood there with two frosty mugs, looking like a beer commercial. "Made you a root beer in an icy glass." He stared at her phone. "Who are you talking to?"

"No one."

He had the audacity to look mortally wounded, tugging at her heart. "You lie to me now? Me, the dad? You lie to the dad?" Oh, he knew how to play his cards.

"No." She huffed. "Reid. A girl from school. I told you about her at dinner."

"She gave you the ride. Cheerleader. Future best friend forever."

"Right." She nodded to the mug, hurrying him along. "Root beer?"

"Right." He proudly placed his creation on her bedside table. "I'll give you your teenage privacy. Don't break the law."

"Glad you told me. Close one."

He closed the door, and she turned back to her phone excitedly.

Did I lose you? the message read. Then another one. *Anyway. Homework. See ya tomorrow.*

Dammit. She sighed, closed her laptop, and lay back in bed. Her wayward brain imagined Taylor Andrews staring lovingly into the eyes of Aspen Wakefield, and her stomach clenched. She imagined them kissing, and it made her turn over in bed. Next, it was Reid's face she saw staring at her with those big green eyes and perfect lips. The rest of her body flew to attention wanting things at a record-setting intensity. She sat up, hand on her forehead. Her cheeks were hot, her lower section uncomfortable.

"Yep. Okay. Got it. Definitely a cold shower kind of a night."

❖

"Two more and that water break is yours," Coach Rogan called as the cheerleaders took yet another lap around the football field. Reid was suffering, but the physical pain was actually a decent distraction from her reality, harsh and wildly off-kilter these days. Her father was packed and spent his first two nights at his new place, a concept that still hadn't settled into Reid's permanent understanding. Each time she remembered that her family was crumbling, it was like relearning the information for the first time, bitter and tough to digest. Mateo, feet away in the midst of football practice, wanted her promise she'd follow him to whatever school gave him the biggest offer. He also wanted to get into her pants. Both of which gave her pause.

"I don't understand why it matters which school it is," he'd said the day before. They'd sat in the grass in front of the school as the sun set, both their practices over for the day, her head in his lap as she gazed up at the sky. "We go together. They're all good schools. I'll play ball. You'll study. We get married after that. *Bam*. Life is great."

He made it sound so easy, but for her, it just wasn't. There was something huge in the way, blocking her progress. She couldn't say yes. "I don't know. I'm still not sure."

She swallowed as he traced her collarbone, each time getting a little closer to the neckline of her shirt, which was admittedly low today. She squirmed and sat up, killing his progress, knowing exactly where this would go. He sighed, put off again.

"What does it matter if we're together and we're getting our degrees?"

"But it matters, a lot. I'm looking for the right fit. You know? I want to do college right."

"Why?"

"Why?" She stared at him. "This is my future. It's an important four years. I can't let you just make that decision for me because you're fast with a ball."

"Fine, dude." He stood. "You go one place. I'll go another. We'll see each other every few weeks. Perfect. I love it."

She stared at him. Hard. "Can you not?"

He dropped his arms. "I'll drive you home." The disappointment dripped off Mateo, who was used to getting most things he wanted in life. Reid felt like she'd let him down. At the same time, how could she simply hand over such a big life choice to someone else? Even if that person was her person. But then again, *was he*? Was this what love felt like? Her head swam. She had doubts.

Hence, she ran around the track that Thursday. And hard. The burn in her throat was a nice distraction from the constant worry.

"She's trying to kill us," Ella said with what little breath she had. She stared down Coach Rogan, who eyed them from the metal bleachers. "We will die slowly while running in a circular pattern around a group of boys chasing a ball. I'm positive. I'm going to keel over dead, and all my deepest desires will be revealed in a dramatic reading from my journal at my funeral." She was routinely dramatic and sucked the other girls onto her train.

"I would never allow that to happen," Reid said around an intake of air. Her lungs burned, but she would not give in. "I'd burn that fucker for you first."

"God bless Reid," Ella called to the sky. "Keep her safe and happy and well supplied with matches, Lord."

"And she's not trying to kill us," Reid said in her calmest voice to the larger group.

"Prove it," Sunny said. "I puked twice yesterday. I get that regionals is not that far out, but shouldn't we try not to run ourselves into the ground first?"

Reid sighed. Her cocaptain sucked at motivational work these days. But Reid wasn't having it. "World class athletes keep their eyes on the prize. I'm not losing to Lancaster again this year. Rogan's trying to get us into shape so we don't fall down dead when full out run-throughs start next week." Running the entire competition routine at full intensity was when the real work began. United had taken the championship trophy home Reid's freshman year but had lost to Lancaster High the last two. This was their last opportunity. She couldn't imagine working so hard for something only to fall short just in time to graduate out of the program. Not after all the hard work they'd put in. Nope. Not on Reid's watch.

"Our fearless leader," Jennifer said, ripping her bouncy blond hair out of the ponytail holder as they completed their second-to-last lap. "I don't know how you do it, ReRe. I want to murder everyone. Regionals can take a back seat to my ass."

"Use it," Reid called back not just to Jennifer, but to her entire fourteen-girl squad. "Rip down the walls of mediocrity."

"Like Maria did?" Sunny asked. Reid's heart sank. That's right. They were down to thirteen now that they'd lost Maria Jimenez. Battered but determined, she'd pushed through practice when she should have called out. Now, she'd blown her ankle entirely, leaving them missing one of their best. The freshman alternate they'd tossed in to fill her spot was woefully young and lacking Maria's experience and ability. Now, they were forced to sacrifice difficulty level if they wanted a clean routine. That would hurt.

"Maybe don't use the rage that much," Reid amended. "But you know what I mean."

"All right. Let's get going!" Coach yelled. "Finish the lap, grab some water, and head to the gym. We have stunts to polish."

"Do we have our new mascot yet?" Sunny asked as they jogged to the gym. They'd turned in their scorecards, but the decision would be Coach Rogan's to make.

"We'll find out this afternoon." Reid plopped onto the floor and began to stretch. The others did the same. They had another ninety minutes of practice ahead of them, and no one wanted to get hurt. Not with competition looming. Not to mention the games they'd be cheering for starting tomorrow.

"Do you think it's going to be that Bethany chick? The one with the handsprings."

Reid bristled at Sunny's tone. "Why do you say it like that? The girl is crazy talented. She tore up the floor with her tumbling. Neither of us could have done anything like that, and in the Kenny costume? No chance."

"Sure, she had a good tryout, but can she back it up?" Sunny offered a dubious snort.

Reid didn't hesitate. Had they not seen the same girl flipping her ass off? "I know she can."

"Big talk," Sunny said and toweled off her face. "Now let's see if we can crush today's full out."

They didn't. They dropped the same stunt three times. Plus, two of their tumblers fell during passes, and the pyramid barely survived.

Rogan stared at the squad for a long time in silence. "I don't know what to say about today's practice." She tapped her forehead with her middle finger. "It was painful, and I think it's time for the hard talk. We have very little hope of taking regionals on the path we're on. Make that zero. Something has to change, or we're going to embarrass ourselves and the history of this program. If that's what you want, keep at it. Really." Rogan sounded like she was tired, frustrated, and held very little hope. Reid's senior year was off to a catastrophic start in more ways than one. "I know we lost Maria. But that just means you all have to pull together and work that much harder to make this thing work. As of now, I'm grasping at straws."

Reid closed her eyes. It didn't matter how hard they worked if the freshman replacement couldn't hit her stunts or make her tumbling passes. They were sunk. She wasn't one to point fingers, but she wasn't afraid to talk to Rogan privately. While her teammates packed up, she decided to do just that.

"Something you want to say, Reid?" Rogan asked as she took her seat behind her desk. The small office with trophies and photos of years gone by flanked the practice gym. She closed the door behind her, aiming to make this conversation discreet.

"Bethany Cahill."

Rogan took off her glasses, which always made her eyes seem so much smaller. "What?"

"From the mascot tryouts. Do you remember her?"

"Oh, right. Keep this between us, but she's a lock. She was fantastic. Give her the badger costume already."

"I don't think that's a good idea."

Rogan sat back. "And why is that? Do you know something I don't?"

"Only that we need her on the squad. Arabella isn't cutting it, and I don't blame her. She's green, and there's not enough time to get her into shape. Bethany can do this now. I know she can."

"Is that fair to the other girls to pull her onto the squad? Tryouts were last year."

"Times are desperate, though, right?"

Rogan seemed to struggle. "Does she even cheer? Would she want to?"

Reid couldn't imagine anyone not wanting to cheer, but she remembered Bethany's disdain for the sport and knew it might take some persuasion. "Leave that part to me. Provided you give me the go-ahead to recruit her."

"Fine, but keep this whole thing quiet until it's official. Deal?"

"Deal." This had been an easier sale than she'd anticipated.

"If she's interested, send her to me for a meeting."

Reid exhaled, pleased with herself for taking the leap. And hopefully, excited for Bethany, too. A good portion of the girls in school would give up their prom date for a spot on the cheerleading squad as evidenced by the size of the tryout last year.

All she had to do was convince Bethany Cahill that cheerleading was worth her time and talent. Couldn't be that hard.

❖

"I appreciate the offer, but I'm gonna go with no."

Bethany had been intrigued and, quite honestly, thrilled when Reid had asked to grab dinner at a cute little coffee shop in Venice Beach. Hell, they even had their own roaster, which was impressive to watch in action. The owner was kick-ass and knew what she was doing. But the last thing she expected was Reid attempting to pull her onto the actual cheerleading squad. Hell, no.

"Before you flat-out refuse, let's think this through." She had on that same perfume today that reminded Bethany of a spring meadow, an incredibly clichéd comparison. It was all she had. Reid made her a walking, talking rom-com character, and she wasn't even sure she minded.

Bethany took a sip from her coconut latte with a rock-and-roller cat on the cup. Reid seemed really intent on making her case, and quite frankly, the gold flecks in her otherwise green eyes really sparkled when she felt something strongly. Who was Bethany to get in the way of that sparkle? "If it will make you feel better."

"I know your initial thoughts on the sport. I respect them." Reid tented her fingers. They were feminine and her nails were a deep pink. It looked like she'd had them done recently. Another indicator of her physical perfection. "But think of it as another way to keep your tumbling sharp. Daily practice." Bethany chewed the inside of her lip and let Reid press on. She was having trouble listening but tried hard. "Plus, there's the fact that you're new to United. This would be a great way to get to know people. If you took the mascot position, no one would ever see your face or really know who you were."

"I'm actually okay with that. I just wanted to be involved in some way. Peripheral is fine with me. I promise."

"Well, it shouldn't be. There's a lot of status that comes with being a United cheerleader."

Bethany was beginning to understand that that kind of thing mattered to Reid. Her social position. Bethany had never had one of those. She valued friendships, and good times. A great slice of pie was high on the list. She cared less about how important other people thought she was. She just wanted to fit in. Make a friend or two to have fun with on weekends. "Why does status matter? Can't we all just be people together? Drink coffee?" She took a sip of hers to punctuate. She felt the cat would agree.

Reid blinked. "You have a really pretty smile." She seemed to forget her trajectory for a minute, which was fun.

"Thanks." She broadened it.

"But it's like you've never been to high school." She sighed, torn. "It's kind of nice. The way you think. Approach stuff."

Bethany leaned her chin in her hand and held Reid's gaze, a view she could stare at for hours. "You don't know what to do with me, do you?"

"Not a damn clue. You're a special unicorn. But a unicorn I desperately need if I want my senior year to live up to the hype." Reid thought for a moment, lost in her coffee cup. "What can I do to persuade you?" Reid raised her gaze and batted her lashes. It was a really good look, and Bethany got lost in her beauty for a moment. Perfect skin. Crazy curls that were just about wonderful. How did she know how to make her mascara subtle but so effective on those lashes? She was ogling. Embarrassing.

"Persuade me? Um…I'm not sure." Her brain was being weird. Not working to capacity. There were tons of pretty girls in the world. Why was this one wreaking such havoc? She had her suspicions.

"I like your hair today," Reid said. The look on her face pulled Bethany. It wasn't a line to butter her up. She could tell because Reid's voice had gone softer and she'd switched momentarily out of goal-driven presentation mode. Bethany had her hair partially pulled back and twisted into a rubber band. "Is it wavy naturally?"

"A little, yeah," she said. "I generally straighten it. Skipped that part today."

Reid nodded, stared, and then blinked as if pulling herself out of something. Bethany's stomach felt tight. Her cheeks heated. Reid straightened. "Anyway, I like it. Where was I? Damn." Look how red her cheeks got. That was something to behold.

"Somewhere around join the squad, you'll love it," Bethany supplied, amused.

"Right. Right. I think you should."

They hadn't broken eye contact in minutes. It was intoxicating. A firecracker they passed between them with an already lit fuse. Bethany was confident she wasn't imagining it either. "I'm listening. You have my full attention." She was harnessing her courage around Reid more and more. Each moment they spent together, either online or in person, put her more at ease. She was herself and not simply trying to impress. Kinda nice.

"Well, we'd get to spend more time together, too."

It was the most compelling argument Reid had made all day. She should have started there. Simply put, joining the cheerleading squad would mean hours each day with Reid. In her hemisphere, around her friends, her world. She couldn't discard it. She was already imagining the various scenarios. Water breaks as they joked off to the side during practice. Working toward a common goal. Laughing together under the hot stadium lights at Friday night games. Lifting each other in the air. Exchanging looks during tense moments. The sound of screeching brakes hit when she realized something that was pretty much a deal breaker.

"I don't have a car, and my dad has no plans to spring for one until I go off to college."

"Good thing I have one. And with my parents more focused on their own personal drama, they've been incredibly liberal with gas money. Anything to keep Alice and me happy."

"Are you offering to shuttle me around?"

"Call me Jeeves."

"Doesn't do you justice." Yeah, she'd gone and said that.

Reid's lips parted before a smile blossomed. "See? You. Me. This could be fun."

Then the reality of what Bethany was actually agreeing to hit, and the fantasy dimmed. Hours of commitment. A room full of competitive girls. Some of them mean. Hair. Skirts. Makeup. Enthusiasm. All of those things lived wildly outside Bethany's comfort zone. Don't even get her started on the sore muscles she'd be signing up for. "I don't know."

"Do it for me. Your new pal." Reid widened her eyes and brought out what could only be described as her puppy dog face. Not fair. How could she not crumble like a cookie in the literal face of such gorgeous persuasion? She wouldn't be the first person who did something ridiculous for a pretty girl.

"Okay."

Reid's mouth fell open. "Really? You'll do it?"

She was terrified and excited by the road ahead, but it felt like the kind of risk that just might pay off. "I think I'm a damned cheerleader."

Reid touched her cardboard cup to Bethany's. "This is an important moment. We're going to look back on this one day and say, *Remember that moment?*"

Bethany was confident she was right. This was a plot point on her journey she hadn't seen coming. "Where do I pick up my miniskirt?"

Reid grabbed her car keys and dangled them. "Follow me."

She didn't have to ask twice. The truth was that Bethany would have followed Reid Thatcher anywhere.

CHAPTER FOUR

Now

Reid hadn't been this nervous in years. She bit her bottom lip and watched the diners at the surrounding tables. A mixture, really. An older couple, who ate in silence using only the best manners. Two women who overlapped their speech, tossing in bouts of raucous laughter, unaware of their volume, and clearly having the best time. A shy, modest-looking couple who didn't eat a lot, stealing glances at each other. Likely a first date.

She sipped from her water, not really wanting any, just something to do as she waited for Bethany to arrive. *God. Bethany.* This was actually happening. Her hand trembled slightly. She placed it in her lap and covered it with the other one.

"Anything for you while you wait?" the friendly server asked. She had three earrings in one ear and only one in the other. Why was she noticing the tiniest details?

"No, thank you. My friend shouldn't be long."

Her seat near the window allowed her a helpful vantage point, a clear glimpse of the walkway leading to the restaurant's entrance. She'd checked it eight times. On the ninth, her breath caught because Bethany, looking stunning in a black buttoned peacoat and red plaid scarf, was hurrying up the walk. She hated to be late. Nothing had changed in that department. She paused at the door, and Reid wondered if she was about to bail on the whole meetup entirely. After all, she'd just barged into Bethany's life after all these years and asked her to dinner. She watched the worry crease Bethany's forehead, the slight purse of her lips, before she took a slow, deep breath and walked inside.

Same, Beth. Same.

The server pointed in Reid's direction, and Bethany followed her gaze, landing on Reid. A soft but guarded smile. That was something. But Beth had always had manners.

"You came," Reid said, standing.

"Yep. Here I am."

For a few moments, they just took each other in. It wasn't awkward or strange. Almost as if they'd silently agreed that this was a necessary exchange after all this time. They were in the same space again, breathing in the same air, and it required a certain amount of measure and time.

"Let's sit," Reid said, doing her very best to behave normally, when there was nothing mundane about tonight. She'd imagined a meeting like this one a million different times under a myriad of circumstances. Actually experiencing it hovered somewhere between surreal and amazing.

"Can I bring you something to drink?" the eagle-eyed server with four earrings asked.

"Wine," Bethany said.

"Is there a wine list?" Reid asked at the exact same time.

That coaxed a laugh from both of them.

"Tell you what," Reid said, studying Bethany. "How about two glasses of the house red?"

"Perfect," Bethany said. And their server was off. It was so odd seeing Bethany the adult sitting before her, who looked so much like the teenage version but also not. Her face seemed a tad thinner, and she came with a very noticeable confidence that Reid had only glimpsed from younger Bethany in clinch moments.

"You're a wine drinker," Reid said. "I wasn't sure."

"Well, I was underage the last time you saw me and hadn't exactly developed a palate yet. But I enjoy a good pinot. A dry merlot. Spicy zins are a favorite."

"So much to learn." She shook her head. "We were just kids yesterday, and now you have a palate."

"Kids? Try babies."

But they hadn't been. Not really. The feelings, the very real emotions they'd shared were anything but juvenile, and the look on Bethany's face told Reid that she agreed. "So...what's new?" Reid asked. It was a joke, but also not. There was so much that she didn't know about Bethany's life, who she'd become.

"Well, I married a nice man and had four kids."

Reid frowned. It didn't fit. She waited.

"Kidding," Bethany said. "But the look on your face was worth it."

Reid took a sip from the newly arrived wine. "I was trying to work that one out, fairly sure there was a punchline coming." She held up her glass. "You're in luck. Spicy. I also hear their bread is baked fresh and served hot."

"Hazel's is known for it." Bethany tried the wine but gave nothing away. "The truth is that I'm married to my job. It's a lot of work to get a practice off the ground. We're young and working to stay above water."

"You have partners?"

"Two. They're amazing, but the workload is oppressive. Wouldn't change it, though. I love my patients."

"You always wanted to go into medicine. But it was always going to be surgery. You changed your mind."

Bethany nodded, giving the menu a quick glance. She seemed to already know what to order. "People grow. Change. But you can't always predict where life will take you. It wasn't meant to be, and I've made peace with that. Not *everything* works out." The implication was clear. *They* hadn't. They'd been so sure of forever. It was still a bit startling that someone who was her everything was quickly gone from her life. "What about you?"

"I teach American Lit to freshmen at Chapman. Newly, as you know, after a four-year stint at Sacramento State while I finished up my PhD. Hoping for tenure at some point down the road, but there are many dues to pay first. It's going to take some time. I'd like to get back to coaching club cheer on the side now that I'm no longer a student. I did a lot of that in my midtwenties."

Bethany shook her head. "Of course you did. You love a good pyramid." The server returned, and they ordered their food. A sirloin salad for Bethany. The shrimp in white wine sauce for Reid.

"You should see them now, Beth. It's insane what these young girls are capable of." She held up a finger. "They have nothing on you, though. But the rest of us? They'd tumble us under the table."

"I'm afraid I've said good-bye to my tumbling days. Do you know how many broken bones I treat for that stuff? Eye-opening."

It made her a little sad, Bethany leaving it all behind. But what use did a grown woman have for a tumbling pass? "Of course I do. But I imagine you're really good at your job." She glanced down at the white tablecloth and the dot of wine that marred its surface before meeting Bethany's gaze. "You were always good at everything."

A beat. She held eye contact. Reid knew the floor was hers. She'd called this meeting and should probably get to why.

"I was hoping to try to understand. So many unanswered questions from back then."

Bethany sipped her wine, noticeably more uncomfortable now. "Understand what? What happened with us? We broke up." Either from discomfort or disinterest, Bethany shrugged it off like it was kid's stuff. It wasn't. Not to Reid. "I think we were just on two different paths."

"It didn't feel like it. We hit a bump in the road. I screwed up, but it's hard to imagine that what I did, what I said, was that unforgivable. And I've spent a lot of years wondering if there was more to it."

Bethany sighed. "Is that why you came to my office? To get mired down in the past?" She smiled. "I have an idea. Let's not. Let's catch up, enjoy spending a meal together, and—"

"Go back to our respective corners of the world and forget this ever happened? Is that what you'd prefer?"

"Maybe." She nodded, her expressive eyes searching for how to navigate this situation. "I don't know. This has all been very over-whelming."

Reid deflated. Sharing the same space with Bethany again really did bring it all careening back. The connection, the emotion, the rush of excitement. All of it. She felt it now. Today. They were still tethered in so many ways. But she didn't want to push, and that's what this felt like. "Okay. If you don't want to talk about the past, we won't." She lifted her shoulders, searching for a consolation. "Tell me everything that's happened since. I really want to know."

Bethany seemed to relax. "I live just outside LA. I like coffee in the morning. In the afternoon. Sometimes the evening."

"Remember that amazing spot in Venice Beach? The roaster. The amazing lattes." She remembered staring into Bethany's gorgeous blue eyes and dreaming about everything ahead. It had felt like the sky was their limit.

"It's still open. I hit it up on occasion."

"Really? And now I have to. Okay, so coffee's covered. What about the bigger stuff? You're not married with four kids. But are you married at all? Have you been?"

She shook her head. "Never really got around to that. Someday. I date. Well, I try to." She put down her glass. "I plan to. There wasn't a lot of time in med school, and I never really got out of that habit."

"The habit of skipping over a personal life?" Reid asked. Bethany's eyes were still so very blue, just like at the coffee shop, almost turquoise in their luminance. They'd always been her most striking feature. Reid had never forgotten those eyes. Her memory of them had been spot-on.

"Yeah, that's pretty accurate. I'd like a more active one. It's on the list for someday soon. What about you?"

"Couple of serious relationships. I almost got married."

"Let me guess. Mateo?"

Reid frowned. "No. Mateo and I...we're in touch, but no. I came out officially at twenty and never looked back." She was startled to hear that Bethany had imagined her with Mateo all these years. "Her name was Kelly and she was great in so many ways. We tried really hard. It just didn't work out."

Bethany stared at her glass. Took another sip. A much bigger one this time. "How come? If she was great." It was hard for her to ask the question. That much was clear.

"It's complicated."

"Ah."

They stared at each other. Reid understood that she might never see Bethany again. There was no reason to hold back. "Let me just be honest. She wasn't you."

Bethany's lips parted. She eased a strand of hair behind an ear. It was just long enough to fit. "Reid."

"Beth."

Her eyes widened. "No one really calls me Beth."

"I do."

"Yes." Her voice went soft. "I remember."

"Good. Then I'm not the only one who does. I was beginning to wonder." It was her instinct to reach out and take Bethany's hand, or cover it with her own. Touch her in some way. After all this time, that reflex was very much intact and flaring, which spoke to the potency of their link. She found it jarring and eye-opening. *Well, well.* After years of feeling like she was limping along, the burst of life in the center of her chest was back like food to the starving. She couldn't stop looking at Bethany, remembering. How she longed to go back there and do it all over again. Maybe this time with a different ending. Was that really so crazy, or was it the wine taking hold?

Their food arrived, and they made small talk, which helped quell the tension and ease them off the heavier topics.

"So, tell me about Alice," Bethany said.

Reid nodded, dabbed her mouth with the cloth napkin. "She's great. Currently single, but I think she likes it that way. A personal trainer, which, let's be honest, we probably all saw coming. I've never known anyone who enjoys running as much as Al."

"Did she tell you we ran into each other a couple of years ago?"

Reid paused, floored, because no, Alice had certainly not mentioned that. How weird. "What? Really?"

Bethany nodded. "I was in line at a deli not far from a conference I was attending, and out of nowhere, there she was. We only chatted for a moment. I had to get back."

Reid couldn't believe her sister hadn't mentioned something that she understood would matter to Reid. She sighed. Except Alice knew what a horrific time Reid had had after Bethany. She might have buried the information on purpose. "I can't believe she never said anything."

The smile on Bethany's lips dimmed. She'd always been so intuitive. "She probably just forgot." A lull hit.

Finally, Reid lowered the curtain. "I had a hard time when we were over."

Bethany frowned. "Why would *you*—" She waved it away. "We said we wouldn't."

"Right. Right."

After they ate, Reid paid the bill, her treat, and they stood.

"It was good to see you again. I'd be lying if I said I hadn't been somewhat curious," Bethany said. "Still you, just all grown up."

Bethany's gaze moved across her face, memorizing, and Reid felt the goose bumps immediately.

"You might say no, but I'd love to see you again. Hear more about medical school. The years I missed. How you're doing, your dad."

Bethany shifted. "Um…I don't know." It wasn't a declaration. She honestly seemed unsure which road to take.

"Tell you what." Reid adjusted the shoulder strap on her bag. "Think about it. It's just conversation. I don't plan to accost you. What can it hurt, right?"

She pursed her lips, which was Bethany for lost in thought. "Okay. Well, I better get back to the office. A mountain of paperwork is waiting for me. But thanks for dinner. I might not have gotten any otherwise."

The formality was back in place almost like a pail of cold water had been dropped on the conversation, separating them on purpose. She could handle it. If it's what Bethany needed. Wanted. "Enjoy the rest of your night." Her heart tugged as she watched Bethany walk to her car. Reid had left a part of her heart with Bethany once upon a time, and for a few moments as they sat across from each other, she'd felt whole again.

Reid didn't expect to hear from Bethany.

But that didn't mean she couldn't hope, at least just a little bit. From within the invisible walls of her bland existence, what did she have to lose? She kept her phone close over the next few days, picking it up quickly and checking for messages if she was away from it for too long. None arrived. The writing on the wall was beginning to take shape. Bethany Cahill would remain part of her past, forever and always.

CHAPTER FIVE

After being pulled into the force field that was Reid Thatcher, Bethany was anxious for the date she'd set up, confident it was just the salve she needed to move herself forward. Reset the board. Get Reid and her perfect voice and soft hair out of her mind for good.

She selected one of those coffee shops with the myriad of board games and books along the wall for the grabbing. Maybe if things went well, they could stay a little longer, explore the place. Maybe the woman played chess and could teach her a move or two. She imagined them laughing, growing more comfortable with each other.

An hour later and Bethany had sidelined the fantasy entirely.

"What do you call it?" Bethany's date asked, her fingers searching for an imaginary word in the space next to her long auburn hair. She'd used that phrase and searched the air for a word five times now, and they'd only been on their date for thirty-seven minutes.

"A coincidence?" Bethany offered, not really loving the find-a-word game but aiming for polite.

"No, no." Helene, the flight attendant, shook her head, pursed her lips, and thought hard. She had just told an elaborate story about meeting her cat on a street corner, a story they'd jumped to well in advance of even the basics about Helene. Bethany still knew nothing about her job, her hobbies, her family, or even what brought her to the dating site. She knew everything there was to know about meeting Hector the cat, however. Right down to what his little cat breath smelled like. She pointed at Bethany in victory. "Kismet. That's what it is. Kismet brought Hector and me together. He's my *furever* cat. Get it?"

"Yes. I love cats. That's a sweet story." Bethany nodded and smiled. "I do believe in that kind of thing. Fate can certainly intervene when you least expect it."

"Has it happened to you? Kismet with a cat? It's the most wonderful thing."

"Not with a cat. No." She tried not to think about her random grocery store run-in with Reid. That wasn't fate assisting. If anything, it was a mean joke designed to shake up her otherwise low-key existence. Especially since she hadn't been able to get back to her life as scheduled since that moment, thinking about the encounter, the dinner, and all of the memories from when she was seventeen and eighteen. It's like Reid had been given a key to her brain and let herself in whenever she pleased. The most potent, wonderful year of her life had come roaring back into the forefront of her everything. She remembered the feelings, the passion, the overwhelming tension and lust, the quiet moments, the wonder of falling in love and just knowing it was going to last a lifetime. Until it didn't. Because she also remembered the way it felt to have her heart ripped out of her chest and everything she lost after the fact.

Helene met her gaze. "Ever?"

"Fate? No, I don't think it's happened to me."

Helene nodded and pushed her long straight hair behind her ears and adjusted the spaghetti strap that had slipped from her shoulder. "That's okay. Maybe it's fate at work right this very second. I always said I would marry a doctor one day. Perhaps this is my dream come true right in front of me. What kind of medicine, Dr. Cahill?" Her voice dropped about three octaves on that last sentence, which pulled an eyebrow from Bethany.

"Oh. Okay. I'm a primary care provider for individuals and families."

"Do you ever do surgery like on *Grey's Anatomy*? I love those doctors. I know everything about them. Quiz me if you want."

"Maybe later. And I don't do surgery. No."

"That's okay. We need doctors like you. You're…what do you call it?" She searched the air with her fingers. Again. "Essential?"

"We try to be there for our patients."

"No, no." She snapped her fingers. "Necessary." She snapped them again. "No, no! Vital! That's you, Dr. Cahill." She seemed pleased.

"Wanna go back to my place now? I might need you to take my medical history if you catch my meaning. Happy to disrobe." She followed that up with a saucy wink.

Bethany sighed, realizing that the dating world was certainly an interesting place full of all types. "Tempting. But I think I might have to take a rain check."

"Rain is so sexy. Don't you think? We could dance in it sometime."

"Um, about that." She finished her coffee in one long gulp. "It was so nice meeting you, and I've had a great time today, but as for romance, I don't think this is going to work out."

"Oh, I love a chase."

Bethany stood. "I'm sure you're great at it, but please don't chase me."

"Call me," Helene said.

"Probably not, though."

"Tomorrow's good. Take care, sexy Dr. Cahill."

Holy Mother of Cadbury. Bethany couldn't get out of there fast enough.

❖

With her forearms leaning against the railing separating the spectators from the students, Reid watched as one girl after the other took a turn executing a run into a roundoff back handspring. It wasn't the easiest combination for girls as young as these. Ten, maybe eleven-year-olds. Impressive. Each one of them. This was Sunny's advanced group. "They're really great, Sun. Dark ponytail is killing it."

Sunny nodded from her spot next to Reid. Flipping Out was a successful tumbling gym that Sunny Lynch operated. Under Sunny's management and expert coaching, the waiting list for classes continued to grow.

It was a mixed bag, seeing her again, her childhood friend with whom she'd cultivated years of wonderful memories from the first grade on, but also someone who'd negatively influenced her, and who'd leveled judgment when Reid needed a friend. It was more than just Bethany she needed to square things up with. Sunny felt like a basket of unfinished business that she didn't know what to do with. Maybe this visit was fact-finding in nature. Sure, she was interested in coaching again and used that to arrange this meetup, but she was also curious about the person who'd made life unnecessarily difficult.

"It must have been, what? Four years since we grabbed that drink in Sacramento?"

"I think you're right. I'd just handed in my grades and could kick back."

"Who would have imagined you'd jump to the teacher side of things. I'd pretend to be offended, but here I am, a coach."

"Who can hardly talk."

Sunny wore blue joggers and a matching blue zip up. Her long dark ponytail hadn't budged since high school, which was a little sad. "Over there. Mariah Tam. She's my superstar. Works around the clock and never gives an inch. She has a lot more to learn, but she's going to teach 'em all a lesson at competition this spring."

Reid straightened. "Wow. A lot of parental support?"

"Some. Family and friends step in, too. Oh, and you know the Tuesday-Thursday pickup. The girl from United."

"More specifically?"

"You know, what's her name? From our senior year squad. You used to run around with her. The one we pulled in last minute when Maria Jimenez went down with an injury?"

Reid was frozen. "Bethany Cahill."

Sunny nodded. "Yes. Thank you. That's the one. Bethany. She used to have a massive chip on her shoulder but seems much nicer now. I don't know. I think she works with Mariah's mom."

"Huh. Interesting." Reid tapped her lips, prepared to enjoy the next few moments. "We *were* a thing back then. In high school. You were right about that part all along."

"Right about what now? Avery, you have to extend your body as you rotate," Sunny called, her hands cupping her mouth. "Get back in line and try it again. Don't give me that face." She then turned to Reid, confused. "What does that mean? Honestly, my memory is awful. You were together how?"

"Romantically. And sexually if you want to get right down to it." There was nothing to hide. She liked who she was now and owned the journey that had gotten her here.

"What? No." Sunny frowned. "Huh. Interesting."

"Oh, I think you knew. You didn't like it. Pushed me back to Mateo. Remember?"

Sunny frowned. "No. I highly doubt that. I think you have your friends confused."

"Do I?" She kept her tone light. She wasn't here to confront anyone, but she did need to start standing up for herself. Better late than never.

"So to summarize, you knew you liked girls back then and were getting it on behind the bleachers with this Bethany chick." Sunny looked like she'd stumbled upon the most amusing gossip she'd ever heard.

"With a little more finesse, I would hope."

"You get yours, Reid. Nice. All I remember was you and Mateo sucking face at those gatherings on Venice Beach. Man, you two were hot."

That would be all Sunny remembered. It was all she wanted to see. Reid and Mateo, everyone's favorite high school couple. They'd even been voted as much by the student body when they weren't even together. "There's more to life than a pretty picture, Sunny."

Sunny nodded. "If you say so. Not that the whole gay thing doesn't work for you. Suzanne! Pull your stomach tight." Sunny inclined her head to the top of the entrance to the bleachers. "You realize she just walked in, right? This is too good. Have you two seen each other since you've been back?"

"Um. Yeah. We have." Reid squeezed the railing. Why hadn't she realized Bethany would be showing up? Sunny had just explained that she picked up Mariah after practice, which by the clock's reporting would be in mere minutes, on a Tuesday no less.

Because she had no willpower, she turned to the gym door and gave herself away. Bethany, who now likely thought she was an out-of-control stalker, had just taken a seat on the bottom of the shiny wooden bleachers. She was wearing her scrubs, which Reid had decided was too good a look to be allowed. The expression on her face was dialed to curious as she watched Reid across the room. Reid held up a hand and offered a wave. Sunny leaned in. "Go talk to her. Reminisce about old times, and get naked together. Why not? Everyone's still young. I've never seen Bethany with anyone."

"Because she's single," Reid said quietly.

"Even better for you."

"I'm not sure she's my biggest fan."

"Don't those things just make the sex all the hotter? Is it the same for women? Penelope Ann, you're killing me with flimsy arms!" She turned to Reid. "I better go. They're finishing up the reps. If you're interested in picking up that Tuesday class next session, let me know."

"Will do. It was nice to see you, Sun." Was it, though?

"Back atcha. Looking forward to more."

Reid partially regretted putting her feelers out with Sunny. Time would tell whether reconnecting had been a wise move or not. There were other gyms in town. For now, she turned her focus to Bethany, deciding to say a quick hello. She'd already ambushed her at her clinic, practically forced her to dinner, and left Bethany with her card at the grocery store. Her phone hadn't rung or buzzed or danced a jig once. That was a clear sign Bethany wasn't interested in reconnecting any further. She probably had enough friends and was content with how things were left. Reid was becoming a bother. Her goal was to simply say hello, explain her presence, and get the hell out of there before making a bigger fool of herself.

"You must be here to hang with Sunny," Bethany said knowingly as Reid approached. Oh, thank God. She'd already realized the legitimate truth.

"I wasn't sure if you'd recognize her." She made a point not to sit. She'd give Bethany her space and resist lingering. "She looks entirely different."

They shared a laugh because nothing about Sunny had changed except for the lines on her face, accentuated by all the screaming she did. "Unfortunately, I'd know her anywhere."

Reid gestured to Mariah. "Sunny told me you shuttle her home after practice. Because Sunny, unfortunately, runs the best gym in town, and Mariah wants the best. How do you know her? She's good."

"Her mom is my best friend, Veronica. She handles our late patients on Tuesdays and Thursdays at the clinic, so I volunteered to drive Mariah home on those. Plus, I like to watch a few minutes of practice."

"That's really nice of you. I bet you have some great tips." Reid glanced at the exit, trying not to linger even if she wanted to. "I'm gonna get out of here."

"Oh." Bethany looked a little sad about it. Was that possible? Had she misjudged? "You don't want to watch for a little while? You can meet Mariah."

What was happening? Her heart rate leaped. "I'd love to." She didn't hesitate. "If that's okay with you."

"Yeah. Of course." She shifted down the bench, leaving a spot for Reid.

They sat together, side-by-side, watching the end of class. Sunny had the group spotting each other on assisted back tucks, an advanced skill for kids this age. "Man, this place takes me back. The sounds, the terminology, the enthusiasm, even the smell."

"Like chalk and sweat," Bethany said, nodding.

"I'll never forget you tearing up the floor in the mascot costume. I still can't believe your talent."

"That should be past tense." She laughed. "I think they'd frown on roundoff back handspring combos in the hallway at the clinic." She smiled, and a little part of Reid sighed with joy. Bethany's smiles were always authentic. She wasn't the kind of person who handed them out just for the sake of camaraderie. Seeing one now helped her breathe a little more evenly.

"Fair enough, but it could be a fun way to enter the exam room." They watched Sunny bring the girls into a final huddle. "I hope I didn't crash your day. Running into an ex is probably not everyone's cup of tea, which I don't even drink."

"Are we exes?" Bethany seemed surprised she'd said it. Reid turned over the question, caught off guard herself.

"Yes. We were together." A pause. "Right?"

"We were. I didn't know if you agreed." Bethany turned her attention back to the action. "I went on a date this week."

"Oh?" That snagged Reid's attention like a bird dog who heard a shot. She tried to imagine an adult Bethany on an actual date, and it made everything feel uncharacteristically warm. She resisted the urge to touch her neck to see if the heat was palpable from the outside. "How did that go?" Was it awful that she wished for a downright disaster?

"Well, I wish I could say incredibly well, but we spent most of the time searching for the right words to describe her cat."

"Vague." She quirked her head. "Also, weird."

"It honestly felt like both. The dating world is a complicated place. Do you date much? Since Kelly, I mean."

"Some. I go through spurts of fully committing and other times when I sit happily on the sidelines. Watch all the other saps try and figure it out first." She shook her head. "My dad is more successful. Can you believe that?"

"So I take it he never married that woman he moved out for?"

"God, no. They ended a year later, and he's been a serial dater since. My mom settled down with a new husband about five years ago. She told me to keep searching. That she's out there somewhere."

Practice was over, and they stood as the girls trotted over to the sidelines to retrieve their belongings. "You mentioned you came out in college. That would have been a pretty big deal for you."

"Right. In college. I practically took out an ad."

Bethany's eyebrows rose. Mariah was on her way over. "I think I need to hear the rest of the story."

Interesting. Where was this going? "Anytime you want."

"We could grab a drink or coffee soon. I'll text you."

Well, blow her over. This had taken a turn she hadn't expected. "Sounds good."

"Hey," Mariah said, slamming her body into Bethany and slinging an arm around her waist. "Did you see my back tuck? It's getting there."

"It's amazing. Soon you'll be doing them freestanding on your own."

Mariah hopped once. "I'm ready. Hi," she said, smiling up at Reid.

"Hi, there. I'm Reid. I'm an old friend of Bethany's."

"She was the head cheerleader at my high school with Miss Sunny."

Mariah's eyes went large as if JoJo Siwa had just danced her way into the gym. "Wow. Nice to meet you. Really?"

Reid nodded. "But Bethany was on the squad, too."

"But she wasn't captain. I want to be in charge."

Bethany shrugged. "See? Everybody loves the head cheerleader. I wasn't alone."

Reid's mouth fell open both in jest and authenticity. She gave

Mariah's shoulder a squeeze. "Well, you looked great out there. Love the tenacity. Maybe I'll see you again the next time I visit."

"Cool. Yes!" She looked up at Bethany as if to make sure she'd heard about this update.

Bethany did her best hugely impressed look. "It's your lucky day, kid." She met Reid's eyes. "I'll message you."

"Okay," Reid said quietly. Their gazes lingered for an extra second or two, in a moment that left Reid's head spinning. She blared the radio on the way home, playing back the moment over and over again, daring to wonder about what might be possible. Her Bethany moments had always been charged—why would now be any different? This afternoon had her a little turned around, excited, and questioning, well, everything. She checked the clock. After-school activities would be getting out shortly, and she had to make a quick pickup on her way home.

CHAPTER SIX

Something interesting happened. Seeing Reid at the tumbling gym, in an environment that was so very them, had loosened something important in Bethany's chest. Before she knew it, she was inviting Reid out. She hadn't planned it at all. Yet it had felt like the most natural thing in the world between those walls. Even the presence of Sunny Lynch couldn't stop her from taking that little leap. Later that night, she took another.

"Why the hell not?" she murmured. She'd had a beer after their clinic's patient rounds at the hospital that night and hit the call button. She was clearly out of control and embracing it.

"Bethany?"

"Surprise."

"It really is."

"I hope it's not too late." Not quite ten. Was that an acceptable call time? She was really bad at this stuff. No practice. She exhaled to steady herself and wandered around her living room to kill the extra energy. Maybe jumping jacks would help.

"Not for me. Just finished grading papers. Was about to have a glass of red. Want one?"

"I killed a beer. Made me brave."

"Aha. So that's what I owe the pleasure to."

"It's strange to think about you as someone's teacher. I'm confident you're great at it. Do you lecture?"

"I lecture a lot."

Dreamy sigh. Bethany held it back. They talked more about their day. Their jobs. The eighty-two-year-old woman who told Bethany that afternoon that the paint colors in the office were offensive, but did she want to come to her house for Sunday lunch?

"I need more clinic stories!" Reid said through laughter. Bethany could imagine her face. The way she dabbed her eyes when she laughed so hard that tears formed. It used to have been a goal of hers to inspire that kind of laughter.

The more they talked, the more stories they told, the more it felt like those nights they'd killed on the phone for hours growing up. It was apparently that easy to fall back in with someone who knew you so well. Like a tall glass of cold water to a dry throat.

The next night, as Bethany thumbed through her mail, her phone rang. She expected her answering service with a question from a patient, or her dad with an awful joke. But it was Reid, and that made her jump in happiness.

"Is this a prank call?" she asked after she slid onto the line.

"Not a chance. I wanted to say hello."

"You picked the perfect moment. My electric bill is up by sixty dollars and I need somebody to rant to."

"You live in a fancy house, don't you?"

Bethany looked around at the two-story living room with the automatic shades. "Are you spying on me?"

"Were you hoping I was?"

"You can't answer a question with a question."

They spent the next ninety minutes going back and forth. Banter. Sincerity. Hints of flirtation without actually going there. But something was simmering on low…just waiting. Reid and their interactions were both terrifying and exhilarating. Yet she looked forward to hearing from her.

Over the next week and a half, their calls became a regular evening occurrence. They happened often enough that they now breezed past any potential awkwardness. Bethany also thought that Reid's voice on the phone made the exchanges a lot less daunting. She wasn't faced with the sparkling green eyes that stole her ability to think. They were getting closer, but from a distance. There was safety in that.

"What about that coffee you promised me not long ago?" Reid asked, late into one of their conversations. Alarm bells. Bethany *had* offered up a get-together back at the gym. That was before she'd nestled into the comfort of their faceless late-night conversations that had her wanting, craving, and wondering about so many Reid-related things. When she went to sleep each night, she was already reminiscing about her favorite parts of their conversation. If they got together, that snap, crackle, and pop on the phone was surely going to burst to life. Then what? There was so much to sort through from years ago. It was surely going to need their attention at some point, and was she really willing and equipped to go there? They'd kept things light on the phone on purpose.

When she didn't answer right away, Reid pushed on. Her voice was less playful than it had been. They were treading into more serious territory. Cinderella's midnight approached. "I think we have a lot to talk through, don't you? I know I have questions. Maybe you do, too." That part alone made her sweat. But didn't she owe it to Reid at this point? "And maybe we could enjoy each other's company over a cup of joe at the same time. In person. What do you say?"

Dangerous. Like walking into a burning building. "Okay. Let's do it."

She could almost hear Reid grinning into the phone. "I know the perfect place."

CHAPTER SEVEN

Why was her hair giving her hell on a night when she actually cared? She slammed her brush onto the counter in a huff. Bethany stared at herself in the mirror that hung above her dresser. Her dark hair, now shorter than she'd worn it in high school, looked too much like she'd styled it when she just really wanted that happy accident look. Why couldn't she have the happy accident look? She ran her fingers through it, huffed, and then put on her glasses, which were only needed for driving. She stared at herself with them, and then without, opting for without. No, with. Then, finally, settling on without.

Here's the thing. She wasn't an insecure person. She also rarely cared about how other people perceived her appearance. She did her best to look nice and took the days as they came, but getting together with Reid was different, and she cursed herself for caring about how her damned hair looked.

"Who are you anyway?" she asked her reflection.

She and Reid had settled on a time and place. It was still against her better judgment, but she had to acknowledge at some point that she was vulnerable to the feelings that swirled when she thought about Reid.

She'd logged on to the fish site to see about maybe going on a second date, a much-needed distraction from Reid and the phone calls, but she wound up scrolling for far too long because her ideas of love were all tied to Reid. Too hard to match. That was something she needed to accept. She was. She'd gone to therapy once upon a time to work on forgiveness and acceptance of the cards she'd been dealt.

She flexed her fingers. Her therapist, Joan, would be proud of her for understanding that Reid was the bar. Acknowledging it was so much easier than fighting. So her only option was to face the most terrifying, exciting, anger-inducing person she could imagine and see about either obtaining some closure, which would free her to live life as scheduled— another therapy gem—or dip a toe in the Reid Pond. And not just on the phone, which had her shaking in her own shoes with terror and hope.

When she arrived at The Cat's Pajamas, Reid was sitting outside on the hood of her red Nissan, which pulled Bethany up short. It was an image she'd seen before. Different car. Same girl. This time a woman. Even more sexy than before. Curly light brown hair lifted by the wind, blown into her eyes and out again. Damn. This was why phones were better. What was she supposed to do with this woman, all grown up and sure of herself? She knew what she *wanted* to do right on that very car but tamped it down in the name of civilization.

"You're late," Reid said as she approached. No move to get off the car. Good. She looked amazing there. Why would she ever move from that spot?

"LA traffic. I continue to underestimate its considerable power."

A soft smile. "Forgiven. It's good to actually see your face. Not that I don't love your voice."

"It's good to see you, too. Too good." Okay, that was honest. She sighed. "What are we doing, Reid?" She held out her arms and dropped them with a frustrated laugh. It was perhaps the most straight-from-the-heart sentence she'd uttered since they'd seen each other at the grocery store. Everything else had come from behind her carefully guarded walls. This was her peeking out from behind them, acknowledging that she was out of her depth, and maybe that was okay.

"I don't think either of us really knows." Reid hopped down. "But I'd like to do a little rehashing. I know it's your favorite, but I've lived for years with a lot of questions. Can we do that?"

Bethany nodded as the daunting task loomed. She didn't think much about those days on purpose. Too much to sort through. She looked up at The Cat's Pajamas. "This seems like the place to start."

Reid followed her gaze. "Where I first persuaded you to join the cheerleading squad. You looked so good that day." She exhaled slowly and gave her head a shake. "I think it was the first time I truly started to acknowledge my crush."

"I had no idea." She stared, dumbstruck. If she'd known that day, she could have been blown over with a feather. "I still can't believe I said yes to your crazy request. A cheerleader? Me?" She grinned. "I would have run into traffic if you'd asked me with those eyes and a pretty please. I was ahead of you. I was already hooked."

"And in that moment, I had zero idea. I was admittedly a little behind."

"Well, you were still figuring yourself out. I knew who I was."

"See? Good at everything. What can I get you? I'm buying," Reid asked as they moved inside. She paused and looked around the interior of the coffee shop. "Wow. It's been updated, but the style is still…loud, bright, and—"

"Exactly the same. I appreciate that. I can count on that cat on the wall to wake up every day, skip getting dressed, and play his guitar. The constant is comforting."

"Dr. Cahill, what up? Shall I make up your dry cappuccino?"

Reid shook her head. "You're here, too! Bethany, she's here."

Bethany grinned. "Hey, Autumn. I brought my friend Reid from long ago. I'd love a dry cap. How are the little ones?"

"Tearing it up in preschool. They put them in separate classes to manage the madness."

Reid laughed. "My kind of kids."

"Right?" She laughed along with them. "We love that pediatrician you recommended. Dr. Baker? Amazing. She caught Will's ear infection before it even got off the ground this time."

"She's the best." She turned to Reid, who was listening to the conversation eagerly. "What would you like?" She pointed to Reid. "She's paying."

"I'll try the lavender latte. Sounds interesting."

"Oh, it is. Just wait. Big fan of lavender myself. We source the flavoring in from a farm in Kansas, believe it or not. None of that retail stuff," Autumn said, reaching for a cup. Reid handed over her credit card. "I'll have these out to you in a few moments. Please grab any old table, but the far ones over there get the best light and have an amazing view of the sun setting. You can nearly glimpse the beach if you work at it."

"And we will," Reid said. As she moved through Bethany's space, there it was. That same unique and wonderful scent that was all Reid.

Flowers in a meadow. Still as cliché as hell. She'd never forgotten it and her body hadn't either, reacting with acute stirring.

They could have sat at their old standard table, but Reid took the lead and led them to the booth near the window that Autumn had suggested. Somehow that felt just. It was a new era, after all. That called for a new table.

Reid sat across from her and tented her fingers. "You're a doctor now."

"You keep saying that."

She shook her head. "Because I'm so proud of you."

Bethany's cheeks went warm. "Thanks."

"Now, let's get down to business."

"You don't waste time."

"Well, we got a lot of surface conversation over and done with the past couple of weeks. I know what food you love for lunch, but less about how we became who we are. So let's start with this. Why did I never hear from you again?"

"Dry cappuccino and a lavender latte for the best table I've had all day." Autumn dropped off the drinks without waiting for a reply. She had a keen sense of what the customers needed even when it was privacy.

"That looks great," Bethany said, surveying the latte once they were alone.

"No. You're dodging the question. Ignore the coffee. Up here." She gestured to her eyes.

"But I like coffee."

"Pretend you don't."

She frowned and took a sip. "So awful. Blech." Reid sighed and Bethany held up a hand. "Fine. We had a thing. It was pretty serious. It changed my entire life, but it didn't work out."

Reid arched a brow. "You're minimizing."

"I know."

"Good. Go on."

Bethany arched one right back, attempting to keep the mood easy. "We both had some feelings about that, probably not great ones, and here we sit. We survived but are likely carrying a few battle scars. What's more to say?"

"I was in *love* with you." Bethany was struck. Reid hadn't lowered her voice or dipped her head for privacy. Out and proud or not, Bethany wasn't used to the new Reid quite yet. She'd said the words with every confidence.

Bethany held up a finger. "But it didn't always feel that way on my end. You're forgetting the graduation party. Your friends. Mateo. What happened had nothing to do with my feelings for you." She heard the way her voice had shifted, now brittle and raw. Just like that with the flick of a memory. This was exactly why she didn't want to do this. Panic flared.

"I tried to make things right again. Was forgiveness really that hard? Couldn't you have sent a message, a carrier pigeon, something?"

"I needed time. And when I was ready to talk…Well, things had changed."

"You're being vague again."

"I'm treading lightly. For both of us."

The table went silent. "Yeah. I know." She closed her eyes and dropped her head. "I'm sorry. For all of it. For who I couldn't be. A lot of this is on me."

Bethany exhaled. "Thank you. I appreciate that. But me, too. I'm sorry because I see things I would have done differently now."

"A couple of vulnerable kids trying to figure it all out."

"At the very least." Her throat felt tight, and she used the moment to take a sip of her drink. The hot liquid felt good going down, soothing her like a soft hand on her back.

"Maybe you had the right idea after all," Reid said with a sardonic laugh. "It's not the easiest to talk about. Maybe we can table it for tonight?"

Bethany exhaled dramatically and fell back against the leather booth. "Thank God on Tuesday."

"I'm sorry, what?"

"Something my grandmother used to say. I'm my grandmother. Did you miss that part? We're getting old."

"We're thanking God on singular days of the week," Reid said, sharing her laugh. "I think we are."

Bethany glanced into her cup, the coffee half gone now. "This cappuccino is amazing as always, but let's find food."

"I forgot. You love those little stands on the beach. You used to go nuts for them. I achieved a contact high just from watching."

Bethany bounced her eyebrows. "Corn dogs. Churros. Slices of pizza. Name your poison. Could be fun." Anything to get herself off memory lane.

"I'm keeping my options open." Reid's eyes danced, and the sunlight lifted the green to a new and brilliant hue. They were winging it now. But for the first time in so very long, Bethany's smile was authentic and whole. She wasn't sure where the evening would take them, but she knew with surprising certainty that she was meant to spend it talking to Reid, looking at Reid, and figuring out if there was something here to hold on to.

❖

Night fell slowly as they walked the boardwalk along the beach. They'd watched the sun beautifully make its exit as more and more people arrived, excited, talkative, holding hands, and laughing. Venice Beach felt like the place to be with the promise of the night stretched out in front of them. So much potential. Reid's world felt limitless with Bethany next to her.

An energy hummed through the streets as streetlights popped on, illuminating the walkways flanked by fluorescent signage, food stands, and shops along the way. Reid had given up trying to smother her smile and decided to just own it. No outing had felt as exciting to Reid as this one did. Well, no adult outing. Walking with Bethany, seeing the sights through her eyes, was all-consuming. It felt like a little part of her she hadn't seen in years had found its way back. Whole. There was no other way to frame it. Reid felt whole when she was with Bethany, and she honestly didn't want the feeling to ever go away. Was there a secret to capturing it? Could she draw a map so she could find her way back to it tomorrow and the next day? Addictive. Wonderful.

"Who's your closest friend?" she asked.

"Easy. The two doctors I work with. I told you a little bit about them, remember? Thea and Veronica. We met in medical school, and I convinced them to move to California and open a practice with me after completing our individual residencies."

"Oh. That's right. You had to do one of those after med school, right? Where was yours?"

"San Diego. I was lucky and had a great match at Scripps Mercy.

Didn't have to go far, either. I said good-bye to sleep, though. Intense times."

"I can't imagine." Reid paused, stopping their progress. "Isn't it interesting that neither of us ever fully moved away from California?"

"It kind of is."

"Think about it. You're not even from here originally."

"You Californians hook us on your weather, and we can't look away. You probably have meetings about it. They have fried dumplings. Look. Oh, wow. They have fried dumplings. They're cooking them right now." Reid followed her gaze to the stand producing amazing aromas of chives, onions, and ginger. She could understand the appeal.

"You had to say that twice. You were that overcome."

"Overcome is a good word for it."

Reid immediately flashed to a time when she'd fed Bethany french fries as they lay on the floor of her bedroom after skipping the last two classes of the day in favor of some alone time. They'd wound up doing more than just eating. Clothes askew, breaths shallow, Bethany had stared up at Reid with those cobalt blue eyes that somehow saw straight through Reid to her everything. They'd burned bright and hard, but never without a depth to their feelings. Reid knew without a doubt that they hadn't been just run-of-the-mill teenage lust.

Theirs was a rare connection. She knew because she hadn't come close to duplicating it. No one knew her the way Bethany did. No one made her feel as much.

She clenched her fists now to anchor herself in the present instead of getting swept away, such an easy happening. The memories had a way of slinking back these days, wrapping themselves around her and squeezing gently. She felt them all over.

"There's something about street food that's so immediate. Like you're a part of breaking news. I'm addicted." Bethany was already searching her bag for a credit card but Reid beat her to it.

"We'll take one order of immediate dumplings, please," she told the vendor, who swiped her card and quickly provided them with a cardboard tray containing six hot dumplings and sauce.

"You have to stop buying everything," Bethany told her, happily accepting the tray from Reid. She practically hopped.

"No, I don't. I'm enjoying myself, and I'll do what I want."

"Here," Bethany said, handing her a fork with a dumpling. "Blow on it first, okay? They're hot." Her voice was tender and their arms touched.

"Thank you," Reid said quietly. She sampled the dumpling and sank in surrender to its flavor reveal. "Okay, okay. I get it. These are worthy of two-time declarations upon discovery."

"Have another," Bethany said, her eyes on Reid's mouth.

Bethany once said how satisfying it was watching Reid enjoy food. "You just get this happy look on your face and it's everything," eighteen-year-old Bethany had said. She declined to share the memory and instead accepted the second dumpling. She pointed at her own mouth. "Too good."

"I'm aware. Let's find more food."

Reid laughed but followed Bethany, playing the role of her dutiful sidekick. They sampled tiny street tacos, miniature hot doughnuts, stir-fried bulgogi, and a couple of amazing double cheese sliders. Forgotten was the coffee conversation that had taken them to difficult places. The night was carefree, easy, and simply humming. She loved the way the streetlights lit up Bethany's smile. Her eyes. The light and shadows alternated, mysterious and beautiful. She couldn't stop looking at Bethany as they walked, stealing glimpses, melting each time.

"I can't eat another bite," Bethany said. "Which is sad. There's another whole group of vendors down there unexplored."

"Oh, this is hard for you."

"The fried food is calling me like sirens in a Greek epic."

Reid laughed. The food had most definitely prompted Bethany to unwind. She was in what seemed to be her happy place. "I won't presume, but maybe someday we'll come back."

"I'm not against that idea," Bethany said, boldly meeting her gaze. "It's hard to know where to step and where not to, so I'm trying to just be a person while I'm with you."

"You're doing an admirable job."

"I'd be lying if I said I wasn't having a good time. I am, so I'm owning that. And I've really enjoyed our calls. A nice way to ease in."

"That makes two of us. I feel the same way." Reid spotted a cute little outdoor bar across the street. She gestured with her chin. "Wanna? We gotta continue our streak somehow."

"I could handle an adult beverage about now. I've eaten like a child at a birthday party tonight."

"Done." Reid took Bethany's hand in hers and tugged her across the street. They scored two seats at the bar that allowed them to look across the low-top tables at the beach in the distance. Funky music played from the bar's speakers. The crowds had really picked up, making for great people watching. Two pineapple habanero margaritas arrived shortly after they'd ordered them, and they touched their oversized glasses. A chunk of pineapple adorned the chili rim of each glass.

Reid pulled her face back just as the wind caught her hair. "Look at us. Out together."

"*Drinking* together." Bethany closed her eyes after the first sip. "Drinking strong beverages together, I should say. Fuck. That hits. Wow. That's awesome."

"Right? I'm not complaining." Reid said above the music. She didn't know the artist. Hell, she couldn't even place the genre, but it was fun and beachy. Some sort of upbeat garage band. Three more pulls from her straw, and Reid knew Bethany was right about that tequila. It packed a punch. Every sweet sip was followed up by the bite from the habanero. She sucked down more of it. "This is really good."

"I need this recipe." The loud music forced them closer together if they wanted to talk. She wasn't complaining. Each time Bethany leaned into her space, her body reacted. Her gaze dropped to Bethany's lips. Her skin tingled with desire after every unexpected touch.

"Be honest," Reid said. "Did you ever think you'd see me again?"

"No. But that just shows that I think I control more than I do. Always been a problem."

"Did you *want* to see me again?"

"No." Bethany winced.

"Ouch. Let me pull this dagger out of my heart for a minute."

"Wait. Wait. Wait," she said, laughing, her hand falling on Reid's thigh. Dear Lord. She swallowed, playing it cool. "Let me expand on that statement. It was a bruise that I needed to keep my fingers from pressing."

"Given. I'm sure it was."

Bethany widened her eyes, taking over. "But now that you're here…"

Reid sat back. "Against your will."

"Now that you're here," she said, chasing her, grabbing Reid's wrist softly, "I'm glad that you are. I mean that." She took a long pull of the margarita. It was sexy and carefree. Reid loved watching her cut loose. "And this generous beverage is helpful in making me say those words." She stared at Reid. "You're also still really, really pretty. See? More courage. It's a little maddening. The pretty part."

She passed a grin. "Well, you're still fucking hot. Always have been. Maybe more so now. Hard to measure." Reid shook her head, feeling a tad drunk. "No. You're definitely even hotter now. Something about the command of your presence. Same amazing mouth, though. It's in the lips."

Bethany grinned. "You like my mouth?"

"I'm obsessed with it. Since I met you. I used to love watching you form words. That's how gone I am." Minor flub. "Was."

Bethany registered it with a raised brow and turned back to her drink. "Well, well."

Reid shrugged. She doubted any of this was a surprise.

They drank. It showed.

"For me it was your hair." Okay, now that had Reid's attention. She swiveled, silent. Hoping to hear more. "You had this way of tossing it, and the curls would rise and fall. I swear you designed that move just to torture me in the middle of practice. Do you know how hard it was to pull off a tumbling pass and fantasize at the same time?"

"Why did I not know about this?"

"Oh, I think you did."

"Maybe." She touched her hair absently. It was a tad shorter now, and the cut tamed the curls a little. Still totally tossable, she thought to herself slyly.

"Don't you dare," Bethany said, setting down her empty drink.

"What?" Reid asked, overperforming the innocence. She didn't toss her hair, but she ran her fingers through it, giving it an innocent shakeout.

She watched as Bethany's eyes darkened on cue. Wow. Would wonders never cease? She'd never realized the power. "Another round?" she asked in a quiet voice, her index finger tapping the back of Bethany's hand.

"I'd be up for it."

She raised her hand to the bartender, who was quick to mix up two new dangerous habanero margs. Drink in hand, she turned to Bethany, staggering their legs, a move you only made on someone you were close with. Sleeping with. Fucking. Bethany didn't seem to even blink. In fact, as they talked about the beach and how often they visited one, her hand made its way casually back to Reid's knee. This time it stayed.

"I always think I'll go soon, but I just seem to get caught up doing other things."

Reid registered the words, but her true focus was on the way Bethany's thumb moved back and forth across her leg. Was she aware of it, and—more importantly—did she know how acutely that thumb was turning Reid the hell on?

"I think it's important to take time for those kinds of excursions. You don't want to wake up when you're eighty and realize that you never really lived, right? At least, that's how I feel lately." She glanced down at the active thumb and back at Bethany, who widened her eyes and pulled back her hand. She'd not realized. Damn.

They stared at each other for an extended beat.

"Old habits," Bethany said.

"Tricky things."

But it was too late. There was this thick tension hovering, a crispness in the air, and Reid felt its effect squarely between her legs. She remembered those hot and heavy days in high school that would surely be topped, no pun intended, by what the two of them would be capable of today. Tonight. As adults. Doing adult things to each other. For long periods of time. Her mouth went dry.

"Should we get out of here?" Reid asked. "Resume our walk, or… something else?" There she went, cracking the door open and waiting to see if Bethany would bust through.

"Yeah, let's walk," Bethany said. She tossed three bills on the bar and waved at the bartender. "Even if I can't eat another bite, we can still take in the scene. Listen to the ocean."

They were a little drunk. Reid felt loose and off-kilter. Bethany lightly touched a chair for balance as they left the outdoor bar. Not only had they killed two of those margaritas each, but the murder had been swift.

"The lights out here are amazing," Reid said, folding her arms around herself.

"I love the buzz of the crowd. Easy to get lost," Bethany said. "Here. Give me your hand." She seemed to offer it in the name of keeping them from getting separated in the throngs, but Reid saw past it. Bethany was on the same page. No sooner had the thought hit, than Bethany pulled her to the side of the masses.

"Where are we going?" Reid whispered as they dashed down a dark street and beneath the awning of a business long since closed for the night. She liked the clandestine adventure. Spontaneous. Exciting.

But no words were needed. They both knew exactly what they were doing. A quick meeting of their eyes, and the restraint was gone. Bethany's lips descended on Reid's, capturing her mouth in a kiss that held nothing back. Bethany held her face in her hands, until her fingers moved into Reid's hair, to her neck, and back to her face again. Here it was. Them again. Their lips sought and clung and held. Everything was familiar and wonderful. Bethany's taste, her technique, the way they *fit*. Something unleashed. The kiss picked up momentum, and they were off in a haze of passion, Bethany's tongue in her mouth, her hands beneath Bethany's shirt, caressing the skin on her back, moving up. Her thumbs stroked back and forth across her ribs. They were about to explode.

"Wait. What are we about to do?" Bethany asked. She stepped back and flexed her hands. They were shaking. She covered one with the other.

"Probably what we've been wanting to do all night." She heard the breathless quality in her voice. Made sense. There hadn't been a lot of air.

Bethany held up her hands and backed away like she'd been burned. "No. Reid. Are we going to regret this?"

"I don't know. But maybe not, and that's big."

"I can't think straight because all I want to do right now—and I can't. We can't. Right?" She was talking more to herself than she was to Reid. It was a glimpse behind the curtain to her struggle. That sobered Reid up rather quickly.

"Right," Reid said, understanding that there was now a grown-up in the room, stopping them from what might have been a reckless, though delicious, encounter. She didn't want to upend the good they'd newly established. So while she very much missed the feel of Bethany's hands on her skin and her lips moving over her own, she understood Bethany's plight and could take a step back. "I guess we should keep our heads on straight."

"But it was really nice to—"

"It was."

"Yeah." They were lust-spun idiots searching for sentence structure in a land where only kissing mattered to them.

Bethany slid her hands into her back pockets, possibly to make them behave. Reid found that unfortunate. She wanted Bethany's hands on her face again, her stomach, her thighs, everywhere. "We shouldn't drive."

"No. I'll grab an Uber and get my car in the morning. Can you do the same?"

"Definitely. I don't have class tomorrow." Reid offered a smile. "Maybe I'll run into you on my walk of shame."

"Can it be a walk of shame without the sex? That doesn't seem fair." Bethany offered a laugh, considering.

Hearing that particular word leave Bethany's lips sent a decadent tremor from her stomach to her toes. "Good point. I'm not assuming the shame without the payoff."

They exhaled and smiled at each other beneath the blue sliver of moonlight that occupied their space. "This was certainly an unexpected night in my playbook."

"I'm glad it happened, though," Reid said, giving Bethany's hand a squeeze. "All of it." The implication was clear—she liked the things they'd done just moments before. She also loved that it was Bethany who'd made the move.

"Just when I think I have you figured out, I wind up in a dark alley so close to you I can't think. I'm never someone who can't think. It's my best skill."

"Sometimes, Beth, it's good to just let go a little. I remember a version of you who was pretty good at doing just that."

Her smile dimmed. "So much changed."

That was the truth. "There's something you should probably know. About me. My life now." The one detail she'd held back was an important one. The drinks, their proximity tonight, the intimacy, all of it gave her the courage to include Bethany more freely in the things that mattered to her now.

Bethany held up a hand. "It's not that I don't care, or even that I'm afraid of more revelations, it's just that my head is a swirly mess right now, and I'm not sure I could properly process anything of importance."

Reid swallowed it all back. For another day. "I get it. Why add to an already eventful night, right?"

"Right."

This was it. They were about to return to their separate lives, but Reid wasn't quite ready. "One more," she said, stepping into Bethany's space, pausing to make sure, and then going in for a kiss she knew would have to last. She made sure it did.

Bethany exhaled slowly as their lips came apart. She had one hand on the back of Reid's head and made no move to drop it. "You really leave an impression."

"I've learned that moments are precious things. Shall we?"

"Yeah, let's get outta here."

Reid busied herself with her phone as they walked back to the throngs on the boardwalk, summoning that Uber, mentally checking through if there was anything she needed in her car. There wasn't.

"Maybe we can talk about your thing next time?" Bethany asked.

"Deal. But I'm holding you to it. That there is a next time. That there is a talk." She'd wanted to spend time with Bethany ever since their grocery store run-in. Now that her wish had been granted, the reality of what she was doing hit hard, terrifying in a manner she couldn't articulate, but that grabbed her by the throat and told her to hold the hell on. This was quite the ride. But she was trying, vacillating between celebration that Bethany was in her orbit again and wallowing in fear of what could happen to her, bare and vulnerable. They were capable of inflicting true damage on each other.

"You don't have to hold me to anything," Bethany said. "I'm here with you. And I want to know everything about you." Unrelenting blue eyes held hers, inspiring a jumble of overwhelming feelings.

"That's all I need to hear." The words steadied her ship. She smiled, squeezed Bethany's hand, and resisted the urge to kiss again right there on the busy street.

It was happening again. The Bethany-Reid magic was taking hold. She let the smile happen fully this time, doing her best to leave her baggage at the door.

Bethany waited for Reid to be picked up first. She was always so careful about Reid making it places safely. In her Uber headed home, it felt a little strange to return to their separate lives, now newly complicated by the smallest chance of rekindling something that had been important once upon a time. But so many questions still swirled as Reid gripped the passenger door handle as the car zipped and turned. Could they overcome what tore them apart years ago? How would Bethany react when she learned more about Reid's life now? And could magic really strike twice?

Her phone buzzed, and she clicked on to the call. "Hi, sweetheart." She sighed happily at the voice on the other end of the phone. "I miss you, too. Only a few more days."

CHAPTER EIGHT

Then

Out of breath, with aching limbs and a bruised torso, Bethany felt like she might just throw up. She'd had no idea how hard cheerleaders worked and, seven practices in, wondered just what she'd gotten herself into. While she was very much aware of the physical demands of tumbling, the rest had been eye-opening. These girls were hard-core athletes, fighting through injuries to keep the competition goal alive. They weren't here to cheer on other teams—that was incidental, a footnote in the agenda. Their true function was to bring home the regional championship in a cutthroat competition of their own. The constant practice, the drive for perfection, and the number of full-out run-throughs the team performed was mind-blowing. She'd say she had a newfound respect for the sport, but there wasn't enough time.

"Take a quick break. Get some water. We're going again in ten minutes," Coach Rogan yelled. These people were machines. Bethany, still nauseous, found a cool spot against the wall to try to find her breath. She closed her eyes and pressed the cold water bottle against her neck. Her calves ached with strain. Her forearms weren't far behind.

"If this is too hard for you, just say so." The voice was sickly sweet, which acted as an arrow sign to the comment's insincerity. Sunny Lynch, her least favorite cocaptain, had quickly become Bethany's own personal critic. Since she'd been announced on the squad, she'd caught looks and comments from Sunny that made it clear Bethany didn't belong. At least in her eyes. Half the squad had welcomed her, but the other half, Sunny's half, seemed to tolerate her presence at best. Yes, she'd had a few learning curves, but she was giving it her all.

"I'm good." She stood, rolled her shoulders to prove it. She wasn't about to let Sunny get to her.

"I'm happy to hear that. A positive attitude is so important for the team to be successful. Wouldn't you say?"

She smothered the sarcastic retort she preferred to respond with in favor of, "Could not agree more."

"And I would never want to criticize, but that last tumbling pass was pretty stoic. You hit all the skills but looked serious as hell when you did it. That's gonna cost us come competition time."

"You're never one to criticize?" Bethany answered, amused.

"Work on your face, okay? That's the takeaway here."

"Just for you, I will do that."

"Also, again, not to criticize but—"

"Of course not. God." Bethany shook her head like that would be an insane concept.

"We generally don't leave our gym bags on the bleachers for others to trip over. We place them neatly along the wall." She shrugged. "Just something to work on."

"And I will. I'll work very hard at the gym bag rule. Nights, even."

Sunny looked like she'd tasted something bitter. Apparently, Bethany's sarcasm was not appreciated. It wasn't like she could help it, though. Not when someone was being so ridiculous when she was already giving so much.

"Good talk, new girl." Sunny strode back to her core group of followers, who seemed hell-bent on keeping her on the outside looking in, probably on Sunny's behalf. She didn't lose sight of the glaring exception, however.

"What did she say?" Reid asked, right on time. She joined Bethany along the wall of the gym, their shoulders pressed against each other. It wasn't an accident, either.

"Pretty much that I'm weak, throw my shit around without care for others, and am not perky enough on my tumbling passes."

"What the hell?"

"She's *your* friend. I figured you'd know what the hell."

Reid sighed and leaned against Bethany's shoulder. She loved it. "Don't you dare let her get in your head. She's just pissed because you're here without having to go through the normal, terrifying process. She's complained to me about it twice already. Something about not earning it. Translation? She's jealous you're so good."

"So if something was hard for her once, it has to be hard for everyone."

"Welcome to life with Sunny. She's always been a gatekeeper. In second grade, she formed a club and brought T-shirts to school for every girl in our class but two."

"So hazing it is. Fan-fucking-tastic."

Reid took her hand and squeezed. "I like your hands."

She smiled, forgetting every trouble when Reid focused on her like this. Touched her. Said things like that. "Thank you. I grew them myself."

"Promise me you will ignore Sunny, and remember you are here because we desperately need you."

"Ignore her minions, too?"

"They're just following her example. Leave them to me." Reid leveled a smile, and Bethany felt herself turn to Jell-O in under five seconds. She was becoming super predictable where Reid was concerned. The drive home together after practice had become the highlight of Bethany's day, when she would get Reid all to herself for a little square of time. Those were the times when Reid let down her guard. They'd listen to music, discuss every detail of practice, and touch each other, a lot. That part was fairly new, and increasing by the day. She couldn't help but wonder to what end. She'd lain in bed awake for hours examining things from every angle. The more comfortable they became with each other, the more they seemed to incorporate little touches. A squeeze of the hand, a pat on the knee—or thigh, if Bethany was really lucky. Just enough to keep her on the edge of her seat, living for the slight intimacy of those moments. She'd graduated to fantasizing about things going farther. Her own little secret. How would Reid's lips taste if she kissed them? How would her body feel pressed to Bethany's? And those curves, how would they feel beneath Bethany's hands, worshipped with her mouth? The fleeting images intoxicated, prompting her body to respond in ways she wasn't sure what to do with. She was a virgin with very little experience with girls. But she knew with certainty that she craved more time with Reid and counted the seconds until she'd get it. Plus, the more time they spent together, the more she actually liked Reid as a person. She was her friend, her confidant. Her person.

"Your hair is pretty today," Bethany said softly, pulling them right back into it. She watched in captivation as Reid touched the brown curls with the sun streaks. She'd pulled it back into a low ponytail, which left small strands escaping, framing her face. Soft. Beautiful.

"Really? Thank you." Her cheeks went pink in under three seconds. Bethany marveled at how a simple compliment from her could have an effect on someone as perfect and wonderful as Reid Thatcher. But that was part of the appeal. Reid, from atop her high school throne, cared about Bethany and what she thought.

"Your curls never cease to amaze."

"I have my grandmother to thank for them. Or blame. Depending on the day and the size of my hair."

"I owe her one." She heard the words before she'd had time to examine them. They gave too much away. Now it was her own cheeks that went hot, but with embarrassment.

Reid turned her cheek against the wall and sent Bethany a questioning stare that softened into quiet understanding. The whole exchange made Bethany want to crawl under her bed and hide for the rest of existence. Now Reid knew that the *new girl* lusted after her. While she walked hand in hand with that Mateo-the-football-star, smiling like the half of the celebrity couple she was, she'd have knowledge that Bethany looked at her a little differently than other girls. Not that it wasn't true.

She would just correct herself, an innocent miswording of a sentence. "Just for the record, I didn't mean that in the way it—"

"Back on the mat! Let's go," Rogan called. And as the other cheerleaders scurried back from break, two remained along the wall, watching each other and figuring out what to do or say next. It felt like a lot depended on it.

Reid dipped her face, finding Bethany's eyes. "You don't have to—"

"New girl. We're waiting. Reid, c'mon!" Sunny yelled, rolling her eyes and tightening her perfect, long dark ponytail. She then flipped around and folded her arms like a four-year-old who'd been refused a second snack.

"Sunny, let me handle it, please. Reid, Bethany, everything okay?" Rogan called to them.

They were still watching each other. Reid pulled away first. "We're coming." She turned back to Bethany and her voice dropped. "Right?" She held out her hand and waited.

The gesture resonated. Reid hadn't scoffed or laughed and moved out of Bethany's space. That was something to cling to in the midst of her horror at the outing of her crush. She placed her hand in Reid's, and they jogged to the mat.

Ella smiled. Jennifer raised her eyebrows as she looked between the two of them. Sunny full-on rolled her eyes. "Our time is just as valuable as yours," she said, aiming the comment mainly at Bethany. Expected and unnecessary.

"Sorry," Bethany said, scanning the group. "Ready now."

"We have one more full-out tonight before we can all go home. Let's make it count," Rogan told the team. "Stay focused. Stay sharp. Remember who it is you support in any given moment and make sure they have what they need. Are we ready to do this?"

"Let's go. United!" the girls chanted in unison. They clapped once and took their spots for the top of the routine. The music blared and they were off. Bethany started as the base of a stunt in which they basket-tossed Ella into the air and caught her. Next, she moved to the corner for a difficult tumbling pass, which she nailed, followed by a dance break, more back handsprings, this time synchronized with two other girls, and finally the pyramid in which she happily hoisted Reid into the air along with two other bases. She smiled just as Sunny instructed, pulling her best cheer face. Above, Reid somersaulted out of her pose, into their waiting arms below. Once she was safely on her feet and into a dance break with a separate group, Bethany blinked and took her spot for her most difficult tumbling pass. This one included punch fronts, roundoffs, forward and back handsprings that led into a back tuck. She ended with an aside to the audience in the form of a no-sweat gesture off her left shoulder before joining the rest of the squad for a final pose to the last note of music.

The most exhausting and physically taxing three minutes of her day.

And also the most exhilarating.

Though it would be difficult to force her to admit it, in just a couple weeks' time, she had grown to love executing this routine. There was something about the music, the timing, the precision, and high-stakes ideology that they strove for as a group. No, she wasn't exactly close with most of these girls, but they were pushing themselves toward a common goal, and that bonded them in a whole separate manner. Underneath it all, that felt pretty damn good. Her days felt purpose filled and, thanks to Reid, exciting and full.

"Best full-out we've had," Rogan said, making her way down from the bleachers. "I appreciate how hard you've pushed yourselves. Let's take Saturday off."

The girls' eyes went wide, and they nodded in appreciation. Bethany's gaze went immediately to Reid, who grinned back at her. They had the whole day free. It was naive to think they'd spend it together. But they might. The prospect had her pushing up onto her toes, the extra energy that flowed through her limbs like a cool current.

The drive home that night was wordless but triumphant. They streaked through the backroads of LA with the windows down, hair flying, and music on full blast. Bethany watched Reid almost as much as she watched the scenery race past. Reid focused on the road diligently but tapped the leather steering wheel with her right hand, carefree and light. Bethany was happy to see it because there was a heaviness that came over Reid whenever they approached home and were forced to say good-bye. The cheerful life she once knew had been traded in for a quieter home.

"It's just this shell of what it used to be," she'd explained to Bethany as they sat against a tree in the park working through their unnecessarily complicated calculus problems. Bethany had the higher grade and took the lead, tutoring Reid as they went, teaching her the little tricks. "My dad sneaks by to say hey, but it's awkward for everyone, and then he's out of there. My mom hides away in her studio assembling floral arrangements or in the kitchen making dinner. She speaks about a third of the words she used to. And Alice? Exists with headphones in until she can come up with an excuse to leave."

"And that's very different than before, right?" Bethany asked with a wince.

Reid nodded. "The complete opposite. My house was the place

my friends wanted to hang out. My parents were warm. Funny, even." She shook her head as if seeing it play out in her mind. "They kissed and laughed. We did everything as a foursome. I don't recognize my life right now." Her eyes had filled until they overflowed, the tears streaking her cheeks. She made no move to wipe them away, staring at Bethany full on, revealed to her.

"I hate that. At least in my case, I don't really remember much before my mom took off on us. I don't have a *then* and *now*. I won't pretend I have these grandiose answers or whatever. But I'm here."

"That's what I like about you. You just listen. You don't judge. You don't try to fix it."

"I wish I could, though."

A smile touched Reid's lips. "And you're kind." They stared at each other for what felt like an eternity, but was likely just a few seconds. "Maybe we should get back to differentiation formulas," Reid said, indicating the book in front of them.

"Do you talk to Mateo about this stuff?" she asked, opening the textbook to where they'd left off.

Reid scoffed, "Definitely not. He's got his own stuff."

"Yeah, but he's your boyfriend. He should be there for you if you need it."

"Maybe." She shrugged. "I haven't really given him the chance. Maybe that's on me. We have fun when we're around each other. It's kind of our thing, so I keep it light."

Bethany nodded knowingly when she wasn't that at all. She hadn't had many relationships, definitely none serious, but that wasn't the kind she would want. It made her sad for Reid all over again.

Tonight, though, there'd been a change in her. Bethany liked the happier vibe. It looked great on Reid, and she needed a break from the problems. When she pulled in front of Bethany's place, she turned to her. "Today was so good. I needed it."

"The practice, you mean? Yeah. The last full-out. We killed it."

"Practice was great. And, um, other things, too," Reid said with a never before seen timidity. What in the world? Bethany was dumbstruck. It was the moment they'd shared along the wall. Was Reid happy to learn that Bethany thought about her in ways that were... less than platonic? But sitting in that car, she had no doubt. Reid was happy, and that particular realization was a powerful jolt that stole her thoughts and words. "Stop," Reid said, laughing. "Don't give me that bewildered look. It's just us in this car."

"I can't help it," Bethany said. "I just…I don't know how to respond to you right now. My words are broken. Mangled."

"Good. Now get out of my car and promise there'll be more days like today."

Bethany laughed and did as she was told. She leaned down through the open car door for one last look. "I hope there will be."

"That's all I need to hear. 'Night, Beth."

She replayed the shortened version of her name in her mind, and her entire body tingled in approval. The nickname wasn't original or unexpected, but it felt intimate coming from Reid. She'd never been a fan of it, but now all she wanted was to hear it again from those lips.

"'Night," she said and closed the car door, unable to say much more. She watched Reid take off into the night after stirring up Bethany's life with less than twenty words. "Good night," she repeated to the empty driveway.

"Hey. You okay?" her dad asked. "You've been standing out here like a statue for five minutes."

"Never better," she told him, meaning it.

"You're smiling like a weirdo." He seemed to be enjoying it.

"I know. It's pretty great."

❖

With a whole Saturday unexpectedly stretched out in front of her, Reid didn't know what to do with herself. Veg in front of the TV? Plan a rager in her backyard? Her mom wouldn't notice. Buy a pony? Her schedule was so often booked solid at any given moment that when a block of free time opened up, her mind raced with all the delicious opportunities she'd never fit in.

"Hey," she said, pressing Alice's door open a touch. "Wanna go for a drive? We can grab a late breakfast, take it to the park like we used to."

"Nope. We used to do that with Dad." Alice clicked her semi-long fingernails on her headphone case. The chip on her shoulder, nonexistent three months ago, grew by the day now.

"So what? Today, we'll do it by ourselves. We're not six and nine anymore. Let's go." She loved the idea of repurposing old traditions. Time to grasp what shreds of life remained. Their house had become a foreign place, quiet and dead. She was ready to wake it the hell up.

"Nah. I'm good. Close the door?" It was the perfect example of the apathetic, short sentences Alice had blessed her with lately. She didn't even recognize her sister, who'd been benched on the soccer team for not attending practice because she'd rather race around town with a group of kids Reid knew to be anything but solid or kind. Two things Alice used to be just a short time ago. She was past worried.

"Hey, what's going on with you?" Reid came into the room and sat on the bed. The walls of her tolerance were crumbling piece by piece. "I know things here suck right now, but it's probably time for us to try to toss each other a rope. I miss you. Let's go to the damn park." She added a smile so it didn't feel like a lecture.

Alice removed one headphone. "I get that you're trying for the whole big sister rocks award, and I agree that you should probably get it, but I'm not *you*. I don't leave here and dash off to my perfect social existence where the world universally adores me. My life is very different, and I'm doing the best I can. I don't want to go to the park. I want to sit here and listen to music."

Defeat. There wasn't much she could do with that. Alice was escaping and needed to. Reid could respect that. "Yep. You got it." She stood. "But I'm going to keep bugging you because you're my sister and I love you to death. Okay?"

Alice kept her gaze on the bedspread and didn't look up, but Reid caught the emotion welling in her eyes. "Okay."

She wanted to hug her, remind her that they were in this together, but got the feeling it wasn't what Alice needed. She walked down the hall to her own room, feeling isolated and not anything like the person Alice described. She still had her whole day stretched out in front of her. Mateo had practice. Alice was a no-go. She should call Sunny. Maybe get their group of four together like the old days. She probably had some ground to make up with them lately. Everything in her screamed for what she truly longed for. Yet fear placed a hand on her shoulder, holding her back. Why? "You know why," she said to her reflection in the mirror. There she stood in front of the childhood dresser, a piece of furniture she'd had since she was four years old. It still showed the chip in the corner from when she'd practiced her softball swing in the house, a constant. It was Reid that wasn't. She was changing in ways that she'd never have predicted. Ever since Bethany Cahill had arrived on the scene, that change had accelerated exponentially. She held eye contact with herself in the mirror, confronting what she'd refused to look at too carefully. Until now. *Just go there*, she urged herself silently. She wanted to be with Bethany most every minute that she wasn't. She wanted to talk to her, watch her think, formulate a response, sip her coffee leaving a faint imprint on the cup, laugh at something with the dry wit she'd mastered. Reid shook her head and straightened. Because it didn't stop there, and she damn well knew it. She wanted to breathe in the same air, open her arms and have Bethany fall into them. Press her lips against Bethany's skin. Her shoulder, her neck, her stomach, her— She took a quick step back, arms falling to her side.

This was happening.

These were her feelings, and a clear obstacle to everything she'd mapped out for herself, her future. What about that?

The open laptop on her bed pinged the arrival of a DM. She whirled around and walked over. The timing was too perfect. She believed in signs.

Do you want to do something today? No pressure.

She blinked. Bethany. She didn't think. Didn't hesitate. *Pick you up in an hour.*

The whole thing felt like a runaway train, but she was desperate to be on it. Maybe the idea of what it would be like to be close to Bethany would be quite different than the reality. Wasn't it up to her to find out so she could put this whole thing to rest? Stop her traitorous mind from all of its fantasies. Stop her body from wanting things so desperately she couldn't sleep.

"Are you a virgin?" Reid asked as they made their way into the park, iced coffees procured. She caught Bethany shifting slightly in her peripheral, but she didn't say anything. "Sorry. That might be too personal."

"No." She straightened. "Was just expecting something a little more to the effect of *Can you hand me my coffee?* or *What did you think of the calculus assignment?* Virginity it is."

Reid laughed. "I get it. I hear it now."

"But it wasn't out of nowhere in your head, was it?"

"No." Reid turned the key, silencing the engine. "It wasn't."

A long pause. "I haven't had sex with anyone."

"Oh." Why was that the biggest relief of her life? She knew. It meant there was no one to be jealous of.

"I realize that makes me a fucking unicorn at nearly eighteen. Well, maybe drop the fucking in that case, since I haven't earned it."

"Stop it. It doesn't make you different."

"When did you lose it?"

Reid only hesitated for a moment. This was Bethany, who made her feel incredibly safe and more like herself than ever before. "Stay tuned." She shrugged. A small smile.

"Not following." Bethany frowned the way she did when they were stuck on a cal problem. "You don't have to say. I only asked because you did."

"No." Reid closed her eyes. "I mean, stay tuned because it hasn't happened yet."

"Wait. No way. You and Mateo haven't…"

"We fool around, but I always stop him before…"

"Wow. Okay." She started about five different sentences before settling on, "That's totally noble of you."

"Is it? Because I'm not sure that's my reasoning. It makes me ask myself why. It's not like I'm waiting for marriage or some grandiose declaration of forever love. Why haven't I slept with him?" She heard the intensity in her voice grow stronger as she spoke.

Bethany hadn't said anything yet. Her one visible ear, the one with a strand of dark hair tucked behind it, flushed with color.

"Oh. I've gone and given you red cars."

Bethany scoffed, "I think I'm just processing it all. Adjusting my outlook." She went ahead and covered that ear anyway. Cute.

"Adjusting it to the new virgin version of me."

"Not gonna lie." Their gazes locked. "Yes."

"I have an idea. Let's walk. Find some space." They grabbed their iced lattes, coconut for Reid and unsweetened for Bethany, and made their way into the park. They were into late fall now in LA, and the temperatures had dipped, making layers a must to compensate. Cold one minute, too warm for a jacket the next.

"What's your dad think of me?" Reid asked as they walked. "He always smiles when he sees me in your driveway but never says much."

"He's making sure you're friend not foe. Extremely protective. A girl's mom leaves, and all of a sudden the rest of the world seems very, very dangerous."

"I can understand that." Suddenly, she felt awful for Bethany. All she'd lost. "I'm sorry."

"For driving me around and becoming my friend? I'm not."

"For your mom. It must have been hard growing up without her. I talk your ear off about my parents' split, and you've been living with only one parent for practically your whole life. I promise I'm not always so self-focused."

Bethany frowned, again always thinking, and then stopped. "My difficult path doesn't have to mean that yours isn't hard."

"Thank you for saying that."

"I mean it. I see what you're going through and wish I could fix it for you. It's frustrating that I can't." The sentiment meant the world to Reid. Bethany cared, and in that instant her gratitude overwhelmed.

"Can we sit?" Reid asked. She was nervous. And also not.

A breeze hit, the trees danced, and they found a spot located far into the park, secluded and pretty. Reid pulled the blanket out of her backpack, laid it neatly on the grass, and settled onto it, her legs crisscrossed. Bethany lay on her back looking up at the treetops overhead. Now that was an image she never wanted to forget. God, she looked dreamy. Beautiful. Heaven kissed.

"There goes your hair again." Bethany stared up at her as the wind hit and tousled her curls. "I love watching it."

"Oh yeah?" Reid said, giving it a purposeful toss. She watched Bethany's eyes dance. "Like it?"

A smile took over her whole face. "You keep it up and I might even give you cheer face at practice."

"Is that all it takes? Some individual hairography?"

Bethany curled an arm behind her head, enjoying the show. "From you? Yeah. I'm easy."

Reid flipped her hair from the front to the back, and Bethany responded with an overexaggerated *wow* face, the same kind they were encouraged to pull during their routine.

"Oh, that's good cheer face right there," Reid said, leaning over Bethany, propped up on her hands and letting her hair fall and tickle Bethany's arms playfully. "Rogan would love it. More of that."

Bethany nodded a few times like an enthusiastic ray of sunshine.

Reid laughed, looking down at her. "Now you're just making fun of us." Instead of climbing off Bethany, she followed her instincts for once and lowered herself onto her forearms with most of her weight on Bethany's body. The smile fell right off Bethany's face. Her own, too.

"Oh," Reid said, surprised at all that happened to her in that moment. Everything stuttered and then burst to life. How many times had she lain on top of Mateo in the very same fashion? Not once had it felt like this, like someone just turned the lights on.

For a fleeting moment, she thought of apologizing and moving herself right off, but the idea was gone just as quick as it had arrived. This was too good. She savored the firing of every nerve ending she owned, the flaring of her body in a manner to which she was entirely unaccustomed. She wanted Bethany to touch her. She wanted to touch her right back, slowly. She wanted to make Bethany feel things and be the cause. She wanted. She wanted. She *wanted*. With everything in her. She watched Bethany swallow, wondering if her body felt half as alive. Did it yearn the way hers did?

The softness of Bethany's fingertips when she reached up and cradled her cheek hypnotized Reid. The moment played in cinematic wonder, like she was watching a movie, only she could feel everything that played out on the screen. She covered Bethany's hand with hers and offered a small smile to see what she would get back. This was such new territory. Were they really doing this? Was this real or just another dream? Bethany gave Reid's face the smallest of tugs downward. Encouragement. A proposal. Reid's eyes found Bethany's perfect mouth, and that was all she needed, moving to it like a beacon. She didn't think anymore. Thoughts would only get in the way of doing what she truly wanted. When her lips met Bethany's she knew she'd made the right decision. Bethany made a noise, one that could only be interpreted as good, a little surprised, like when she tasted a wonderful bite of ice cream. Her body squirmed beneath Reid's. Her lips pressed back, accepting the kiss, holding them there, Reid hovering close to heaven.

Then it all changed. Bethany's mouth began to move. Holy fuck. Reid's lips moved with her and the effects were staggering, like she'd been hit with a warm wave on the beach. Out of necessity, she pressed her hips closer. She could feel Bethany's curves beneath her, the swell of her breasts, which was enough to make her brain nearly explode. It was getting harder to breathe normally and kiss and feel. The heat coursing through her had nothing to do with the sun. Their tongues touched and then Reid's was in Bethany's mouth in an adjustment so satisfying that they both moaned their approval. Unlocking the secrets of kissing Bethany only made her want to do more. She wanted to slip her hands beneath Bethany's shirt and place her fingertips along the smooth skin she'd find there. She wanted to touch Bethany in intimate places, see her naked, explore every inch. It was all so overwhelming.

"Reid. We're outside."

Her jumbled thoughts began to slow and she decoded the words, all while Bethany still cradled her face.

"Yes. Outside." It wasn't an eloquent response, but that would have been asking too much, given the most recent five minutes. She distantly understood that they should stop and why. It just took a moment for her body to receive the *turn off* message, for her to come back to herself. The ache between her thighs remained insistent. She sat up a little drunk, a little shocked, and blinked.

"I didn't see that coming," Bethany said, her gaze still very much on Reid's lips. That was cruel. Especially when all Reid craved in this world was to be kissed more by Bethany. Now that she knew firsthand what that entailed, how could she not?

"It was starting to feel inevitable." Reid straightened her hair. "Are you okay?"

Bethany nodded. She attempted a weak smile, but they were both in recovery mode. "I'm better than that. I'm happy. I want to make that part clear."

Relief. "Me, too."

"But here's the thing," Bethany got that thoughtful look on her face, just like when they hit up a difficult homework assignment. She was trying to work all this out. Reid didn't blame her. She was, too. "You have a boyfriend." Her brows dropped. "So…"

"I don't have the answer." She searched for the perfect words. Came up blank. "I just know that I feel something for you."

"And him. Your boyfriend."

"Right." She sighed. "It's different. I wish I could describe it." When she was with Mateo, she'd always been happy. Loved their relationship. But she didn't crave his touch, or stay up late thinking about his smile, his wit, his body. That was Bethany. She wasn't quite capable of saying all of that out loud. Even after the best make out session of her life.

Bethany searched Reid's face and seemed to make a decision. "You don't have to arrive on the scene with all the answers. This is new. But maybe start searching for them? For both our sakes."

Reid nodded. "Kind of important. I know." A long pause. "I just want to kiss you again." She watched Bethany's throat and caught the thrum of her accelerated pulse.

Bethany swallowed. "It's all I've thought about for weeks now. You. Like this."

"Why didn't you say so?"

She laughed and her eyes went wide with incredulity. "Are you serious? Tell the head cheerleader I have a crush on her. I'm sure you figured it out, maybe even before yesterday."

Reid touched Bethany's hand, turning it over in hers. "Yesterday was telling. I didn't know before, about you. Only what I was feeling."

"I don't know how that's possible."

"Why?"

"Because I've caught myself staring. Coming up with ways to be near you. You had to have noticed."

Reid shrugged. "Friends do those things." She intertwined their fingers, studying their hands pressed together.

"Are you sure about that?" The tone of her voice and the arched eyebrow said it all.

Reid had to laugh. "No. I'm not, actually. What is it with us?"

Bethany scooted closer. "I wish I knew. But it's like fire. And it's spreading fast. Every day I feel it more than the day before."

A long pause. She dropped their hands into her lap. "What am I going to do?"

Bethany pulled hers back. "Well, for one. We're going to be good. I definitely don't need Mateo and his entire football team upset."

"He's not like that."

"Yet. He's never had his girlfriend kiss someone else in the park." She tilted her head, and one side of her mouth pulled. Reid loved it when she offered that face, the sly half smile. Why was she so damn hot? "And secondly, we'll just enjoy today. Hang out."

Reid semi-pouted. "Without kissing?"

"Without kissing."

"That was a much easier prospect an hour ago. We opened the door already."

Bethany's eyes flicked to her mouth and then quickly away as if having broken a rule. Reid held back a smile. She could really get used to the way she was feeling right now. On a high as everything buzzed pleasantly. The world seemed bright, colorful, and full of life.

They spent the afternoon lounging in the park, listening to music, sharing headphones. The kissing had been put on hold but that didn't mean they couldn't look at each other. Smile. Occasionally Bethany would squeeze her wrist, or she would give Bethany's hair a gentle tug. Reid went home in the early evening with a smile she couldn't wipe away. She checked herself in the mirror to see if she looked any different. Surprised that the changes on the inside hadn't manifested in a drastic change on the outside. She kept her eyes on her DMs for any little message from Bethany, smiling to herself when she'd receive a *Hi* or *What are you doing right this very second?*

"You're certainly in a better mood," her mom said, when she emerged from her studio and began tossing a few ingredients together for a simple dinner. Make your own tacos with a big bowl of sour cream and another of guacamole. Good enough for Reid. They hadn't been eating around the table too often, unfortunately. Another new normal. With just varying combinations of the three of them, self-service from the stove had become their routine. Grab and go.

"It was a good day. Mom, I think I really needed it."

"Really? Makes me happy. One of us needs some fun in her life." Her mom touched the back of her head. "Out with the girls again?"

She kicked her hip against the counter as she watched her mom pour the seasoning packet in with the browning meat. The sound of the sizzle underscored their back-and-forth. "One. Bethany Cahill. Remember I told you about her?"

Her mother closed her eyes. "The new girl on the squad, right? The really good tumbler."

"Yes," Reid said, smiling at the accurate description. "We've gotten pretty close. She's awesome."

"Bring her by sometime. And Sunny and the gang, too. I haven't seen them in so long."

She nodded, wanting to say more. "It's just…I don't know. She's different. To me. Than the others. You know?"

Her mother went still. "Is this some sort of news I should be picking up on?" She squinted. It was a friendly squint. But it came with concern for Reid, too. "There's something you want to say, but aren't."

Her mother knew her too well. "I don't know." She couldn't take it any further. Out of nowhere, this little shred of doubt crept up her spine, reminding her of who she was and all of her plans. Did she have to upend her life? How did she make it all work together? Until she knew, it felt better to hold on to her feelings. "No. Not anything major." She snagged a chip with some guac.

"And Mateo's still around, right? Because I love Mateo."

She deflated a little. "Everyone does. Yeah, he's still around. Practice today."

"Thank God. I was worried I'd missed a big chunk of your life because I'm working through my own issues. Never marry a golfer."

"That's specific."

"Maybe just my PTSD." Her mom dropped the Teflon spoon and turned. "Are you sure there's nothing I should know about Bethany? And you?"

"Nope. Basic stuff." Reid sighed, suddenly aware of the changes she was facing and daunted by their scope. How quickly her emotions could shift. She'd gone from celebratory to terrified in the span of five minutes. "I'll be in my room."

And there she sat, listening to the rumble of the heater in the hallway and plotting her next move. It almost felt like a game of chess where her opponent had her cornered and there was no where to go.

The high she was on earlier in the day felt foreign now. How did she get back there? What happened that afternoon felt like it changed everything. She knew what it was she wanted. But did she have the courage to reach out and grab it? She was feeling less than confident and instead, curled up in bed, dragging her quilt up to her chin and clutching the fabric close. She now choked on the happiness that had just been hers hours before. There had to be a way forward. But in this moment, Reid felt trapped by her own life.

CHAPTER NINE

Bethany sat on the front porch of the little white and green house her father had purchased for them upon their move to LA. It had two steps that led up to the small porch, and she spent more time sitting on them than any piece of furniture inside the eclectically decorated home. Her dad liked knickknacks. That was for sure. But the porch was open and breezy. It helped Bethany organize her thoughts and grounded her somehow.

She liked watching the world go by. Her neighbors from two doors down, whom she stalked regularly for sport, were two thirtysomethings. They were constantly heading off on foot and coming back with various bags, which pulled her interest. Take-out food. Groceries. Dry cleaning. He generally carried whatever they picked up. She held the leash of the grumpy bulldog who didn't want anyone too close. Their life looked close to perfect from her spot on that porch.

She wondered now about falling in love. When did those two decide they simply couldn't imagine walking with bags alongside any other human? Because right now, she got it. She missed Reid. There was no one else she wanted to kiss or talk to or think about. Was she falling in love? She had to be. There was no other explanation for the emotion that lived in a tight little ball and burst forth wonderfully anytime they were together. And that kiss? She could still feel it all over. Her lips buzzed pleasantly. Her limbs were loose. The couple, on their way somewhere, nodded and smiled at her. She waved as she always did but carried new appreciation for them now. They shared a secret understanding.

She wanted what they had, one day.

Longed for it. She imagined walking hand-in-hand to the store with Reid. Talking about their days. Making plans for the weekend. The beach. A drive. A movie. Who knew? Didn't matter. As long as they were together.

"You ready for dinner? Or do you want to stare at trees a little while longer? Your pick. I can get behind either," her dad said, poking his head out. He'd been cooking, which translated to opening up a variety of cans and boxes and heating them all on the stove.

"Sure. Yeah. I could eat."

She slid into her spot at the oval shaped dining room table he'd picked up secondhand when they'd arrived in town. "You've been quiet today. Where's your smart mouth?"

She grinned. "I was saving it for dinner. You're welcome."

"Things still good with you lately?"

"Even better."

"And that cheer competition you're spending so much time on?" He sliced a chicken nugget into four sections. Only her dad. "That working out?"

"Yeah. It's not bad actually. Much harder than I thought. But surprisingly, kinda cool. I could see us winning the whole thing if we work hard enough."

He shook his head and stabbed another section of chicken—he was burly enough to fit three nuggets in his mouth at one time. "I thought you hated that skirt and pom-pom thing."

"I do. Have you ever done something to be near someone else?"

"I learned to write poetry," he said without missing a beat. "Your mom liked it, so I learned what a goddamn stanza was. I still know. I can write sonnets all over the fridge. Just need some alphabet magnets."

"Did she also ask you to cut already small pieces of food smaller?"

He grinned, jolly and big. "No. That was all me."

"Well, there's a girl I really like. She cheers. She wanted me to."

"It's Reid with the blue car." He didn't ask. He proclaimed by pointing his fork at her and had the nerve to look rather proud of himself.

"It is Reid with the car," she told him. "We kissed. Now I'm a weird puddle. Is that normal?"

"Ah. Yep. I remember that puddle part. When your knees are weird and you turn into a lovable cartoon character. Are you the character?"

She reached for the spicy ketchup. "I believe so. Any advice from a former cartoon to a new one?"

He set down his fork, his grin waning. "Be kind. The love roller coaster is a scary one, and everybody is doing the best they can. Sometimes when it takes a twist or a turn too fast, people get scared and hurt each other. Don't do that if you can help it. That's been my takeaway."

She sobered. "Okay. I won't." Her phone buzzed where it sat across the table. They ignored it and continued to eat, Bethany honoring the deal that she would—quote—*put the damn thing away during dinner*.

But after four more buzzes, he shrugged. "You can get that if you want."

"Thanks, Dad." She checked her messages. The cheerleader group thread was hopping. They'd only added her out of obligation, but now she got to see the workings of socially viable teenage girls up close and personal in a way she'd never been privy to before. She found she hadn't been missing much. Nails, hair, and boys. Those were their favorite three. The actual sport of cheerleading was relegated to fourth position. She scanned the multitude of messages flying back and forth. The crux was that it was Saturday night and Sunny was inviting people over to *chill or whatever we want to do in my backyard. The place is empty tonight.* She set the phone down and thought on it. Sunny wouldn't want her there, in all likelihood, but in her defense, she had just been invited by way of a group message. Reid had been involved in the back-and-forth and was planning to be there.

"There's a gathering," Bethany said. "A bunch of people are going to this one girl's house. Sunny."

"And you want to go and get your teenager on?"

"Is that okay?"

"Tomorrow's my day off. I thought we'd eat Cheez Whiz and devour Civil War biopics." He frowned. "So this is a bit of a hit."

"You did not. I don't even know what Cheez Whiz is. It doesn't sound promising."

"That's the fun part." He dropped his napkin in mock resignation. "I will go it alone. Take your leave. Frolic with the youth. I'll represent on the couch for both of us."

"You're a pal."

"Home by midnight or no dice."

She tapped her lips. "Right. So…since you're in tonight, can I take the car?" Reid hadn't exactly reached out and offered her a ride, which was strange, but she decided not to focus on small details.

He fished the keys from his pocket. "Be safe. Don't touch a drop of booze, or I will lock you in the house like Cinderella."

"Rapunzel?"

"Your hair's not long enough."

"Valid." She raced upstairs and agonized over clothes, finally settling on a navy pair of jeans, a black scoop-neck top, and a blue and black plaid shirt left open. She surveyed herself in the mirror. Boring. She grabbed a silver necklace with a small heart that used to be her mom's and smiled. Better. Softer. Maybe someone might think she was pretty, even.

When she arrived at Sunny's, after purposely passing the house three times to get a feel for the event, it was clear that this was more than just a few people getting together. Music floated from both inside and outside the home at an uncomfortable decibel. As she approached, she could feel the *boom, boom* of the bass beneath her feet. There were kids on the porch, the sidewalk, and walking toward the two-story house located on a steep hill. Sunny clearly came from more money than she did and had parents that apparently left her to her own devices. Charming. She was starting to understand the roots of the entitlement she dealt with daily at practice.

As she followed a group of unknown kids into the home, fear coiled and crouched. She looked around for familiar faces. She saw Sebastian from her English class, whom she'd met on her first day and had barely spoken to since. And obnoxious Ryan Leonard who'd taken the mascot job when she'd forgone it. They nodded to her because as a cheerleader, even a low-ranking one, she apparently had a little social credit in the pipe. The house, though sprawling in one sense, was overflowing with small rooms, and Bethany found herself moving through them like a maze until she finally spilled into the backyard without even meaning to. What kind of weird pinball machine was this place?

Surrounding a perfectly square pool lit up midnight blue, she found the United elite holding court—cheerleaders, football players, the basketball stars, all popular for a combination of looks, talent, and confidence. That group was certainly intriguing. On one side of the pool she saw a group of boys chanting, in some kind of beer competition. On the other a letter jacket clad couple made out in a pool lounger. In the far corner, she saw Reid and her friends. Finally. She breathed a little easier.

As if she sensed Bethany's presence, Reid turned and broke into a smile, and all felt much better. The intimidation drifted away in the California chill. She was going to be okay. She smiled back. Except, instead of waving her over or moving to Bethany's side of the pool, Reid turned back to her conversation, hand tucked into the crook of Mateo's elbow. Bethany waited. Tried to figure out what to do with her arms because they felt weird and cumbersome. After another couple of minutes of surveying the action, her discomfort level blew up like a balloon. An awkward one. Did people notice that she was just standing there? She felt a few curious stares in her direction.

"Is that that new girl from Canada?" a nearby voice said. She squinted because that was only half right.

"Yeah. Made cheerleader because the coach is sleeping with her dad. It's a whole thing."

She scoffed and turned, but there was no indication of who the unfamiliar voices belonged to. She decided to move out of the space, made a lap around the yard and a big show of admiring the white twinkling lights and the gazebo on the far right. Oh, look at that. The white fence had little points at the top! How interesting! Anything to look busy. Reid, strangely, hadn't passed her so much as a glance, even when she attempted to catch her eye. On the flip side, Reid'd given lots of attention to Mateo. She now wore his red and white letter jacket, oversized on her frame. They laughed, *howled* really, at some memory from a party the year before. He had the group's focus, and she interjected details into his story like a well-rehearsed duo with their public looking on.

Just as she was ready to pack it in, humiliated and feeling silly for crashing the cool kids' party only to be ignored and ostracized, Reid appeared at her elbow.

"Hey." Her voice was quiet.

Bethany shifted her weight. Her head felt heavy, her muscles bunched. "Ah. There you are."

"What do you mean? I've been right here the whole time."

Bethany nodded. "With your friends. I get it." She turned to go but not before nodding in Mateo's direction. He was in the midst of a handstand for reasons only God knew. "You two are a striking couple."

"Whoa. Whoa. Whoa. Where are you going? Don't. I'm having fun. Is that a crime?"

That's when she caught the alcohol on Reid's breath. It also explained the extra-loud storytelling. "Not a crime. Continue, please. I'll see you at practice. I'm going home. Where I should have stayed in the first place."

"Why are you being like this?" Reid closed her eyes, giving in. Acknowledging. "Listen. I'm sorry or whatever."

"Right. Or whatever." Annoyance flared. Bethany couldn't tamp it down. She felt humiliated. Unimportant. It hurt exponentially more after the time they'd spent together in the park. She'd thought it might have been the start of something special. Instead, Reid had doubled down and invited Bethany to see her real relationship firsthand. Well, message received.

She headed back into the obnoxiously loud maze of rooms, getting shoulder-checked by drunk people because there was zero room to maneuver. It only took a few moments before Reid's soft hand tugged on her shoulder.

"Can we try this again?"

"It's a little late for that." She tossed the words over her shoulder and kept moving.

"Reid! What are you doing? Get back here," a female voice called. One of the minions, surely.

"I'm sorry," Reid said. "I was an ass. I just don't know what I'm doing."

They landed on the front porch, which cut the noise level in half. She whirled around and found her gaze stumbling into beautiful green eyes. "Yeah, well, please figure it out first. I'm a person who would rather not be crushed like a bug. You have kind of a lot of power right now, and you wield it however the hell you want, apparently."

Reid swallowed. "I know. I just—"

Bethany held up a hand. "You don't have to. Good night."

She found her car keys as she hurried down the sidewalk and

clutched them like a lifeline, her thumb moving across the cool metal as her throat ached with raw emotion. The stares. The way she felt when Reid's hands gripped Mateo's. The group laughter. The comment about her dad. Bethany felt sick and wanted nothing more than the safety of home. Cheez Whiz. Her bed. She touched her chest as she drove, rejecting the tears that attempted an appearance. She would be fine. She always was.

❖

Reid had screwed up. So very badly.

She stood on Sunny's porch like a statue as kids moved in and out of the house around her, hating herself for ignoring Bethany, the one person she longed to see above all others. When she'd arrived at the party, her reality loomed in front of her. Kissing Bethany had unleashed a whirlwind of feelings, and now she was going to *see* her. In public. In front of her friends. Her boyfriend. Surely everyone would know. See right through her. And there was a part of her that simply wasn't ready. She was still absorbing this new detail herself. How was she supposed to explain it to others?

"Hey," Jennifer said, appearing next to her. Sunny's Mini-Me. "Don't let that girl bother you. Shrug it off. We're your friends."

"I don't understand," Reid said. She looked back in the direction of the sidewalk. "What has Bethany ever done to you? Any of you?" She was killing the messenger and she knew it. Jennifer was inconsequential, but she stood for a lot more. Didn't matter.

"Sweetheart, we love you. But it's what she's doing to you." She shrugged. "People are talking about her. You don't want to get pulled down, too." Jennifer touched her arm, but it felt like a warning. She pulled hers away just in time to see Sunny cross her arms where she stood in the doorway.

"Jenn-Jenn, someone is asking about how you scored that leather jacket from Nordstrom. They're desperate to learn your ways."

Jennifer's eyes flashed excitement. She loved a good fashion tale, and Sunny damn well knew it. When they were alone, Sunny stepped forward. "Don't worry about Bethany," she said, coolly. "You'll make her feel better later, right?" What in hell did that mean. "She's not used to these kinds of gatherings, and I know you're trying to be a good captain and all by making sure she's included, but she's a big girl. Let her do her own thing." She brushed a strand of hair off Reid's shoulder. "It's not on you. You focus on Mateo. You don't want him to notice."

Reid, the weakling that she was, nodded. "You're totally right. I just get caught up."

Sunny placed her arm around Reid. "That's why we love you. Bighearted Reid. Always taking in the strays."

She wanted to push back, to set the record straight. She opened her mouth to do that, but the porch shifted, the alcohol working its evil magic. She wasn't a drinker. She'd only agreed to the shots her friends offered because the night felt like too much to handle. She hoped it would take the edge off. Another mistake.

"You good?" Sunny asked in her ear. "No one has to know what you do on your own time. But focus on what matters. Your future. And he's over there waiting for you. You don't want to blow this."

"Right. Okay." Sunny knew way more than she'd given her credit for, and maybe she really was trying to help.

"And we're okay, right? I know we butt heads, but I love the shit out of you."

"I love you, too, Sun. Things are just confusing right now."

"It's why you have me. Captains for life?"

"For life." Sunny took her hand and gave her a twirl. She'd come a long way with Sunny. She wasn't perfect, but she had Reid's back and always would. Reid latched onto that kind of reliability right now, especially with her dad up and leaving them.

"There's my girl," Mateo said. "Wondered where you ran off to." She smiled at him and his perfectly styled dark hair.

"I'll leave you two before you give me a goddamn toothache. Jennifer! We need more drinks."

"Hey," he said in Reid's ear. "Wanna get out of here? I want to do things to you." He'd had a few drinks of his own, and now he wanted alone time. Within minutes he'd have them parked somewhere with his hands all over her body as they made out, her back uncomfortably wedged against the passenger side door until she'd finally have to speak up and pull the runaway train to a stop. She'd lived that night one too many times, and after today, she just couldn't fathom going there again. An impossibility.

"I don't feel well," she said, tapping him on his chest. "Take me home?"

"But I don't want to take you home." He got really close to her neck. His breath tickled her skin, and she shifted away.

"Everyone's watching," she said quietly. It was pretty much the theme of their relationship. For show. They played their parts. Went home. And played them again. At least in Reid's brain. "Don't embarrass me."

He sighed, straightened, and nodded. "Whatever. I'll take you home."

"Thank you. But there's no way you can drive, and don't you dare try."

"Fine. Ryan what's-his-name is driving people places. Designated himself."

"Great. Let's find him."

Did she feel bad for breaking up with Mateo in the back seat of Ryan Leonard's Toyota Camry with Ryan eavesdropping like an eager little chauffeur? Yes. But did she see any other way? Not exactly.

"So it's like that?" Mateo asked when she'd finished her we're-headed-in-different-directions speech.

"I think it's for the best," she said, amazed at how guilt and horror at her own actions could sober a person up rather quickly. "Clean break, you know? You have your whole college career ahead of you, after all." It hurt to part ways with Mateo, but it also didn't. That was telling. "We can still hang out. Be friends. I want that."

"Okay, dude, but you're gonna regret this and change your mind. Probably by Monday. I know it."

"Ryan, you'll get him home safe?"

Ryan turned like a deer caught in a trap. "Yeah. Uh, I will definitely get him home." She offered a wave and went inside.

She wasn't sad about the way the night ended, but she did have a lot of regret for what happened in the middle. If she was in Bethany's shoes, she might even hate her for what she'd pulled. She couldn't begin to guess what Bethany was thinking. She tried to sleep, but when it wouldn't come, she fired off a short message.

I'm an ass. I'm thinking about you. A lot. I hope you'll forgive me. Please?

Reid went to sleep with a pit in her stomach, hoping that she'd wake up feeling more in control, free from her relationship and stupid social pressures to be a certain person. But what she hoped for most of all was to spend more time with Bethany. *Beth.* It was her image that haunted her just before she finally drifted that night. A garish mixture of the hurt she'd put in Bethany's eyes, her lips just before she kissed them, her incredibly genuine smile, and the echo of her angry words from the sidewalk.

She'd sort it all out soon.

She hoped. There was no other choice.

CHAPTER TEN

Now

Thunder rumbled in the distance, and the pitter-patter of large raindrops echoed. Bethany was on call that night for the practice. The three of them rotated. She'd already been woken three times that night by the answering service referring patients in need. She'd dutifully called all three and sent two to the emergency room. Sleep. It was quite the obstacle on a night like this one. At four a.m., she'd just abandoned the concept altogether and put on some coffee. Her right hand hurt, a common occurrence, exacerbated when she slept on it, and she had. She turned it over in her left and massaged the muscles, popped some ibuprofen, and did her best to put it out of her mind.

"You okay over there?" Thea asked later that day in the break room. "Not that you're regularly an overly chatty Muppet, but you're hyperbolically quiet."

"I realize that." She straightened, depositing the coffee creamer back into the cabinet where the office manager demanded it remain. "Damn rain."

Thea nodded. "And nothing else?"

"I made out with Reid. Not sure how to rationalize that one."

Thea's mouth made the shape of a silent *oh* and she sat, realizing this talk might take more than lingering in the doorframe allowed.

"No, no, no. Nothing dramatic. We had drinks and it opened some doors."

"Sexy doors. Sexy *kissing* doors." Thea's eyes went wide like she'd stumbled upon her pot of gold.

"Too sexy for their own good. Damn doors." Bethany shook her head.

"Are you improvising all this?"

"Yep. My life is like a four-year-old telling a story, making it up as they go."

"But maybe that's okay. Are you embracing it, or running around like a crazy chicken woman?"

Bethany let her head drop back before raising it again. "Both. Even though I don't know what that second one means. Am I really going for it again? This big, huge, ridiculous leap? Am I a chicken woman? And if I'm not, I probably need to get in front of what this is now, and not lead either of us down a path I can't complete."

Thea squinted. "Haven't you already tried that?" She touched her chest. "I feel like we've tried that and gotten nowhere."

"Don't say smart things right now. Play dumb with me. Act like I have a choice."

Thea stretched. "It wastes time. Let's cut to the crisis like the chicken women we are. The love of your life is back. That first one is always a doozy, and yours was the dooziest. She's kissing like an expert these days, looking just as good as back then, and you're hooked." She wiggled her shoulders, sinking into her chair for the haul. "Let's get down to it. Why didn't it work before?"

Bethany didn't like remembering the wall tumbling down, which had been juvenile, or the unfortunate events after, which were not. But she had no other choice. "She was an ass. I was a brick wall. The rest was a runaway train."

Thea squinted as if trying to see through mud. "Sounds simple enough."

"I can only speak to my part. As a kid, I was incapable of working through the trauma in order to fix anything. I didn't have the skills. If I had, things would have ended very differently."

"Is it possible that she *also* didn't have the skills, and now that you're grown adults, you can talk about it with the *new* ones? I mean, I feel like I've just solved it."

Bethany nodded, absorbing, because that was honestly what they had been doing without the label. But mapping things out the way Thea just had, analyzing their meaning, helped a logical head like hers. "We have *new* skills. Good point."

"See? Adulthood has a few perks." She checked her watch. Their conversations midday were never very long, sandwiched between admin and patients. "And you're still into her."

"It's only been physical once, but wow. Yeah. Four alarm. Kissing Reid was bang-on-the-table good, more so than it was in high school." She covered her eyes. "Which I can't even imagine explaining to my high school self. Her head would combust." Bethany shook her head, searching for a stray clinic-breeze to cool her heated face at the memory of Reid's gorgeous lips moving passionately over hers. The precision. The heat. The need.

Thea slammed the table, and her brown Bambi eyes went even wider. "If the kissing is good, just imagine other things...naked, hot, torrid things. Do you think she has naked skills?"

"I already know she does. And please don't put images like that in my head when I have to work." She smacked her forehead. So much smacking happening. "Now look what you've done."

"And welcome back to Turned On in the Middle of the Workday," Thea said into her imaginary microphone. "This is Skyler Ruiz, and we're here with Dr. Cahill, who just needs to get a little already."

Veronica blinked from the doorway. "She's doing her Skyler impression again. You might be a little obsessed."

"She's just so charismatic," Thea said, marveling. "I think we'd be best friends."

Veronica searched their faces. "What in hell is happening? And why am I missing it? Again."

Thea, always one to commit, held tight to her invisible mic. "Sexy Thoughts in the Workplace would like to interview you, ma'am."

"No," Veronica said, pointed at Thea, and then pivoted to Bethany. "Why are you fantasizing midmorning?"

"I'm not. Well, I wasn't." Bethany pointed at Thea, arm outstretched. "She did it. Now we're chicken people."

"Typical," Veronica said and floated out of the room again.

It had been three days since she'd kissed Reid, and the potency had yet to wear off. It wasn't going to. She knew that now. The kiss had also dispelled the myth that their relationship felt so big because they'd been kids first discovering love and lust. That was not the case. They were huge on their own, an always lingering spark set to ignite at any given second, like the other night. The power of their connection was still undeniable and trampled any other connection she'd attempted to make in her lifetime.

There were certainly differences between the then and now. They were quieter now in between meetings. Messages weren't flying between them all day like they had been back in the early days. In many ways, that made her crave Reid all the more. Think about her. Wonder what she was doing. Wearing. Musing about. There was no way out of it, but did she want out? The remarkable part was that she wasn't searching for the exit anymore.

After work that day as she walked to her car, she ran her thumb across the screen on her phone, feeling the energy. The idea of talking to Reid beckoned her like the sweetest sounding siren song. Giving in, she placed the damn call. Reid answered on the third ring, and at the sound of her voice, with their connection clicked into place, she felt whole.

"Beth. You called me."

She closed her eyes, enjoying the use of the nickname she'd only ever accepted from Reid. "Hey, last minute notice, but you wanna grab dinner? I thought I might keep it simple tonight after a long day at the clinic. Let the professionals cook." She smiled and waited.

"Oh wow." Silence. "Um…that sounds really nice. I want to. I wish I could, but I'm tied up. Busy week."

"So is that no to tomorrow, too?" It was a joke. A half joke. Not a joke at all. She was putting herself out there and it wasn't going well. *Fuck.*

"Sadly, yes."

"Oh. Gotcha." A pause. She was dangling from the cliff of humility and disappointment. "Totally okay." Bethany went into recovery mode, attempting to climb her way back to safety. Everything in her prickled with discontent, but she couldn't focus on that right now because the only thing worse than being rejected was the sidecar of embarrassment that came with it. "I completely get it. Don't worry." She sounded nonchalant, right? Please, God, let her sound like she was living in the land of no-big-deal and loving the real estate.

"Listen to me. This is not a blow-off. I know it sounds like one." Concern seeped into Reid's voice as she hurried to explain. "I just have a full plate this week, or I'd be there."

"It's okay. Dinner is overrated. All that small talk." She hoped she'd successfully faked a casualness she didn't feel.

"Bethany."

"Yes?"

"I'll call you soon. Promise."

"Yep. That'd be great." She said a fast and furious good-bye and clicked off the call. If Reid wasn't blowing her off, what in the world had her unavailable but also vague and cryptic? This didn't feel right. Did she dabble in espionage? Insider trading? Was there a parole hearing she needed to attend? Bethany admittedly didn't know a lot about Reid's life as it stood now. She taught at the collegiate level. She was interested in coaching at the tumbling gym someday. Never married. Still crazy, beautiful, and kind.

But there was so much more to find out, and in spite of being shot down tonight, maybe it was time she started listening, learning, and asking. She vowed to herself to make the effort. This second chance they had was growing in its importance with each hour. Tonight, she would eat alone, but perhaps that wouldn't be the case forever. Hope was a powerful and daunting tool, but she was no longer going to live in fear of its presence. She *needed* hope and planned to tuck it away, keep it close to her heart, right next to Reid Thatcher.

"One step at a time," she murmured to herself, phone to chest.

❖

Weekends back in town were fun. There was so much of her old stomping grounds that Reid excitedly revisited, while still continuing to venture to the new and unexplored. It meant she and Mason had the days stretched out before them like blank slates ready to be filled with any kind of adventures they chose. She had a couple ideas in mind for this particular Saturday and set off to find her partner in crime and get his take. She found him on the couch, zoned out to the world, lost in the action of his graphic novel.

She came up behind Mason and paused, her hands on the back of his shoulders. "Hey, bub. First choice, I was thinking we could do the museum. See the dinosaur exhibit you were telling me about. That or a movie. Third choice, one of those escape rooms."

"We always solve those. Dinosaurs get my vote."

"Done."

"Pepperoni pizza after? With extra cheese?" her son asked. Mason loved pizza almost as much as he loved dinosaurs.

"I think I can manage a pizza date with you if you promise to be a good conversationalist."

She knew that would get him. He set the graphic novel aside. "That's one of my strengths," he said, sitting a little taller. "I talk a lot." He was a smart little guy for a nine-and-a-half-year-old. The school administrators approached them about moving him midyear from the fourth grade to the fifth. His grades were high, and he was likely getting bored with a curriculum he'd mastered. While the academics might have suited him more, they'd worried about the social pressures. He already faced more than his fair share of bullying in and out of the classroom, and they were worried that a grade change might unsettle him further. He wasn't interested in sports or popular songs or recognizable name-brand sunglasses. Don't even get her started on the money LA kids shelled out for fashion. Science was his current passion, most specifically, learning about the Earth and the solar system, and that didn't match up with too many kids his age. She tried her best to be his friend but could tell he was lonely, and it ate away at her. She lay awake at night and said a daily prayer to the universe that he'd make a friend and have people to sit with at lunch. In fact, it made her rethink her entire social existence when she was younger. She should have done more to befriend the less popular kids. She very much regretted that now.

"You're right. You do talk my face off. I'm less worried."

He hopped off the couch and followed her through their petite dining room and into the kitchen composed in deep browns and tall cabinetry. It was the one room in the house that made Reid feel a little fancy. When they'd moved in, she'd replaced the cabinets, redone the floors, and picked out new fixtures. She didn't have a ton of money, but she provided what she could for the two of them, and that mattered most. The house wasn't big, but they each had their own rooms and space. It had really started to feel like home. Though Mason spent time at his dad's place, for the most part, he was with her. The two of them were a team, a ride or die. Without Mason, she didn't know where she'd be.

"I was thinking. Maybe for my birthday we rent a race car."

Reid paused. "Not sure race cars are rentable."

"And I drive it."

"You don't have a license."

"I thought you'd say that."

She sighed, ready for the argument he'd clearly prepared in advance of this conversation. "Yeah, I bet."

"The thing is when you're talking about birthdays, most of life's, um, rules, don't matter. So maybe this license one should go right out that window over there."

"Is that true, though? I think rules are rules." She made up water bottles for both of them for the museum outing. She'd learned to be prepared, and *I'm thirsty, Mom* was a common complaint.

"I think it's true. Wait. Where are you going?"

She turned back. "Museum. Pizza. Let's hit the road."

"Okay. But about that rental race car."

"Out of luck on the car, pal."

"I tried hard, though."

She bopped his head, which was covered in a mass of thick brown hair. "You did."

As they drove, Mason disappeared into silence, and it gave her mind space. She hadn't been able to shake the call from Bethany the night before. The tentative exchange. The *awkward*. God. All she'd wanted recently was for Bethany to let go of reluctance, her nerves, and maybe even give them a glimpse of a second chance. And then as soon as she showed the first glimmer, Reid covered her cards and retreated? She hadn't found the right moment to tell Bethany about Mason and his conception, and that was on her. She could have said as much on their call last night. *Hey, I have a son and he's pretty great. I wanted to tell you, but the time hasn't felt right. Now that we're closer, I wanted to share.*

But after that head-spinning, corner-turning kiss, Bethany deserved transparency. She needed to know more about Reid's life, what she'd been through, and how it made her the person she was today. She was no longer that lost and confused soul working through her own coming out at the same time her parents blindsided her with the divorce card. Or worse, the shell of a person she'd been as she headed off to college, confused and drowning. Mason had helped with all of that. He'd changed her life for the better, and she wanted Bethany to hear his praises from her. Reid's heart sped up at the thought. What if the revelation drove her away? Reid knew from years ago that Bethany liked kids, thought of having some herself one day. Didn't mean she'd be interested in Reid's. The idea made her want to wrap Mace up in a little ball and protect him at all costs. Could she do the same to her own heart? Because it was becoming attached to the one person it had always longed for, and the fall was so very far. Whether she'd planned on it or not, she was back in it. Invested in Dr. Bethany Cahill with so much on the line.

"The brontosaurus exhibit was my favorite," Reid said two hours later, holding a huge slice of pepperoni. "They're so peaceful. Especially when they move with the herd."

"I much preferred the T. rex. He had those huge toenails. The recreation of the toenails was impressive."

"Oh, you *much preferred*, did you?"

"Vocab word from last week. I got a hundred." A small smile appeared behind his slice.

"That's the way we do it." She offered and received a high five, then captured his hand and kissed the back of it as he beamed. He was such a sweet guy, and celebrating his victories was important for his self-esteem. His round cheeks went pink and he pushed his dark brown glasses farther up onto his nose. He'd already polished off three slices of pizza and was eying a fourth. Food was his comfort zone, and though she tried to keep things healthy for him at home, restaurants were always a place to splurge, and she happily encouraged him. Kids needed pizzeria-extra-pepperoni-pizza. That felt like a parenting basic when times were tough.

"This looks like a fun table."

Reid raised her gaze and went still. Her heart rate leaped. Standing at the host stand a few feet from their table stood Bethany and two other women. She smiled widely at Reid and then at Mace, waiting for a response. She should formulate one soon, but this was very unexpected. Not what she'd planned for.

"Hey." Reid gave her head a shake, trying to wake it into expert action. "I wasn't expecting to run into you." Good. That was the truth and a nice start.

Bethany seemed casual, unaffected. She wore jeans and a white blazer with the sleeves rolled up. Delectable. Not that it mattered in a moment as charged as this one. "These are my friends, Thea and Veronica. I told you about them. We're also partners at the clinic." From a few feet behind her, both women waved in choreographed unison. She mustered a wide smile and waved back. "Nice to meet you both." The one Beth had introduced as Thea leaned in, biting her lip. All that was missing was the popcorn because they seemed intensely interested in her exchange with Bethany, making her understand that they'd been briefed. She also realized that it was her turn for introductions. This so wasn't how she'd imagined telling Bethany she had a child, but fate had other ideas. She swallowed and went for it.

"Right. And this guy is my son, Mason. We just came from the museum."

To her credit, Bethany only paused for a beat as the information melted in. Next, she broke into a wide grin directed at Mason. If she was angry or alarmed, she certainly wasn't going to take it out on him. Thank God. "I happen to love that museum. Did you check out the dinosaurs? Only here for another couple weeks."

Mason took a minor break from his slice, immune to all of it. "T. rex has great toenails."

Bethany nodded, thoughtful. "I appreciate the tip. It's a good one." She paused. "I'm partial to the pterodactyls."

He set his slice down entirely on that one. She had him. "Interesting choice. Not a lot of people appreciate them."

Bethany seemed amused, as most adults were when talking to Mace. If only the other kids could see his sparkle. Maybe one day. Bethany turned to her. A shrug. A question mark. Her surprise was clear. "I had no idea."

"I know. That's on me."

Bethany opened her mouth and then closed it. In that moment, she apparently made the decision to focus on Mace. Admirable as always. "Maybe we can talk dinosaurs again someday. Sound cool?"

Mason nodded, super casual. "Sure. Anytime you want. I know a whole lot. Even some secret stuff."

"Well, now you've got me hooked."

Mason beamed at Bethany, and she beamed back.

Reid's brain raced. None of it was supposed to have played out this way. On the one hand, Bethany had been simply perfect with her son. Patient and friendly, tapping into his interests even. On the other, Reid had no idea what she was actually thinking. This was probably a lot to learn without warning or explanation. That part was all her fault. Was Bethany angry? Hurt she hadn't been told sooner? Recrimination bubbled and swirled. She should have told her about Mason on that very first day. But something within her had desperately needed to protect him until she understood what the situation actually was. It didn't excuse the time that had continued to tick by. She'd have to find the words to explain this. Later.

"It was good to see you guys," Bethany said, indicating with a thumb that she needed to join her friends, who were being led to their table.

"I'll call you later. I mean, if that's okay." A check-in to see if she was still welcome, secret keeper that she was now revealed to be.

"I would like to…chat," Bethany said. "Learn a few things." She waved energetically at Mason, who waved back. "Bye, dinosaur guy. Enjoy that pizza."

"It's really good. California does pizza right. Something about the crust. I haven't figured it out yet. I will."

Bethany laughed. "Well, let me know."

Reid smiled at her son, pride blossoming. She hoped he was always as earnest. They'd had a good day together, laughed a lot, and now had a successful meeting with the other most important person to ever grace Reid's life. Mason had met Bethany, at last. Wow. She'd need some time to absorb. In the meantime, Mason would stay with his dad that next weekend, which meant she would soak up as much Mace time as possible during the week. This had been a good start.

"Shall we head home and put our feet up for a while?"

"Yes, I'm parched."

"Do you mean exhausted?"

"Yeah. Wrong word?"

"Points for trying, though."

She paid the bill and drove them home, already thinking through possible afternoon movies they could relax to. They were a tight knit pair and had been since the moment of his birth. Mason was her very best friend. Still, she tentatively imagined a third person sharing their afternoon, tried it on in her head, reliving the brief exchange at the pizza place and wondering how far that rapport stretched.

"I liked your friend," Mason said unprompted from the passenger seat.

She grinned at him, feeling hopeful and full. Maybe prematurely, but she didn't care. She planned to hold on to this moment. "Me, too, Mace."

❖

Veronica eyed Bethany around their towering pineapple and prosciutto pizza on a stand, a favorite from their med school days. She then eyed Thea, who joined her in eyeing Bethany. "Why are you staring? Am I that beautiful today? I did use a new shampoo." Bethany touched the back of her hair and grinned. "Well, thank you." And went back to her plate.

"You're either experiencing the best pizza of your life and need silent reverence, or something important is on your mind," Veronica said with a squint.

"Can it be both, though?" Back to her plate. The solid white color of the porcelain helped anchor her thoughts, which, to be honest, were in some sort of race with her flying feelings.

"I appreciate you copping to it," Veronica said and tucked a strand of long dark hair behind her ear.

Bethany shrugged. "Not like I can hide anything from you two."

"So, that was Reid," Thea said in a singsong voice that a mother would likely use.

"The one and only," Bethany said.

"And was that her little boy?" Thea took a delicate pull from a straw. "You didn't mention she had kids."

"No." She shook her head. "You're right. I didn't. Because I didn't know."

Her friends went still in a comically perfect pose. Thea's mouth was open midbite, pizza slice suspended. Veronica was just about to speak. Now they sat before her like animatronic characters who'd lost power.

Finally, someone plugged them back in. "Wait," Thea said. "So you're just finding out today? As in, over there a few minutes ago?"

"That would be correct."

"But why?" Veronica asked.

"I will have to get back to you on that. Though I have my guesses." That set them off in a flurry of speculation.

"She wanted to get to know you again first." Thea nodded thoughtfully.

"Make sure there was something substantial there," Veronica pointed out.

"Find the perfect moment." Thea shrugged.

Veronica gasped in realization. "Maybe she's been burned in that department before."

Bethany chewed, considering. "Yeah. Maybe. Any of it." But inside her own brain, she knew that Reid was in self-protection mode and holding parts of her life back. Bethany was, too, so she couldn't blame her entirely. They'd done a number on each other, and before they could let go of their inhibitions, they were likely going to have some triage and work to do.

"Can I offer some unsolicited advice?" Veronica asked delicately.

Bethany sobered and perked her ears. She'd always looked up to Veronica. She was their leader, the wisest friend she had. "I would very much appreciate that, actually."

"If she matters to you—"

"She does," Bethany said without moving a muscle. She felt Reid all over. Even now.

"Then you try not to judge each other for the things you do to survive."

Bethany exhaled in relief. "Good. Because learning about Mason is jarring, but at the same time, I might have handled things the same way. Withheld at first. Figured out what this was before leaping."

Veronica squeezed her hand and Thea nodded along. "And you liked him?"

"He seems adorable and smart. I don't have any issues with kids. Especially great ones. I can't imagine Reid raising anything but."

"Don't take this wrong." Thea held up an apologetic hand. "Is it possible that the other parent is…still in the picture?"

Bethany frowned. "No." A pause. "I can't imagine that would be the case." She thought about the cryptic, vague phone call, which could easily have been because she had Mason and couldn't get together. But yeah. Maybe she had this whole secret life that Bethany knew nothing about. "Well, damn."

Thea winced, her big brown eyes apologetic. "My bad."

It was all so unlikely. Bethany knew as much, but for the next few days, it felt like she was holding her breath waiting for Reid to reach out. When she finally did, Bethany all but jumped at the chance to unravel the mystery. The call came late in the day on Friday. She had just finished up with a patient with a strawberry rash. Alone in her office, she stared at the word *Reid* on her screen in big white letters and, finally, slid her thumb across the glass.

"Hi."

"Hi," Reid said, followed by an exhale. "Long week."

"Jam-packed."

"Just gonna jump in. I want to see you. I need to." Bethany took a slow inhale, steadying herself against the power of Reid's words. They had a way of enveloping every inch of her.

She closed her eyes. "Okay. Um, dinner. Are you free? I can come to you if you have your son."

"With his dad for the weekend."

"Oh. Okay." So the dad lived elsewhere. That was something to celebrate. No hidden families. Not that Bethany truly believed that was the case.

"I'm sure you have questions."

She remembered the one she'd just asked herself. "I might." She sighed and let her head fall backward against the cool leather of her chair, her emotions banging down the door until it splintered and cracked wide open. "Okay. Yes. I do have questions. And regrets. And fears. And probably things that I need to say to myself and you." Yep. There it all came.

"Sounds like I should maybe buy a bottle of wine."

"Or eight."

Reid laughed, and she let herself simply soak up the sound, transported back in time. Only they were right here in the present, better versions of themselves. There was no happier sound than that laugh, and after a week with virtually no contact, she craved more and it wasn't in her power not to. Would it end differently this time? And if not, what in the world had she gotten herself into? Reid Thatcher 2.0 was poised to break her heart all over again if she wasn't careful. She tried not to think like that. They were going to get through this. They mattered to each other, and there was nothing she could do about that part. Whether together or individually, they would survive this tangled-up time.

"Tell you what," Reid said. "I'll send you my address. You bring the eight bottles."

"You're on."

CHAPTER ELEVEN

Then

It was one of those sleepy Sundays where not a lot happened. When the day took its time and there wasn't much to do. Bethany had been making a spaghetti dinner for herself while her dad worked some reshoots at the studio lot when she'd heard the doorbell. Expecting a delivery or a neighbor, she wiped her hands and pulled the door open, surprised at who she saw.

Reid extended the single red rose. When Bethany accepted it, Reid pulled a white T-shirt from her back pocket and waved it like a flag on the end of her fingertips that sported pink polish. When Bethany didn't say anything, she proceeded to drop her chin and offer the biggest puppy dog eyes Bethany had ever seen. She wasn't playing fair.

"Stop it already. I can't take it."

Reid took a step closer, nearly in Bethany's space. She could smell Reid's shampoo, flowers in a meadow. Her proximity made Bethany's skin tingle and her resolve weaken. Gone were the puppy dog eyes and in their place was guilt, plain and simple. Reid felt bad. "I was an ass last night. Am I forgiven?" she asked softly. She took Bethany's hand and gave it a soft squeeze. "Say yes."

"Yes." Bethany wanted to explain all the ways her feelings had been hurt the night before. But the look on Reid's face right now said she understood. "Can we not do that again?"

"I have zero plans. I broke up with Mateo. It's done." She stared at Bethany, who was speechless, rooted to her spot in shock. She hadn't seen that coming, and the words were on delay. "You did? Why?"

"I don't imagine that he's the one for me. You and I both know that." She seemed nervous now. Her cheeks colored pink, and she shifted her weight. Reid was never nervous. In fact, she was always the one in control, calling the shots. This was a new look.

"Does this have anything to do with…"

"This has everything to do with…" Reid hadn't hesitated or even moved a muscle.

She tamped down the spark of excitement. Not yet. "So, what now?"

"Can we take our time? This is new." She ran her fingers through her sun-streaked hair. "I'm a little out of my element."

Bethany granted permission for the grin to take over her face. Maybe the night before hadn't been such a bad thing if it kick-started Reid to affirm their legitimacy. "Yeah. We definitely can. I've not exactly been here before either. At least, seriously."

"I don't know that I'm ready to take out an ad about us or anything. Especially with Mateo and the breakup being so fresh."

"No, no. Discreet it is." She glanced behind her. "I'm making my famous spaghetti. It's widely reviewed or whatever. Interested?"

"The whatever was a fantastic selling point."

She opened the door and led Reid inside. Reid'd been inside a handful of times when picking up Bethany, but this would be her first official hang-out-inside visit. Bethany saw the bland, small single-story home through Reid's eyes now. Not too much to write home about. White walls. Lots of photographs. Her dad was big about printing and framing important moments, including one of her mastering the balance beam for the first time at five. Some of the furniture they'd brought with them. The rest was secondhand stuff he'd found once they arrived in LA. It made for a mismatched space of different colors, textures, and wood tones. But it did have one thing going for it. It was homey and warm. He did that for them, and she liked their little place together.

"I love this kitchen," Reid said. "And the fact that you're cooking in it."

"It helps quiet my brain. I like it in here."

She took in the space. Her father had lined the counter with a couple of spindle-backed barstools so they could hang out together while one of them cooked. Reid slid onto one now, and Bethany got to work on the other side, assembling two bowls of spaghetti with the small meatballs she'd baked. Her dad's recipe. She felt Reid's gaze on her hands as they moved, which added a thick layer of tension. Excitement, too.

"I'm seeing a whole new side of you right now. Maybe you'll open a restaurant one day."

"Not likely. I'm planning on medical school." She slid a bowl to Reid and passed her the dish of freshly grated Parmesan. Her father insisted it was the only way to top spaghetti. None of that lackluster stuff from the jar.

"This looks ridiculous. Confession. I can't cook."

"Then I guess I'll have to do most of it." She watched Reid take in the comment and swallow. She was glad she made it, bold as it was for her to assume there'd be a future them. Reid's recent actions had bumped her confidence up a few notches, and she was running with the newfound power.

"You seem pretty sure about medical school. You got this determined look in your eye. The same one you get right before a killer tumbling pass."

"I've known since I was young that I want to be a doctor. I've grown and changed, but that part I've never wavered on."

"Well, you certainly have the math and science part down. You're my favorite person to go to for the answers."

She basked in the compliment. "It certainly helps. And I only give them to you because you're pretty." She offered a wink to let Reid know it was only half true. They smiled at each other as they ate, Reid from her spot on the stool, Bethany still standing across from her against the counter, twisting her spaghetti into round little forkfuls from afar. It was almost like she was afraid to get any closer, now that she had semi-permission. The flirtatious looks they occasionally passed as they ate and talked were underscored by The Skips, the band that Reid recommended on that first ride home. Appropriate. She played them more often than she should because the music made her think of Reid, which was all she ever really wanted to do. And now here Reid was, wearing a yellow sweater, form-fitting enough to highlight her curves, the neckline low enough to offer the small glimpse of cleavage, making it hard to concentrate on anything as mundane as noodles and sauce. She'd never lusted after another human the way she did Reid Thatcher. It was astonishing how much she thought about kissing Reid, running her thumbs up Reid's rib cage, exploring her body, and taking liberties she'd never taken with anyone in real life before.

"You drifted away just now, Dr. Cahill," Reid said with a point of her fork. She slid the bowl forward. "Killed it. You have many talents."

Bethany raised an eyebrow and Reid raised hers right back. The air crackled. They were quiet for a moment. "I want to kiss you again." The sentence was so simple that it didn't match the level of lust that it inspired. Reid stood, offering a better view of the yellow sweater of temptation. Her boobs were clearly announcing themselves. Reid pointed at the couch. "Over there." She walked the short distance and took a seat, waiting patiently like a present to unwrap. Bethany blinked. Her shoes stuck to the floor. None of this was what she imagined she'd be doing with her Sunday night on her own.

She rolled her lips in, which bought her time to get her head right. "As in now? You meant this moment?" Could Reid see her pulse race from the spot on her neck?

Reid nodded. She clearly had so much more experience with this kind of thing.

She had to figure out how to take what she wanted. And she did *want*. Bethany somehow found a way to the couch, took a seat next to Reid, and allowed herself a much needed breath. Reid's gaze was unwavering. Her bravery astounded, giving Bethany much to work toward. Reid's eyes met Bethany's, then dropped to her lips. With one finger, Reid swept a strand of Bethany's hair from her forehead with precision. It sent a shiver. "Do you want to kiss me?" Reid asked in a near whisper.

Bethany nodded and gathered her courage. This was not the moment to be shy. She tilted her head and leaned in. At first, she brushed Reid's lips with hers, tasting the lip gloss she must have applied on the sly after dinner. Berries. It made her body tighten and ache. It also made her deepen the kiss, needing something from Reid that she couldn't quite articulate as she slipped her tongue into Reid's mouth. It felt so good that she had to steady herself. Her hands trembled. *Go slow. Go slow.* Reid moaned quietly. Not helping. Bethany felt hot. Noticeably dizzy. A lot wonderful. They were lying down. How? She wasn't sure how that had happened, but she had a feeling she'd taken them there. She was on top, and with Reid's body beneath hers, she felt things that she wasn't quite prepared for. Her center ached, and an intensity came over her. She had to do something or she was going to bust apart. Her shaking hands slipped beneath Reid's sweater as they kissed. She stroked the skin at her waist with both thumbs, itching to go higher, dying to, holding herself back. It was a full-on war with her hands, but she wanted more than anything to be respectful.

"It's okay," Reid said, her breath tickling Bethany's lips. "You can."

Bethany nodded. Words failed. She watched in awe as Reid sat up, prepared to do the work for her. A gift. She pulled the yellow sweater over her head to reveal a light pink satin bra that offered a more than generous dip in the front. She wanted her lips in the middle of that line of cleavage. Reid extended her hand, beckoning Bethany, which she wholeheartedly accepted, allowing herself to be pulled back down.

Everything was different now. With Reid in nothing but a bra and jeans, it was clear that the rules had changed, and they were actually living her fantasies. Only better. Everything felt intimate, forbidden, awesome. They continued to kiss as Bethany's fingertips skated across the smoothest skin she'd ever encountered. She placed featherlight touches up Reid's rib cage that became more insistent with each second that passed. Their legs staggered in a wonderful tangle, each pressing against the other to get closer, then closer still. With Reid's tongue in her mouth, her breasts so close, and her thigh between Bethany's, it was almost too much. She went white hot at the onslaught of feeling that sprang from her body, every nerve ending at attention, tight and pressing. The insistence between her legs grew by the second, and her brain stuttered to process the sensations flying its way.

"My turn," Reid said, intuitively taking the reins. Bethany blinked. *Wait, what?* She was at Reid's mercy and in awe of her confidence, her moves, the way she carried her body. Bethany treasured every moment, even if most of her own body wasn't working correctly. Reid bit her lip in apparent concentration, her gaze locked on Bethany's chest as she slowly pulled Bethany's shirt up over her head. She didn't stop there. That was the crazy part. Kissing Bethany's neck and then breathing hotly against it, she unbuttoned her jeans. "Can I?" she whispered, to which Bethany nodded. The feeling of Reid's hand sliding down the front of her pants into her underwear was one she'd never forget. The world tilted beneath them. Reid's forehead rested softly against her neck as she began to stroke Bethany slowly.

Reid's breathing became shallow, labored, and the knowledge that she could affect Reid in that manner shook her. Nothing in her life or fantasies had ever felt so off the charts wonderful. Floating in over a ballad by The Skips came the noticeable sound of an engine in the driveway. Her body's response to Reid's touch was too much to ignore, however. She couldn't stop. Her hips rocked, and she pressed herself against Reid's hand, which rhythmically moved with her. Her dad was home. What? Why? Didn't matter. The pressure climbed systematically, a machine, until she thought it might kill her. Nothing had ever felt more intense than that climb. It had only been a few seconds of intimacy, but she was already there, dangling over the precipice, threatening to topple. She heard Reid moan. Bethany held on to her shoulders. She also heard the key in the door. That's when she shattered, light bursting forth behind her eyes. Pleasure hit hard and fast to a level she didn't know existed. The wonderful sensations consumed her and rocketed through every nerve ending, all brought to her by Reid. That was the amazing part. The house had a decent sized entryway that her father would putter in for a moment, storing his wallet, phone, and keys. Reid was already losing the wrestling match with her inside-out sweater. Bethany's own pants remained unzipped.

"Hey, you guys. Whatcha doing?" Bethany turned and stared at her dad, who was standing in the entrance to the living room holding a newspaper folded in his right hand. It only took him about three seconds to get it. His face went red. He wasn't entirely sure what to do with himself. "We wrapped our day early, so here I am." His voice was too loud. He looked at the walls. The framed picture of Bethany standing next to the Easter Bunny when she was four. All the while, Bethany did her best to register the things happening around her while recovering from the most potent couple of minutes of her entire existence on Earth. So far, that sweater had only made it onto one of Reid's arms. She now fumbled for the rest. Her dad whirled around, giving them his back. "Fuck. God. Pardon me. I'll be in my room for a few moments. Pretending I saw nothing and hoping to scrub it from my brain." He gestured to Bethany without looking directly at her. "Fly's down, pal. I'm out."

"Oh," Bethany mumbled, righting her zipper.

Once alone, Reid turned to her, mouth agape. "Oh my God."

"I can't believe that just happened."

A small smile played on Reid's lips. "Which part? Because…"

Bethany's brain was still mush. Her body sang the song of lazy satisfaction. And her bones were still liquid. "All of them. I can't believe all the parts happened."

"I think he's onto us."

"He's totally onto us. His face was red."

"I'm mortified about that, but also you're really cute right now," Reid said happily. "In spite of everything. I had to say that."

"Because it wasn't *your dad* who caught us—"

"Half dressed and breathing like sprinters who just won a race?" Reid looked incredibly proud of herself. "He won't kill me, will he? I wouldn't blame him. His daughter. His couch." She sighed.

"He won't. He might try to give me the birds and the bees talk, though. We somehow skipped that part growing up. I'm self-taught but earned an A."

"Oh, I'll say," Reid offered and fanned herself. Victory.

"Don't make me laugh right now. This is a serious situation." It was also an amazing one, if you took the dad part away. Bethany closed her eyes, still reveling. The physical side of her was very much still clinging to five minutes ago. "I've never felt that before."

"I've never made that happen to someone before." They exchanged a smile that felt important. A link between them. New territory. Her heart swelled. She interlaced their fingers and gave Reid's hand a squeeze.

The regrettable part was that they'd been cut short so soon. She'd not had the chance to touch Reid the way she had been touched. She wanted to, flashing to the image of her discarding that yellow sweater, skin on display, cheeks pink, lips full and swollen from being kissed.

"Excuse me, world!" her dad bellowed. "I'm on my way into the living room, which I will pass through on my way to the kitchen for a beer and snack. Do you hear that, world? Here I come! Teenagers have been warned appropriately and with volume."

"Not necessary," Bethany said simply, sitting two cushions down from Reid and folding her hands in her lap like a dainty flower. They were both the picture of prim and proper. Just two incredibly chaste friends staring at a dark, motionless TV screen. Totally normal. "We were just watching a movie."

"On that?" he asked, hurrying through. "You two have talent. Want food?"

"Had some," Bethany said. "Leftover spaghetti in the fridge."

"I knew there was a reason I had a child."

"Hi, Mr. Cahill. I meant to say hi earlier." Reid nodded nine times. An overkill. They'd have to work on burying guilt.

"Good to see you, Reid. Did you get any spaghetti?"

"I did. Five stars."

"Generous. I'd go with four point five. She always skimps on garlic."

Bethany sighed. "Everyone's a critic."

"I should head home," Reid said quietly to Bethany. "Still have that paper due in English tomorrow. I'm relieved we're better. Moving in the right direction."

"Okay. Me, too." She didn't like the idea of saying good-bye. Reid had broken up with her boyfriend, showed up on Bethany's doorstep, and rocked her entire world in under two hours. She followed her to the car anyway, lingering like a shy schoolgirl hopeful for a crumb of attention, which she apparently was now. "I'm glad you came over."

"Does this mean we can put last night in the rearview mirror? As in officially? I'm really still so sorry."

"I think we can."

"Confession on the way. I'm still a little lost and not so great with change."

"This is kind of a big one," Bethany said. "I get it. I didn't like the way last night made me feel, though. Can we not go back there?"

"I promise you. We won't." Reid leaned in, closed her eyes, and brushed Bethany's lips with a gentle kiss. "I'm kissing girls in driveways. Just look at me. Growing by adventurous leaps and bounds every minute." She sighed, playing with the ends of Bethany's hair. "I'm afraid I'm addicted to you. No. I know it."

"May you never seek help."

"See? Your dry wit is a big part of it. And your intelligence. And the way you look. I can't stop staring at you during practice in those stretchy tank tops. It's all on display. Muscles, curves, skin." She took a deep inhale as if deeply affected. "And I love the way you talk. And smell."

Bethany laughed and made a keep-it-coming gesture.

"I like a lot of things about you, okay?" Reid said loudly in defense.

"Yeah, well, have you spent any time with yourself? My list is probably more exhaustive. I'll send you an annotated copy one day, popular girl. See you at school?"

"You better. And stop being so hot." Reid slid into her driver's seat, the same car that had taken Bethany home the second day of school. How far they'd come since then, as evidenced by Reid's hand down her pants. But damn, she looked really good behind the wheel. Reid opened her mouth to talk, paused, then went for it again, seeming to bite the bullet. "For Mateo's sake, can we downplay things when we're around other people? Just for a little while."

"Oh. Yeah. Of course." A deflation.

"It's nothing to do with sexuality or me being afraid."

"Aren't you, though?"

"A little. Yes. But this is more about Mateo's feelings because he's a good guy at heart, and I don't think he saw this coming. Just want to put a little space out there before he understands all this."

She felt a little better about that. "A respect thing. I get it." Bethany could be patient and honor the request. Honestly, she'd walk to San Francisco and back if it would make Reid happy. That's how much she cared. In the midst, there was a tiny kernel of concern that wiggled its way into her conscious thought. She tried to move past it, but it ripped through her newfound happiness, elbowing its way. She shifted her weight as Reid drove away. She could play by those rules. She kicked a pebble, struggling with her warring emotions. The true question remained: How long did Reid plan to keep her a secret?

❖

Daunting. That's what this week felt like as it loomed in front of Reid. There would be fallout, questions, and maybe even accusations coming her way regarding her breakup, and she'd have to be ready. Nothing happened quietly at their school, and every action had a social domino effect on everything else. Reid knew as much, but the reality still rocked her. After only taking about six steps down the crowded United hallway that Monday morning, she was flanked by Sunny, Ella, and Jennifer all wearing very determined expressions. The trio of doom.

"Why didn't you call us?" Sunny asked, matching her quick pace. Reid was late because Alice had insisted on eating a third bowl of Golden Grahams, in literally no hurry at all. She could have killed her sister but held her cool, given the difficult time she was clearly still having. This wasn't about Alice, though, and she knew it.

"We would have been there for you," Ella offered.

"Talked you off the goddamned ledge," Jennifer said. "Because now you're splattered on the ground in a bloody social mess. No one can help you now."

"What?" Reid balked. "Harsh."

"Accurate," Sunny corrected.

"Listen, I love you guys," Reid said. "And maybe I should have called you. It's just that Mateo and I, we've been moving in different directions, and in that moment, I just couldn't see a way forward. So I improvised. This is for the best, you know?"

"No," her three friends said in unison.

Sunny took over. "I mean that's everyone right now. We're all overthinking. You're not alone. We're each panicking about the future. And colleges. And regionals are literally next week, which is a fucking head trip on its own. You're probably just stressed." Her dark brows were low and her voice insistent. It was clear she was worried this move might somehow impact her social world, bottom line. The truth was, it just might. That couldn't influence Reid. At least, she tried not to let it weigh on her. She'd known all along that there'd be fallout when she ended things. But she hadn't let herself think about it too much. Until now that it was here, in her face, literally walking her down the hall like an armed escort.

"You can fix this," Ella said, tapping Reid's shoulder gently.

"What if I don't want to? What if this is what's supposed to happen?"

Jennifer's eyes went wide as they arrived outside the door of Reid's first period English class. Sunny placed a hand on Jennifer as if to say, *Let me take this one, novice.* Her voice dropped in deep warning as she said, "Don't do something stupid. This is your future we're talking about. Mateo is the guy every girl at this whole damn school dreams about. You're the one they want to be."

She exhaled slowly. Was she even that girl anymore? She felt like her, but not. Both an exciting and jarring realization. This was new terrain, unmapped, terrifying, and mysterious. "I gotta get to class. Try not to worry so much about it."

"Reid," Sunny hissed. But Reid didn't look back. She was starting to get it. Her friends weren't just upset on her behalf. They felt betrayed because she'd turned on one of their own.

At practice that afternoon, they pushed themselves to the brink of exhaustion. With the clock ticking on their route to regionals, they were still dropping stunts, and that was simply unacceptable. Which meant they went again. Another full-out. Another chance to exhaust or injure their bodies. They lived on fumes and pushed harder. Bethany, in particular, had an incredibly hard track in the routine, and the full-outs had to be killing her. She didn't let on. After practice, Reid checked in.

"Looking really good out there. You might be the only one who hasn't missed all afternoon. You okay?"

Bethany unwrapped her ankle and rubbed the back. "Just need to ice is all."

"How you holding up, Cahill?" Coach Rogan asked over Reid's shoulder. "Need the trainer? Be straight with me. You need to let me know if we're pushing you too hard."

Bethany forced a smile. "I'm okay. Just feeling the strain a little. Nothing that's going to stop me."

Reid had no doubt about that strain. If she had Bethany's tumbling passes, she'd be feeling it, too. Bethany's difficulty level within the routine surpassed everyone else's.

Sunny, from a few feet away, folded her arms. "The last thing we need is you not taking care of yourself." Her voice was ice. "We all suffer if you go down. If you're hurt, say so. We can't lose another tumbler."

"She says she's okay," Reid said.

"And you speak for her now." Sunny's eyes narrowed. "Predictable."

Rogan bristled. "Stop it. Set an example. You're captains. Bethany knows her body better than anyone."

"Got it, Coach," Sunny said, her voice now dialed to supportive team player.

Rogan clapped her hands. "Circle up. Let's chat about logistics for regionals. Send me your roommate requests. If it matches the other person's, you're all set. After that, I'll make the remaining assignments. Tatum and Christina, you're not together anymore after the shower flooding incident last year, so don't even try."

Sunny's gaze landed on Reid. They'd always roomed together in the past. It made sense. The cocaptains. The leaders. She passed back a smile. But beneath it all, she knew who she wanted to room with, and it definitely wasn't Sunny. This would be a tricky maneuver. She was going to have to play her cards right in order to not make waves.

As they walked to their gym bags at the conclusion of practice, Bethany sent Reid a look she wouldn't quickly forget. The heather-gray Nike tank top and the ponytail with her dark hair escaping in wisps around her face certainly didn't help Reid's concentration. The look, however, communicated so many things, and all of them had Reid's skin tingly and warm. Her midsection flip-flopped. She remembered Bethany flushed and bothered on her couch and it bolstered her determination.

When the roommate assignments were posted on Rogan's office door two days later, Sunny exhaled loudly and whirled with a hand on her hip. "What the hell? Why am I with Jasmine?" Nearby, Ella and Jennifer fist-bumped at the news they'd be rooming together.

Reid played innocent. "That's weird," she said, squinting. "I bet Rogan wants us to buddy up with the new girls. Show them the ropes of competition. So you're with Jasmine, and they have me with Bethany, looks like."

Sunny folded her arms and stalked toward the mat. "I hate this fucking year."

Reid swallowed a smile and found Bethany in a corner of the gym warming up her back handspring before practice. She paused and marveled at Beth's form. The way her body rotated with perfect precision beneath sheer power. Watching her was everything. Better than any movie ever made. Strong, beautiful. Never boring.

"So, we're rooming together at regionals. That okay with you?"

Bethany pulled her foot into her palm and stretched. A smile tugged her lips. "I can get behind that. I mean, if I have to."

"Funny."

"I can be a lot of things." She dropped her voice. "Want to find out?"

"I do."

Reid stood there with her hands on her hips, enjoying the moment. They hadn't had a lot of one-on-one time this week with the flurry of end of semester exams and competition approaching. She felt starved for Bethany time in the best and worst ways, especially since they'd upped the intimacy factor. It's all Reid thought about. Teenage lust was apparently not the cliché she'd always imagined. These quiet exchanges were water in a desert.

"I'm sorry you have to room with her," Sunny said later that afternoon, as they returned to the mat to finesse a basket toss that continued to land too far left. "It's also not great for your reputation, which is already fucked."

"Bethany? It's fine. Just one night."

"She's your charity case. We all get it. I don't envy you, though. At least I got Jasmine."

That pulled Reid the wrong way. "Can we get down to it? What's your issue with Bethany? Beyond the fact that she didn't try out for the squad with the rest of us. Pay her so-called dues." She put her hands on her hips and waited for an honest answer.

"She's got an attitude half the time. She acts like she's this awesome tumbler."

"She is."

"Still. And"—a hesitation—"she's pulling you into her world."

"You mean she pushes back when you haze her? Wouldn't anybody with a backbone? I think it's admirable." She ignored the other part of Sunny's accusation. Too close to home to touch. She *was* deeply entrenched in Bethany's world. She just wasn't ready to shout about it yet.

Jennifer must have overheard their conversation from her spot a few feet away. She approached and leaned in as if sharing something personal. "You should know that she's also into girls. Not that it's a bad thing. But I just want you to be aware. Especially now that you're sharing a room." She tossed a glance behind her to make sure they weren't intruded upon.

Reid blinked at Sunny, who was surely responsible for passing that bit of information around. Her heart thudded, thunder in her ears. "Why would something like that bother me? What year is this?" She looked around in mystification.

"It shouldn't bother you. I'm an ally, too. I went to Pride last year." She held up a palm in pledge and placed the other one over her heart. "Just…maybe change your clothes in the bathroom, you know?" She passed Reid a knowing look that sent ice water surging through her veins. That kind of sentiment applied to her every bit as much as

Bethany, and it made her want to run screaming from these people, this school. All she wanted in the world was to be herself, but was that how things would be for her? Her own teammates talking quietly behind her back and nervous in a locker room, but smiling to her face while waving a rainbow flag? The audacity astounded.

Rogan took over practice, effectively ending the conversation. Reid tried to put it out of her head, to no avail. Nausea assaulted her for the next two hours, and she hated herself for it. She longed to be strong enough to put her friends in their place, let the words roll off her back. Hell, she wanted to announce to the world just exactly what was happening between her and Bethany, because it was just that awesome, but a part of her wouldn't allow it. Why? What was she afraid of exactly? This wasn't back when her parents were kids. People were openly gay, lesbian, bisexual, nonbinary, and more all the damn time. They lived fantastic gay lives. Coming out was just another Thursday for so many of them. Why couldn't she manage the same breezy approach? Say to them all, *Hey, I'm into girls now, too. And this one happens to be the most amazing thing that's ever happened to me, so shut up about us already because we happen to be really happy. What's for dinner?*

This was exactly what was going through her brain when she dropped Ella in the middle of a stunt and then took a knee to her own face. Hard. "Fuck." That was gonna swell.

"Grab some ice," Rogan called out. Someone killed the music, and there were a lot of faces staring over her as she lay there, flat on her back with a throbbing face.

"Ella okay?" Reid sat up slowly. It was her own fault. Her head hadn't been in it, and that's exactly when bad things happened. "My bad."

"I'm fine," Ella said, waving at Reid. "My knee is sorry about your face."

"Yeah, well, tell your knee we're cool." She held the icepack to her cheekbone as she stood. Bethany was by her side immediately, taking her arm. That made this a little better. She softened. But just as quickly, Sunny appeared.

"Move. I've got this," she said to Bethany. "Stay on the mat."

"No," Reid said, feeling brave. "We're good."

Sunny took a step back as if she'd been burned. Her eyebrow arched and her facial expression was dialed to *really?* Reid had embarrassed her, and that wasn't going to play out well. She couldn't worry about it. She knew how to handle Sunny and would do damage control later. For now, she felt dizzy.

"Come on. Let's sit you down," Bethany said quietly. She was always the picture of calm. "What do you need?" Just her voice made Reid feel better about the last five minutes. It was a mystery how she did that.

Reid took a seat on the glossy pullout wooden bleachers. "Nothing now. Thank you." She met Bethany's eyes, and their connection clicked into place, like a light in a dark room. She'd let Ella knee her in the face daily if it made those soft blue eyes look at her that way.

"And on that note, why don't we wrap up for today?" she heard Rogan say. "Give you guys some rest time." The girls started to scramble, and her voice rose to top them. "Don't forget your permission slips. I need them by tomorrow. Regional championship, here we come!"

"Go, go, go, fighting badgers!" the squad chanted.

"I'm driving," Bethany said, scooping up both their bags. "Don't argue. Won't work."

"Do you even have a license?" Reid asked, following behind her.

"Cute. And your head wound makes you hysterical. This will be fun. Now come on."

As Reid trailed Bethany out of the gym, she absorbed the extra-interested stares from her friends and fell back by another couple of steps, increasing the physical distance between her and Bethany. She despised herself for doing it.

When they were alone in the car, she felt every part of her relax from head to toe. She turned her cheek against the headrest and took Bethany's hand. "Hi."

"Hi, injured cheerleader. You hanging in there?"

"I'll pop two Tylenol and rally like a champ. Just wait. How are you?"

"I'm your hotel roommate. That's how I am." Her eyes shone, and a victorious smile broke out. Perfection.

Reid laughed. "Oh, I see. You like that, do you?"

Bethany beamed. "You have no idea how much."

"You can't look at me like that when there are several days to still wait. Stop it right now."

"Okay." Bethany started the car. "Only because I have to drive, or else you'd be getting the eyes." Reid laughed. Bethany had a comedic side that she didn't show to a lot of people, and that made Reid feel special, important.

Reid's house was dark when they pulled in. Alice was out with her friends, and Reid's mom had a craft fair at which she showcased and sold her arrangements. She and Bethany could have done…whatever they wanted. But there was something about the day, her injury maybe, Sunny, that made her want to curl up and let go. Bethany must have felt the same way because they wordlessly wound up on Reid's couch, snuggled together, watching TV. Reid was tucked on top, her face beneath Bethany's chin. It felt so natural, so wonderful. She didn't want to move from this spot…ever.

"I think we were supposed to work our way into each other's lives," Bethany said quietly an hour later. "When my dad said we were moving here, I didn't complain or get upset like I usually do. I think, somehow, it was because I was being pulled to where I was supposed to be."

"Me." Reid lifted her head, struck by the concept. "I think so, too." Her mind sorted through all the new feelings that came at her, a welcome rainstorm. Since Bethany had arrived on the scene, she felt less aimless, no longer someone going through the motions. Bethany made the very difficult time of her family breaking up bearable. The perfect escape. She'd saved Reid when she'd needed it most, and only a true blessing did that. Bethany was hers.

She placed a soft kiss on Bethany's lips, melting just like always. She smiled against her mouth and snuggled back into the most wonderful oasis from the stresses of the real world. She was whisked away from the drama with her friends, Alice's troubles, her parents' divorce, and the breakup gossip. She was just Reid on the couch with Bethany, watching a show. Yeah. She liked this version of things. She stroked Bethany's arm with her thumb. Every few minutes, Bethany stroked her hair, her touch calming in the best way. The thought that rose far above the pain in her face and all her stresses? She could definitely get used to this kind of life.

CHAPTER TWELVE

The National Cheer Group held a regional competition every year in La Jolla, and the trip had become not only tradition for United, but a rite of passage for all competitive high school cheer teams. Bethany knew this because Reid had filled her in on practically every detail of the three regional competitions she'd attended in the past as she'd played with Bethany's hair on the floor of her bedroom. They'd have a short time on the mat in advance of their competition slot to familiarize themselves with the space, the bounciness of the floor, and all other environmental conditions. There'd be tension, suspense, camaraderie, and if all went well, a trophy at the end to bring home.

"You ready for this?" Reid asked with a glimmer. She lived for this stuff, and it was becoming contagious. All the hard work, the squad traditions, the precision had Bethany invested. She was in. Bethany Cahill was a damn cheerleader and embracing it.

When the day of the trip came, they loaded up early in the morning with only a sliver of sunrise peeking over the horizon. The chartered bus ride was lively. Her teammates alternated between singing, chatting loudly over the rumble of the road, and seriously discussing what they had ahead of them.

The prep day at the regional competition went by in a flurry of activity. When they arrived to register, the convention center was flooded with overly made-up girls in miniskirts, and it was a little crazy for Bethany to realize that she was one of these people now. She had to admit it. The culture had a way of sucking you in, and she wanted very much for their team to take home the towering trophy on display in the lobby. More than for herself, she wanted it for Reid, who focused on little else. Their team was entered in the midsize squad bracket, and according to Rogan would perform second to last, which meant they needed to keep their energy up.

"These things come down to a fraction of a point," Ella said, gesturing solemnly to the blue mat in front of them. "One little error is all it takes to move us out of contention."

Reid shook her head. "If we lose our senior year, I don't know what I'll do."

"Our last chance," Sunny said quietly. "I don't know about you guys, but as far as I'm concerned, that trophy is ours to lose. We keep it tight and clean and leave it all out there on the floor."

That afternoon, Bethany's stomach fluttered with the wings of a thousand butterflies as she pulled her suitcase down the hall of the hotel, looking for number 1202. She didn't want that one little error they spoke about to be hers. The pressure loomed. Reid was in the lobby answering questions for a few of the freshmen, so she picked up the key and went ahead. She found the room and let herself in. Not too shabby. Two queen-sized beds with a calming beige and white pattern. A high ceiling, small desk, a fancy looking TV, and a really cool painting of what looked to be a jazz trio onstage. Go United High for forking over the money for a nice stay. She slid her suitcase onto the padded bench and practically face-planted onto the bed near the window. It wasn't long before a key activated the lock and Reid appeared. She closed the door behind her and leaned against it.

"Hi, you."

"Today has been forever. Come here," Bethany said, extending an arm in invitation from her spot on the bed. She'd waited hours to just be them for a little while.

Reid grinned and crawled onto the bed and beneath Bethany's arm. She buried her face in her neck, and Bethany sank into the warmth and perfection of them pressed together. "Missed you."

"You use so many words to express yourself," Reid said. "Stop it already."

"What can I say? I'm someone who just has to gush."

Reid laughed, probably because they both knew Reid was definitely the more outgoing and talkative one in their relationship. Their *relationship*. That's how Bethany thought of them, but they'd truly never talked about a definition for what was happening between them, other than to say something definitely was. They spent nearly all their free time together to Reid's friends' annoyance. They kissed like experts, messaged constantly when they were apart, and shared, well, everything. It was a relationship whether they'd formalized it or not.

"Do you think you're gay?" she asked Reid.

"Well, that's out of nowhere. As opposed to bisexual or non-labeled?"

"Yeah. How are you feeling about that kind of thing? Have you figured it out yet? Where you might fit." Bethany raced to put Reid at ease. "Not that you have to. I just kind of want to know what *you* know. No pressure to declare anything." She stroked the back of Reid's neck beneath her hair, her favorite soft spot and the one that made Reid push her head closer to Bethany for more.

"No, it's okay. Um…well, I think we've established that I'm far from straight."

Bethany smiled. "I was leaning that way given my very memorable encounter with you."

Reid gave Bethany's stomach an affectionate scratch. "Ya think?" She exhaled. "I feel pretty gay these days. I've never experienced this kind of wanting with a boy. I actually didn't realize there was more to it all until…"

"Until?"

"You."

A beat. "Oh. I don't know whether to take a bow or apologize for shaking up your world."

"Righting it, you mean. Definitely take the bow. Life and relationships and sex? They all make sense now."

Bethany tightened her arms around Reid. "I know what you mean. I think I just got there quicker. I was eight years old on the playground, trying to understand the boy-appeal as they ran around smashing into each other. I failed miserably, and here we are."

"I think you're lucky. I wish I'd known sooner. It might have solved a few confusing issues for me. Took life a while to tap me on the shoulder."

"It's a really hot shoulder, though," Bethany said. Reid raised up and arched a brow. "It's true." Bethany sent her a sly smile.

"Look at you," Reid said, shaking her head. "So proud of yourself."

"You should reward me. Probably right now."

Reid sat up, which left her straddling Bethany's stomach. "Hmmm. What would make you happy?"

"You could always take your top off." She was joking. Her attempt at flirty banter.

"I would certainly oblige except we have to be back in the lobby in thirty minutes for dinner and my hair needs desperate attention. Have you seen it?"

"I happen to like your hair when it's extra curly and wild like this." She touched the soft ends that fell in every which direction. A Reid staple. In her opinion, no taming required.

"Well, now I have to reward you." Reid lifted her shirt over her head to Bethany's astonishment. "For you. But maybe don't touch. I can't get lost in you right now, as much as I want to."

Bethany sat up taller, mesmerized by the view. A baby-blue satin bra this time. Generous curves. Soft, smooth skin peeking out above the fabric line. Cleavage. It was a lot to absorb with perfect lighting in the middle of an afternoon.

"Look at that focused attention," she heard Reid say. It was distant, though, a commentary on the fact that Bethany's gaze had settled on Reid's breasts and had not wavered. "You're a boob girl, aren't you?"

When she adjusted her position, Reid's nipples pressed against the fabric. Bethany nodded slightly, attempting to answer the question. Too busy, though. Her body roared to attention. Her hands itched to touch. To anchor them and obey the rules, she placed them safely on Reid's waist.

When she raised her gaze to Reid's, she saw she wasn't alone in her desire. Those green eyes were hooded. Dark. This playful exercise had turned Reid on just as much as it had her. As their eyes held, the heat level seemed to quadruple. "Yeah, okay, we should stop," Reid said seriously, pulling her shirt back over her head. A damn shame, too.

"You're beautiful," Bethany said quietly, once Reid was dressed.

"Thank you."

She watched as Reid hurried into the bathroom to do whatever she needed to do to make herself happy with her hair. "You're safe with me—you know that, right?" Bethany said. She needed to make sure Reid understood.

Reid stuck her head out from the open bathroom door. "It's one of the best parts of us."

With that reassurance, Bethany hopped up and went to Reid. She put her arms around her waist from behind and found her in the mirror. "I happen to really love us."

Reid smiled, and it looked like her eyes filled. "Me, too." She turned, took Bethany's face in her hands, and kissed her. "Are you really mine? It's starting to feel like it." Bethany nodded. "And I'm yours, okay?"

She nodded again. "And that's not going to change."

"Is this what all love feels like?" The vulnerability that crossed Reid's features when she said the word spoke volumes. She meant it.

Bethany took a moment because this was the first time either one of them had mentioned love, but that's what it was. She'd never been more sure of anything.

"It's not like anything I've ever felt before. No."

Reid looked thoughtful. "That would make it too simple, too everyday."

"You're definitely not that for me," Bethany said.

"Good. That's how I want it." Reid touched her cheek, seeming to absorb as much of her and this moment as possible. "I better get ready."

"I'll see you out there."

"Beth?"

She turned before opening the door to find Reid moving quickly to her. "One more." She pulled Bethany's mouth to hers for a deep and thorough kiss that left every nerve ending Bethany had dancing. "So much better now. As you were."

Bethany decided then and there that she never wanted to leave a room any other way.

❖

The pizza joint Rogan had picked out for them had a lot going for it. The red and white checkered tablecloths were accented with black curvy chairs and white napkins. Photographs of what could easily have been the cast from some mobster flick hung on the walls along with all sorts of framed newspaper clippings, various car silhouettes, and sepia photos of people making pizza crust. The place had a lot of clichéd personality. It was also under cheerleader attack. Not only was *their* long table made up of teenage girls in letter jackets but most every other table in the place was as well.

"Lancaster is the table near the door," Sunny advised the group quietly.

Reid looked over at the group of girls who appeared strong enough to toss an ox. There was a champion caliber energy to them, too. "That's what we need," Reid said. "Swagger."

"I have it," Sunny said with a mouthful of pizza. She had her hair pulled back on top, showcasing its length along with her steely brown eyes and large hoop earrings.

As much as Reid hated how arrogant Sunny could be, she was right. She walked around like she owned the world, and that was how you won championships. She needed to borrow a little bit of that swagger for tomorrow. In fact, she would.

"We're gonna crush Lancaster." She gestured to Bethany, seated to her right. "Plus, we have our secret weapon."

"Make us proud, new girl." In a surprising show of solidarity, Sunny lifted her glass and touched it to Bethany's. "Counting on your mad floor skills."

Reid beamed, proud of Bethany and happy to see the small gesture of support from Sunny. The rest of the team was watching and would take that cue. She saw several nods and grins in Bethany's direction, making her heart swell.

"You got it," Bethany said, like it was the easiest thing in the world. She had the swagger, too. Always had. Only on her, it was sexy as hell. Good God.

Over the sizable roar of teenage chatter, they exchanged a variety of private glances over a dinner made up of some of the most impressive pizza Reid had ever tasted. She went easy because competition loomed, but the extra cheese, thick crust, and large pepperoni made the splurge worthwhile. The looks were better, even more decadent, and laced with possibility.

"I need each and every one of you to go to bed early tonight," Rogan told them in the lobby an hour later. "Big day tomorrow. We've worked too hard to throw it all away." Next to her Bethany nodded and gave her shoulders a roll. She was nervous, which was totally understandable. Reid could think of ways to make her relax. Yes, they were sharing a room and would be alone. But she wasn't entirely sure what Bethany's intentions were.

In fact, when they headed down the hallway, she became incredibly quiet, seemingly lost in her thoughts. Reid let them in. More silence. She swallowed, not sure what to do with the lack of flying words. Where was that swagger she needed now? It wasn't like they hadn't shared intimate moments. They had, even just a couple of hours earlier. But they'd been contained encounters, stolen, and isolated. They had the night to themselves. A room. A bed. What in the world happened now?

While Bethany changed in the bathroom, quiet as a mouse, even more than usual, Reid pulled on the cotton shorts and navy top she'd brought to sleep in. She knew for a fact that the short-sleeved top hugged her tightly. She'd intentionally packed it. To cover the lack of conversation, she threw on some music from the bedside radio provided by the hotel. Not exactly The Skips, but the music was mellow enough to fill the room without overwhelming.

After a few moments, Bethany's voice floated in loudly from the bathroom. "Are you trying to seduce me?"

Reid laughed, which helped her relax. "With the music from the friendly doctor's office. Yes. Am I that obvious?"

She walked into the room, hands on hips. Black cotton shorts that hit at her upper thigh and a plain gray T-shirt that looked so sexy on her that Reid went still for a moment. "Tip—you don't need mediocre music."

Reid slid beneath the covers, the bedside lamp on. She was beyond nervous but also quite sure of what she wanted. She also didn't want to push. "It's pretty late." It was her way of offering Bethany whatever out she might want or need.

Bethany stood at the foot of the bed looking very much in thought. "I don't want to go to sleep."

"Me neither." That did it. Reid sat up and met her gaze. Bethany nodded. Important information passed between them without so much as a word. Reid wanted Bethany. Bethany wanted her back. They wouldn't be letting this night go by unexplored. And God, how very badly Reid wanted to explore. She tried to overthink, or worry about the skills she likely did not have. She'd tried education-by-internet but everything looked and felt different up close and in person. What she did have was instinct, and she sent up a silent wish that it did not fail her.

Bethany pulled the covers back and sat on the opposite side from where Reid lay.

"Get in here," Reid said, sliding over to make room.

Bethany laughed and slipped beneath the sheets, her legs immediately moving to Reid's. They'd gotten in the habit of intertwining them whenever they were alone. Only with less clothes this time, the very familiar position took on a whole new level of heat. She could feel the smooth skin of Bethany's thigh pressed to her own. Her stomach rippled. She ran her fingertips along the back of Bethany's leg up to her thigh to the seam of her underwear. It didn't take long for Bethany to squirm beneath the touch and push against it. Reid smiled to herself, knowing it had turned her on. That made two of them.

They should go slow. Reid wasn't sure she was capable. The knowledge of what they were about to do consumed her. Every touch felt exponential.

"Wait." Bethany killed the light before returning to Reid, this time fully settling on top, her hips between Reid's legs. "Oh, okay," she said out loud to the onslaught of sensation that hit with Bethany pressed up against her center. "That's a lot." Bethany paused. "No. In a good way."

"Oh. Should we start with—"

"Yeah, let's just…" Reid reached up and cradled the back of Bethany's neck. Why were they awkward all of a sudden, when they'd never been anything but smooth? She shoved her thoughts to the side and asked herself what she wanted. And easily, she knew. She raised her head and kissed Bethany, slowly, softly, focusing on just that one thing. Systematically, she felt Bethany's muscles relax into her one at a time. She was liquid, light as a feather, moving with ease over Reid. She lost herself in the smell of Bethany's mango shampoo. The longer they kissed, the more heated she became. The sparks were soon flames, raging hot and wild. They were on the twelfth floor and kept the curtains open, which allowed the moonlight to hit the back wall, enough for her to see. That's what she wanted next, to *see* Bethany. Fully. Nothing between them.

As they kissed, she inched the gray shirt up Bethany's back, exposing the extra-soft skin there. Feeling the tug, Bethany sat up and pulled the shirt over her head, presenting two perfect breasts for Reid's viewing pleasure. Not large. Not small. Reid sucked in air, taking in all she saw, amazed that this was real life.

"Can I?" she asked.

Bethany nodded. "Yes."

Reid followed her up. She took Bethany by the waist, wrapping both arms around her middle, and with her tongue slowly licked a circle around one nipple, a fantasy she'd held on to and could now act out fully. She watched Bethany. Was she enjoying herself? Bethany's eyes were closed and lips slightly parted, telling Reid that what she was doing was welcome and working. A relief. She let herself explore. Touching each breast. Tracing with her finger, holding in her hand, kissing it fully, and finally pulling each nipple into her mouth and sucking gently until Bethany physically stopped her, a wild, determined look in her eye. She liked that look very much and understood that the driver's seat had just been commandeered. Not a problem at all.

Bethany undressed her now, turning the tables. She removed Reid's blue top, her eyes going immediately to what lay beneath. Next, she slid her shorts down her legs, kissing her thighs as she went. Reid realized distantly that the soft rock from another era still played on the radio. The air conditioner hummed unromantically in the corner. Didn't matter. Reid's desire smashed her awareness of both because Bethany was now removing her underwear, leaving Reid stark naked and wanting. There was what felt like a heartbeat between her legs, insistent and uncomfortable. She wanted to be touched and soon. Before she burst. Reid had never imagined there could be so much want in one person. Bethany hesitated. She understood. This was all so new.

"It's okay," Reid said, encouraging her. Her voice sounded different. Breathy. Strangled. Was this what sex did to a person?

Bethany flashed a nervous smile. "This is new for me."

"Us both."

Bethany nodded. She caressed Reid's thigh with featherlight touches that became more confident moments later. The proximity to her center was torturous. She closed her eyes to steady herself as Bethany's fingers inched closer. When they slid between her folds, she began to pump her hips slowly, amazed at the quick shots of sensation that seemed to top the ones before. As much as she wanted to go fast, she kept the movement of her hips slow and rhythmic, concentrating, memorizing the way she felt, until slow was no longer a choice on the table. Bethany pressed inside of her and the concept was too much, the fullness too great, and desperation set in. Their pace shifted. Frenzied. Reid couldn't control herself, and in just seconds she was careening, awash with warm pleasure that had her shaking. Reveling. With her faculties stunted by the power of the orgasm, she was powerless to do anything but ride it out. She didn't have the chance to see Bethany's face, or join their hands, or any of the things she'd planned on when she imagined this moment. This barrage of feeling was so overwhelming that she was only distantly aware that she was using her voice. She was calling out, a cry of pleasure and shock. Her hips slowed, but the pleasure continued. She'd never imagined so much or achieved it on her own.

"Beth."

"Right here." A soft touch to her cheek. That helped steady her, offered an anchor. As she gradually drifted back to her mind and body, she was able to enjoy the soft caresses. Bethany's arms went around her, her warm skin pressed to Reid's.

She turned and found Bethany's lips, desperate to kiss them, to bring them together, to express this welling up of emotion. She was on top now, her tongue in Bethany's mouth. She ran her hand down Bethany's side, to her stomach, behind her shorts to cup her ass. "Can we take these off now, please?" An unrecognizable urgency laced her voice. Bethany nodded, and Reid slipped off just enough for Bethany to remove those shorts and the underwear beneath. Driven by pure instinct, she parted Bethany's legs and nestled her hips between them. Bethany murmured quietly, and her breath tickled Reid's shoulder. Another moment to memorize. She pressed herself firmly up against Bethany and began to rock her hips.

Bethany moaned from deep in her throat. "Keep going," she said, guiding Reid. "Just like that."

Reid didn't have to be asked twice, and as she fell into rhythm her own need returned, startling and strong. Bethany's hands were on her breasts and the pressure became too intense to manage. If she kept going she was going to— "Bethany," she hissed, going still and arching against Bethany as she came a second time in a fast burst of white light. Bethany watched her with a reverent expression on her face. Reid, never one to abandon a mission, took a few steadying breaths.

"Slight detour." She offered a wink and looked down at feminine curves that had sent her soaring in the first place. When she touched Bethany intimately for the first time, she was surprised by so many things. How soft she was and how turned on, how ready. She'd done that to Beth and wore it like a badge of pride. She stroked her softly, let her fingers move in lazy patterns until muffled whimpers greeted her. So sexy. So different from the put-together girl she knew. She let Bethany lead her, set the pace. Reid entered her softly with her fingers, not wanting to hurt her in any way, and began to move. The warmth that enveloped her was unreal. She closed her eyes and paid close attention to the cues until she lost herself in their hypnotic connection. They were creatures of desire, bound together as one. It wasn't long before Bethany grabbed her wrist and bucked. She went tight and rigid as she cried out, attempting to muffle the sounds with her hand but finding little success. She'd done that to Bethany. Her.

Full of wonder and with her hands still shaking, she rejoined Bethany on her pillow and watched as her breathing leveled to peaceful. "I feel like we left this room and came back," Reid said. "That was so different than what I expected."

"I hope better," Bethany managed, returning to herself.

"Yes, but also so much more *important*."

"It was. I'm glad my first time was with you," Bethany said.

"I can't believe we didn't do that weeks ago. I like you naked," Reid said, tracing her breast. "I love getting to do what I am right this minute." Bethany stared down at her finger.

"If you had told me at the activities fair that you'd be doing that right now, I never would have believed you."

She had to laugh at that. "Neither would I. Tell the truth. Was it... okay?" Reid knew they'd had their clunky moments as they learned each other's bodies, but they'd also easily surpassed most every expectation she had of sex. She needed to hear Bethany's thoughts.

"Was it okay?" Bethany echoed. "Is that comedy?" Bethany pushed herself up on her forearm, which caused her breast to dip and rest on the pillow. Reid would never grow tired of her topless. This was a whole new world to explore. "That was the most satisfying, amazing experience of my life, and we're still naked in the bed together, which means it isn't even over."

Bethany placed a hand on Reid's hip, and she resisted a shiver.

Her touch was magic. No wonder people made such a big deal about sex.

"Good. I loved it." A pause. "I love *you*."

"I love you, too."

Her heart squeezed and blossomed. This was real and all-encompassing. She was Reid but a more exciting adult version, experiencing happiness in its truest form. Just her and Bethany together. She knew the next thing she wanted. For always. "I know tomorrow is a big day and we need to sleep, but do you think you could hold me?"

Bethany nodded and kissed her softly. "Come here." She lifted her arm, and Reid snuggled in, amazed at the events of the evening, and ready to embrace this new aspect of them. She wasn't a virgin anymore. And she was in love with the most wonderful person. The world wasn't any less complicated than an hour ago, and she would have to figure out how to maneuver the new terrain. That could wait. Tonight, she had everything she could possibly want. She raised her head and placed a kiss on the underside of Bethany's jaw before settling in to sleep.

CHAPTER THIRTEEN

The warm-up session had gone by in a blur, girls with extra energy trying to keep themselves focused. They'd had a chance to run their routine and walk through their individual tracks. Bethany felt different. Off. Like her muscles were stiff and unbending, causing her to over-rotate twice on tumbling passes. Not only that, but the floor felt weird. Not awful, but also not the same style of floor they'd been practicing on for weeks leading up to the competition. She hadn't really expected that. The blue floor set up by the convention center had a lot less give to it, leaving each of her passes with a lot more height, and giving her more time in the air. She would need to account for that.

"How'd that feel?" Rogan asked her quietly as they walked back to the holding area. They had ninety minutes until their competition, and Bethany planned to use it to stretch and prepare her body to avoid injury.

"Great. I need to make some adjustments in my head for that floor. It's weird."

"Right. I noticed that, too. Bouncy. But you're smart, and you'll make it work."

"Thanks, Coach. I will."

She placed her hand on Bethany's shoulder and led her away from the pack a few feet. "Hey, I want you to know that you've done a fantastic job this season. You work hard. You show up, and you don't complain. A true athlete."

Bethany absorbed the compliment, feeling her face warm. Reid watched them from a few paces away, grinning proudly. That part felt great, too. "That means a lot."

"And I don't know what your college plans are, but anything you need from me, just ask." Coach gave her a clap on the back. "Get ready to kill it out there. I'm gonna let the officials know we're good."

Reid hurried into the spot Coach vacated. "She rarely gushes. She saves it for the important moments. Huge deal."

Bethany couldn't stop smiling now. "That's pretty cool."

Reid bumped her with her shoulder, her voice quiet. "My girlfriend is a superstar."

Girlfriend. The word almost knocked her over. She absolutely treasured hearing the word from Reid's mouth, especially after their night together. She'd woken up with Reid in her arms, warm and amazing. She had longed to stay in that bed forever.

Bethany looked over at her. The others were chattering away, lost in their own world as they boarded the buses. "I love you," she mouthed.

"I love you, too," Reid mouthed back.

They stood on the mat a short time later, the crowd cheering loudly. Parents, friends, supporters. Her dad hadn't been able to miss work, but Reid's mom and sister were in the crowd. United was well known in the cheer world, a contender, and the only possible spoiler to Lancaster's shot at the championship trophy. Bethany was all nerves and adrenaline, nearly to the point of discomfort, but decided to use the extra energy to make the next few minutes of her life important ones that she'd always remember.

United, in their red and blue uniforms, took their places and waited for the music. When the first note blared on the loudspeakers, they were off. Bethany counted herself in and took off on her first tumbling pass, diagonally across the mat and in front of the stunts happening center. She landed the final back handspring in the combination to thunderous applause. That had gotten their attention. It was one of her most difficult and she'd slayed. On a high, she moved through the routine, tossing and catching one of the freshmen, jumping into the group dance section, and returning to the corner of the mat for her next tumbling pass. Roundoffs, back handsprings, a full into a back tuck. Nailed it. The no-sweat sign to the audience. But something was wrong. The crowd didn't scream the way they had on her first stuck landing. She kept going, turning back to the center just in time to see Reid midfall, on her way to the ground from the first section of the pyramid. And with her, she brought down half the team in an unorganized, disastrous crash to the mat. This was bad. Her brain shorted out as she tried to think what this would mean. *Keep going. Just like practice. Smile through it.*

They went into recovery mode, modifying the pyramid the way they'd practiced, but from there it only got worse. On Reid's three skill tumbling pass, she missed the landing and hit the floor on her ass. Another gasp from the crowd. They pressed on even though the prognosis was grim. The deductions would be huge, unrecoverable. Every cheerleader on the mat would know that. Bethany stayed focused, finished the routine, and nailed her final back tuck in sync with the group. She held her pose until the music cut out and relaxed out of it. Her teammates forced smiles, patted each other on the shoulders, and waved to the crowd. All things they'd been instructed to do in the face of a poor showing. She saw Coach Rogan, her face stricken, leaving the front row to join the team. Once they were out of the judges' line of sight, the tears hit. Bethany stood off to the side, searching for Reid in the crowd of her teammates. She was behind the huddle, sitting on the floor, knees pulled to her chest, shaking. Bethany, heart thudding, moved to her immediately and sat down.

She placed her hand on Reid's back. "It's okay. We gave it everything we had."

"It was me. I dropped the stunt. I brought the pyramid down." She shook her head, sad and mystified. "After that, it was like I couldn't get out of my own head. I just lived my nightmare."

The whole series of events felt surreal to Bethany, too. She never would have imagined that it would have been Reid who stumbled. Their captain, solid as hell. But all she could do was be there for Reid. She put an arm around her and gave her a squeeze, but Reid immediately moved out of the touch.

"I can't right now."

"Hey," Sunny said, kneeling down. "It's okay. We gave them all we had. Chin up." But then she was up and away, hugging and consoling the others. Her words had been calm at best, but the terse quality hadn't been lost on either of them as they stared after her. She was pissed that Reid had brought their score down, and she likely wasn't the only one.

"I can't believe this happened," Reid said, staring at her hands that still shook. "After working so hard for so many months, and I'm the one who ruins it for everyone. Perfect." She laughed sardonically. "I'm really sorry."

"You don't have anything to be sorry for. Mistakes happen. Maybe Lancaster will make a few of their own."

But they didn't. Lancaster's routine was flawless and strong. When the winners were announced, not only was Lancaster handed the championship trophy, but United finished third in the rankings, an entire place lower than the year before. The ride home was long, painful, and quiet. Gone was that anticipatory excitement. The group didn't sing songs or participate in road trip games. Bethany sat with Reid, who wasn't interested in much conversation either. She kept her gaze trained on the passing scenery and earbuds in her ears.

"I'll call you later," Bethany said in her driveway, bag over her shoulder.

"No need. I'm gonna go straight to bed," Reid said. It was dark out, but still pretty early for Reid. "But I'll see you at school tomorrow." She blew Bethany a kiss, which made her feel a little better. Her heart hurt for Reid, who'd been pretty unreachable since the crash and burn routine. This competition had meant everything to her. She understood, though. Had Bethany been the one to sink their chances, she would have been overcome with similar guilt. She tossed a kiss back and waved as Reid drove away, eyes forward.

They had just a few weeks until graduation, and then she'd be on her way to Colorado. Her summer research program kicked off early in an entirely different state from the person she loved. She desperately wanted to make the most of every minute they had together. That meant getting Reid back to herself again. She would need time and TLC, both of which Bethany was prepared to offer her. If only the last day of their lives had gone differently.

❖

The next few days of Reid's life were brutal. She woke up every day remembering her stunning failure in acute detail. She saw herself falling from both her own perspective and watching from outside her body. She replayed all the things she did wrong, the crowd's reactions, her teammates'. She imagined going back in time and undoing it or, better yet, nailing every moment of the routine, coming away the hero. But when that alarm clock went off, she was thrust into the harsh reality of her new existence as a failure.

"I've been thinking about it. You shouldn't beat yourself up anymore," Ella said. "Some things are just written by the Fates. We weren't meant to win. The power of the stars decided to use you as their instrument to bring us down."

Reid blinked at her friend over a chicken burger she had no appetite for. "When did you get so new age?"

"I saw a show on crystals." Ella nodded proudly. "They're real. Anyway. I don't think it was in your hands."

"Then whose hands brought the pyramid down?" Sunny asked, joining them on the wall during lunch. Bethany had a make-up quiz in history, and Reid missed her already. They'd started stealing a couple of lunches a week to eat together on the lawn away from the masses.

"Harsh," Reid said. "It's not like I think about anything else, as it is."

"Yeah, your year has been rough." Sunny winced as if to imply she was glad it wasn't hers.

Reid stared blandly. "You noticed, huh?"

"Everyone's noticed," Ella said. "You are one hot topic. The social collapse of the decade." She held up a hand. "It's not that bad."

"Really, because it sounds awful." The words didn't sit well. She tried to shrug them off, but the thought of being looked at as an epic loser pushed uncomfortably on her chest like a load of bricks she couldn't budge. She studied the chicken burger with too many pickles and couldn't bring herself to take a bite, opting instead to leave it on its tray.

"Well, think about it," Sunny said, biting into her own sandwich with a loud crunch of the lettuce. "And this is not to say we don't love you. We do. But to the masses, you were the girl who had it all. Perfect family, leadership role on the squad, and one half of the golden couple on campus. Bit of a contrast now."

Reid laughed loudly, though there was nothing funny about it. "No, I get it. Just hearing it mapped out like that, though. Wow. Yeah, okay."

She hated her fall from grace. She also hated that it mattered to her when she had another amazing component of her life she should be entirely focused on. Why was she so shallow as to need the adoration of others? But she did, and it was awful of her.

As she walked the halls later that afternoon, she realized how right her friends had been. Gazes were flicked her away and then immediately pulled back in error. A smile to the person they were walking with. A whisper. She'd been removed from the social ladder altogether and made a decision then and there to do something about it. She said hello to the next person she passed, and the next, and the next. There weren't a lot of spaces that carried happiness for her these days. She needed school back. Home was desolate. Her friends didn't call as much. She had Bethany, at least, a huge bright spot in her world. But even their relationship felt strained lately, and that was all on Reid. She'd been struggling within herself, leaving little left over to give. Not only that, but the clock was ticking on the time they had remaining before graduation and Bethany leaving for school. Reid would then head off to the University of New Mexico, and they'd be apart for months. The idea alone made it hard to breathe.

"Hey, kiddo," her mom said as Reid came through the front door. The house smelled of coffee, an aroma Reid always associated with warmth and comfort. She appreciated it now, and to her own shock it prompted a rush of tears. Embarrassing. Her mother, who was seated at the dining room table going over bills, immediately set down her cup and moved to Reid. "Oh no. Come here, my sweet girl." Reid crumpled into her mother's embrace like a third grader and clung. "What's wrong? Bad week?"

"Things just aren't going so well," she finally managed to croak out. There was just something about the comforting arms of a parent that allowed her to just drop it all at her feet.

"Then we can sit on the couch and cry it out. Sound good?"

"Okay," Reid said, nodding. Before she knew it, she was seated on the fluffy worn-in sofa with her mom's arm still holding Reid against her body. The words flew from her lips, tumbling out in a jumble. All of it. From the looming divorce, to the competition, to Mateo.

"That, to me, sounds like a pile-on, and you're underneath it all."

"Yeah." She wiped her nose and took a deep shuddering breath. "That's a good way to put it."

"Find your lifeline. What is the one thing that you can grab on to right now?"

"Beth."

"Good." Her mother nodded. "Then start there. Focus on your friend."

"We're more than that."

To her credit, her mom didn't react. "Okay. Focus on your *girlfriend*." A pause. "Did I get that right? I'm so sorry that I didn't know about this."

"It's not like I let on." She shrugged. "I was nervous. Still am."

"I should have asked more questions." Guilt streaked her features. "I've been so caught up in money and lawyers and my own feelings that I just…" She sighed.

"Mom. It's okay. Until Bethany, I didn't know either." She leaned her head on her mother's shoulder. "I know you've got your own pile of stuff, too. I'm sorry about that part."

"We're a pair."

"Why is there a cuddlefest on the couch?" Alice asked. She hurried in and plopped down, leaning against Reid's back. Reid grinned, inflating, because she'd seen so little of Alice these days and had missed her.

"We're wallowing in self-pity," Reid informed her.

"Good. Me, too."

"What's yours?" her mom asked.

"Tryouts for next year's team are this week, and I suck."

Reid turned back. "You don't. You're an amazing player. You just need to sharpen up. Everyone says you're MIA from practice."

Alice sighed. "I was. Gotta get back on track. I'm sorry I've been all over the place."

Reid ruffled Alice's pretty blond hair. "We've all been. We all suck."

"New pact," their mom said. "We start checking in with each other and spend more time doing stuff like this. Hanging out on the couch. Watching movies."

"Popping buttered popcorn," Alice supplied with a grin. It was really nice to see her happy.

Reid nodded. "Definitely."

They sealed it with a three-way fist bump and each received a smacking kiss from their mom on the cheek. "Let's have dinner together tonight."

"I'm in," Reid said. "Can we do loaded baked potatoes? Carbs cheer me up."

"God, yes," her mom said.

Reid exhaled, able to breathe just a little bit easier. She craved time with her family, time with Bethany, whom she'd kept at arm's length the past few days. She would remedy that. After a much needed dinner full of good food and lively chatter, the first in months, Reid decided not to wait.

"I'm gonna run over to Bethany's house. Say hi. That okay?" she asked her mom.

"Of course. And bring her by soon, huh? I'm apparently very late to the party."

"You got it."

She swung by Scoops of Joy, picked up Bethany's favorite mint chocolate chip shake, drove the eighteen minutes to her home, and knocked.

Her father answered, scratched his bushy beard, and stared at the two shakes in her hands. "For me? Damn it all. You shouldn't have." Before she could answer, he popped open the door and bellowed over his shoulder. "Bethany Amelia, your ice cream is here." He turned back to Reid. "Enter!"

He was a character she could get used to. She stood in the entryway, the shakes freezing her hands off. Bethany appeared and broke into the best smile imaginable when she saw Reid.

She glanced at the ice cream. "What's going on?"

"I'm surprising you with a milkshake because you deserve it for putting up with my gloom. Here, let's inhale these bad bitches." She craned around Bethany to Mr. Cahill in the kitchen. "Mr. C, I would have brought you one, but I didn't know you'd be home."

"I'm tortured inside," he grumbled, before passing her a smile and a gesture that said he didn't care. "Hey, how's your dad doin'?" She'd talked to him once about her dad's passion for golf when she'd learned Mr. C had played on his high school team. Who would have guessed that one?

"Living with his mistress, but we're working on forgiving him one day at a time."

"Well, this just got a little awkward," he said, setting down the plate he was washing.

"Nah, just part of my life now. I hear his swing is being weird, though. Karma." She held up a hand. "Sorry. He's not a bad person. I'm just working through it."

"Hey," he said, coming around the counter, hands still wet from the dishwater. "I'm an oaf, but if you ever need a clap on the back, I can put my surrogate dad hat on and clap you one."

It was a really generous thing to say. Bethany was blessed with this guy. "That actually means a lot. Thanks, Mr. C."

Bethany put her hand on Reid's back. "We're gonna sit on the porch now, as much as I hate to break up the goodwill train." She offered a smile in thanks to her dad.

When they were alone, Bethany seemed to relax. "God, I'm happy to see you," she said, beaming from her spot on the front step. "You didn't even have to show up with gifts, but please always do."

Reid laughed. It felt good. "I will do my best to always surprise you with food."

Bethany nodded. "Always my favorite." She exhaled. "You look really pretty."

Reid winked. "I put on lip gloss for you. At least, I've started with it. You generally kiss it off."

"Proudly. I know all your flavors."

"See if you can decipher this one," Reid said, then leaned in and brushed Bethany's lips softly with hers.

"Easy. It's the peach one. I forget the name. You were wearing it the first time we kissed at the park."

Reid nodded. "Very astute." She dropped her tone. "If your dad wasn't around, we could reenact it a bit more thoroughly." This was fun. She felt more like herself than she had in a while.

"I'm headed out for a drink with a pal," Mr. Cahill said, emerging onto the porch and heading down the stairs between them. "Don't go milkshake crazy on me."

Bethany turned to Reid with an arched eyebrow. In under two minutes they were pawing each other on Bethany's bed, french kissing like the lust-driven teenagers they were. Limbs tangled, shirts half off, hands on the move. It was perfection.

"We have to be fast," Bethany said between kisses. "One drink could go quick."

"I know. And I need to be home in half an hour."

Two orgasms and some gasping for air later, they lay beneath the cool sheets, cheeks against the pillow, basking.

"This day turned the hell around," Bethany said quietly, stroking Reid's cheek with one finger.

"I started doing the math." Reid touched Bethany's soft hair, while her own body attempted to return to itself. "And we have so few days left. I didn't want whatever it is I'm going through to rob us of time. Plus, I just need to see you, touch you. Do exactly what we just did."

Bethany slid closer, her arms loosely around Reid's waist. "I try not to think about that part. Leaving you?" She shook her head. "It feels unimaginable right now."

"Which is why I try not to think too much about it."

Bethany's eyes went soft. "You're my person. I can't talk to anyone the way I can talk to you. Not just right now. For always." She stared at the ceiling, searching. "Do you know what I'm trying to say?"

Reid knew exactly what she meant. "The forever factor. Infinity. That's one we've yet to study in school. It's real, though. It's us."

Bethany smiled and it reached her eyes. "I like the sound of that. You and me. Forever. School is temporary."

"We're not." Reid ran her finger around Bethany's breast in a gentle circle that slowly shifted to the infinity symbol, a perfect figure eight. She couldn't believe it had taken her this long to understand her acute attraction to the female body. So soft. Smooth. Wonderful in its complexity. And now that she'd been with Bethany, she'd unleashed something potent. This craving for Bethany, this attachment to not just her body, but her entire being. She couldn't get enough. She thought about her day and night, fantasized about things they'd do the next time they were intimate. Such shockingly new territory. While connecting with Bethany was the highlight of a difficult year, it also would have been the highlight of a fantastic one. She was a constant, and Reid could no longer imagine her life without her. "Forever. You hear me?"

Bethany kissed her and smiled against her lips. "You got it."

CHAPTER FOURTEEN

Now

The forever factor. Reid remembered the night of mint chocolate chip milkshakes with a startling intensity. Every detail came rushing back as if it had only happened yesterday. She wanted to wrap those two girls up and keep them just like that, unaffected by the heartbreak ahead. Safe and happy and in love. Their lives would have been something to behold. She was confident of that much. She assumed her share of the blame, which was a lot, but none of it seemed fair. They'd been kids grappling to maneuver a once-in-a-lifetime love with teenage sensibilities. The sound of her doorbell startled her out of it. The present was calling, and it was a lot more complicated.

"Hi," Reid said. Bethany wore black jeans with a red sleeveless top and silver necklace. "Red is your color."

"Kind of you to say. I didn't want to shout passion, murder, or red-light district, but I thought I'd give it a go."

"Only you would say that. So literal. Objective."

"That's my left brain talking. It rarely shuts up. I'm nervous, so it's extra talkative." Her eyes scanned the space behind Reid, probably attempting to get a look at her life. She could help with that.

"We both are. Come in." She backed up and brought the door with her. "Welcome to my humble abode, and I do mean humble." Bethany took in the small space, hands slid into her back pockets. Reid tried to see it through Bethany's eyes. She would likely appreciate the updating Reid had done. That was something. Bethany was by no means a snob, even though she surely had a lot more money than someone chasing a distant tenure.

Bethany held up a bottle. "How quick do we pop that cork?"

Reid laughed. "Seconds would be too long. Follow me. Excuse the skateboard."

Bethany glanced down, stepping over the sideways board with the words *Santa Cruz* on the back. "A whole new Reid. You have a kid living here. He has a *skateboard*."

She exhaled and grinned. "I know we haven't talked much about that portion of my life, but it's pretty great, actually. *He* is."

"Well. It looks really good on you. And your house."

Reid paused, mid-cork pulling. "Thank you for saying that. It helps." They stared at each other, and the invisible fire flickered. Still there. Memories swirled and filled. Reid's little life update hadn't extinguished the always intense connection between them. Their own personal special sauce.

"So, let's go. My first question is why didn't you tell me?"

"You want to get right down to it."

"I feel like I have to." Bethany was talking faster than normal. "I don't know if I sent some kind of signal that I wouldn't want to know about every part of your life. Or if you think I don't like kids, for some reason. Neither would be true."

She poured two glasses, keeping her eyes on the task, absorbing Bethany's words as she went. "I wish I had a clear answer to give you." She straightened and handed off a glass to Bethany, who held it to her eye line.

"That's a really hearty pour."

"Is it?" she asked innocently and tossed a wink.

She tried to explain again. "Things between us felt precarious, like too sudden a move and you'd race for the hills. Mason felt pretty big, so I wanted to ease in. For him, too. I have an ex that I told you about. He liked her a lot. She moved in. And then suddenly she's not a part of his life anymore." She shrugged. "So I go slow when it comes to him. He's important."

Bethany nodded, sipped. She took Reid's hand and interlaced their fingers. "It feels so strange to do this," she said, examining their hands. "In another sense, it feels like I never stopped. Are we dipping our toes in?"

Reid swallowed, so many emotions rushed over her, like a wave crashing in the ocean. "Seeing you again has made walking away harder than I'd imagined."

Bethany closed one eye. "Let's be clear. The kissing didn't help."

"Our specialty."

They grinned at each other, sharing that little source of pride. Bethany dangled her glass from her fingertips and moved to Reid's brown sofa with the newly purchased white and maroon striped throw pillows. "I want to hear about it. How you became a mom. I imagine the traditional way."

Reid faltered slightly. It wasn't a bad memory but it also wasn't a great one. "I was lost at school. Having a truly hard time. I missed home. I missed *you*. I didn't know if you'd ever take my call again, and then, there he was."

"Ah. A popular guy on campus. A boyfriend."

"Mateo."

Silence hit. Bethany shifted. Nodded. "Okay. That tracks, I guess. I should have just done the math."

"It's all quite peaceful. He's married now to a wonderful woman who enjoys his comedy and tolerates his ego. They have two other children, a boy and a girl." She hesitated. "Mateo loves Mace, but I think he has trouble connecting with him. He's not the son he imagined. Mateo is all sports and adventure, and Mason would rather read a book or watch a show about, I don't know, the migration patterns of the Monarch butterfly."

"Well, it's important we know their habits."

"Don't say that to Mace. You'll be stuck in conversation for two days. You've been warned."

"Or challenged." She touched her temple. "Math and science mind, remember?"

"I couldn't forget. Those calculus tutoring sessions in your bedroom come to mind." She sent a smile.

"Oh yes. The ones that often achieved very little calculus."

"And ended with us half dressed." Reid flashed a victorious smile. "I had a great tutor. What do you want me to say? Some true Hallmark moments."

Bethany laughed. "Hallmark would blush. Never be the same again."

"That part's true." They were flirting again, sending Reid to an exciting and recognizable zone. Yeah, she could linger right here forever. Toss her a snack every now and then for nourishment, but she could do this for days. But were they doing this? There was this giant lingering question mark because they'd not formally talked it over.

"Well, rewarding you for your effort was important."

"I'm still a hard worker and quite poor at math. PhD in English, remember?" Reid said, knowing how incredibly saucy that line was. She saw the change happen behind Bethany's eyes. Registered. Bethany stood, took the two steps that separated them, and before Reid knew it she was being good and kissed. Oh, dear stars smiling down. They'd just catapulted from flirting to living room lust in a lovely split second. One hand went to the top of her head as Bethany held her tightly at her waist. The walls of her home had never witnessed anything so perfectly decadent. She knew what kissing Bethany was like, but older Bethany had new moves, and confidence for days. Too sexy to process. It was the best combination, new and old. At Bethany's touch, Reid had come to life like the welcome notification on her laptop. Her skin sang. Her center pulsed. One thing was for sure, she'd never felt so damn invigorated. She was now pressed up against the island of her kitchen in receiving mode because Bethany very much occupied the driver's seat at the moment. Driver's Seat Bethany was her very favorite version, too. Steely, serious, determined.

"How did you just get more beautiful?" Bethany asked, going in again. And praise the heavens she did. No more dramatic conversations were needed in this moment. No rehashing of the past. Just good old-fashioned lust in a quiet, redecorated kitchen. Bethany pulled her mouth away again. A shame. What wasn't a shame? The feral look in her eye when she began unbuttoning Reid's shirt. A sexy woman on a mission, and Reid didn't mind being the goal. Once her shirt hung open, Bethany kissed her neck with an open mouth as she cradled it from behind. Next, her fingertips grazed Reid's breasts through her bra. They were fuller now, up a cup size from college. Surely Bethany noticed. But she didn't dwell and expertly freed the front clasp. A quiet intake of air when Reid was more fully revealed. A moment of reverence lingered before her lips caught Reid's just as her hands pressed and lifted her curves, sending a storm of feeling to her skin, her midsection, and beyond. She was beginning to ache, her desire escalating by the second.

"Are we going here?" It was a dumb question, as she stood topless beneath the fluorescents, searching for air. "I want to," she added.

"Me, too."

Reid took Bethany by the hand and led her the short distance to her bedroom, the very one she'd straightened meticulously just in case. The audacity to have planned paid off. They kissed their way into the wall, then the dresser, bouncing around like a pinball in a machine until *bam*—Reid's back hit the mattress, followed down a short moment later by Bethany, grinning. "Hey."

"Hi."

The world slowed down. The dust settled. They stole the moment to, in no other terms, drink the other in. Bethany looked down at Reid, her thumbs on Reid's cheeks, and Reid smiled up at her. Tension on simmer. There was a tenderness between them that couldn't be discounted or rushed over. They needed this exchange. She cherished it the same way she cherished Bethany, and the memories they'd made. Her person. "Here we are again," she whispered.

Bethany blinked, searching her face. "It's like there's no other way."

She remembered the day she traced the infinity symbol on Bethany's skin, and every inch of her tingled. Being here together now felt ordained. She latched on to those deep blue eyes before pulling Bethany's mouth down to hers. In this moment, she needed Bethany like she'd never needed anything in her life. Body, mind, and soul craved this other human, and all she could do was get out of her own damn way. She flipped them, shrugging out of her shirt entirely as they went. She sat on top, straddling Beth's hips. Her hair was down. Maybe a little wild. Probably. She didn't care. It's how she felt. Like a part of her that had been locked away for years was free. She rolled her hips, pressing downward. Even that small rhythm took her need to fast and powerful heights. Hunger and need raced toward her, unbridled. Uncaring. Bethany sat up, pulling Reid close in her lap, sucking on her breast. She swirled her tongue around a nipple as Reid moaned. Half naked in Bethany Cahill's arms was a concept that had her mind blown, but her body on fire. But never had she felt more herself. This was right. They were. She knew it with every fiber of her being. She went up on her knees, and Bethany easily helped her out of the rest of her clothing, sliding her underwear down her legs. She was ready to even things out and pushed Bethany's shirt up, kissed her stomach, and then went to work on her pants. Moments later, she was caressing those still very toned legs, tantalized by smooth skin that begged to be kissed. She could oblige. She kissed up to Bethany's thighs, parted them, and let her lips and tongue caress their insides to the soundtrack of quiet gasps, whimpers, and cries. Wanting to enjoy this part as long as possible, she climbed back up Bethany's body and leaned over her, supported by her forearms. Bethany's gaze was immediately on her breasts, which was hot and amusing. Some things never changed. *You're a boob girl, aren't you?*

"Come here already," Bethany practically growled, hauling Reid down on top. Sparks flared. For someone who'd always been adventurous and a leader in the bedroom, she apparently had no problem being topped by Reid, which she happened to love. Reid nestled her hips between Bethany's and began to move, bringing their bodies together in a dance that had her eyes slamming shut with tantalizing sensations demanding satisfaction. The payoff wasn't far away. Bethany's body stole her ability to last very long. As they rocked, skin on skin, the pressure between her legs grew to new painful levels. She was wet and in need. A hand between them, Bethany's, pressed against her center. The rhythm, short and fast, sent her up onto her knees. Bethany followed, her shoulders acting as Reid's support. As soon as Bethany pressed inside, it was only a few thrusts before she spilled over, shooting helplessly into an oblivion of wonder and pleasure. She continued to grip Bethany's bare shoulders as her body shook and bucked, overcome with the force of gratification.

She fell back onto the pillow and tugged on Bethany's hand so that she fell back with her. Her arms automatically encircled Bethany's neck and their foreheads came together. Breathing in the same air. Clinging to each other. Bethany's hand was at the small of her back, moving in circles. She found her way between them and began to stroke Reid intimately once again. Reid opened her mouth to protest, to explain that she was simply too sensitive, there could be no more, when familiar stirrings stopped her efforts. "What are you doing to me?" She rocked against Bethany's hand, quietly asking for more, opening her legs. When Bethany's mouth found her, she nearly melted. Bethany's tongue coaxed her along expertly until Reid was certain she'd explode in a much needed burst. Her body was pure heat at this point, and the climb was magnificent torture. Bethany pulled her into her mouth more fully, sucking softly and then with more pressure, until Reid broke free a second time, clawing the sheets and holding on helplessly through the ride. She didn't try to stay quiet. Instead, she let her cries echo in one of the most liberating experiences of her adulthood.

Sweet God.

Bethany appeared to her when she opened her eyes again, still looking down Reid's body, observing it with a reverence that made her feel appreciated, tracing her breast, the curve of her thigh, her stomach. Finally, as they lay facing each other, Reid's own focus shifted. She'd waited for years to touch Bethany, convinced they'd likely never see each other again. She had no intention of squandering the moment, its importance too great. She turned the tables and gently circled Bethany's nipple with one finger, watching her inhale sharply, lean her head back, and close her eyes. *Yes, perfect.* She continued the attention, lazier circles, tighter ones. The undersides of her breasts next, her neck, collarbone, rib cage. Featherlight touches that left this gorgeous woman squirming. She spent a good deal of time kissing her thighs, parting them slightly, touching the soft skin there. It wasn't enough. She slid up the bed, delaying what Bethany craved most, and kissed her stomach, moved on to her breasts, capturing each nipple in her mouth. Good God, this exploration was everything. With a soft hand between Bethany's legs, she played gently. Soft gasps greeted her.

"Reid."

"I'm busy."

"You're cruel."

"I'm enjoying myself."

Another gasp. *Jackpot.* Bethany rocked her hips, finding a quick rhythm. The air in the room disappeared as Reid watched this beautiful woman beneath her touch. She slipped her fingers inside, holding Bethany steady with an arm around her waist. Anchoring her. Bethany moaned. Reid closed her eyes, holding the sound. She slid down the bed and tasted her, teased her, before going to work with her tongue.

"Yes," Bethany whispered, interlacing their fingers. "God. Please?"

Reid smiled against her, pressing firmly with her tongue, a move she remembered as very effective from years ago. Bethany went still and called out. Her body went tight, and all Reid could do was look on, enraptured.

"We didn't finish the wine," Bethany said, moments later.

Reid burst into a laugh, her body sated and warm. "We didn't get close. Maybe next time."

Bethany grinned and shook her head. "I'm still just trying to figure out what just took place. You should know that I'm never that responsive. Ever. Well, not since…"

"Us."

"Right. I thought it was just that I was older now. It was harder to get turned on. Not the case."

"You seemed very amenable," Reid said, touching Bethany intimately and watching her eyes react. "In fact, I think this is an experiment we can continue, if you'd be up for it."

Bethany's eyes flashed with understanding. She was energized. "I was so focused on this that I didn't think about the concept of a next time."

"Is that presumptuous of me?"

"Nothing is at this point. We're a little unpredictable."

Reid pushed up onto her forearms. "You're so wrong. So very, very wrong."

She dropped her eyebrows. "Explain yourself. And keep doing it naked." Her eyes dipped to Reid's body and back. She didn't mind the objectification.

"I can *depend* on you always captivating me. I can count on my body always wanting yours. I know without hesitation that when I kiss you, I will lose myself and not want to be found."

"Oh."

"That's all I'm saying."

"You said it really well. Say it again. I wanna watch."

Reid climbed on top, and Bethany caught her at the waist. "You stop teasing me right now."

"And now you're all bossy. I love it. This just gets better and better."

"Damn right I am." She snuggled her hips between Bethany's thighs. "And I think if I keep it up, I can pull a little more noise from you this time." She rocked her hips and watched Bethany's lips part.

"Are you challenging yourself?"

Reid kissed Bethany's neck slowly. She let her tongue taste its way up to her ear. "Thoughts?"

Bethany's eyes were closed, and her visible pulse had tripled in intensity. "What?"

"Exactly. Hold on." She meant it, too. She took liberties this time. Explored. Gave in to herself, lingering, pressing, and sucking her way to a second orgasm for Bethany that seemed to top the first, if one could judge by reaction alone. And the fact that Bethany didn't speak for a good three minutes after.

Finally, Bethany covered her eyes. "How do you do that? You play me like an instrument."

"Well, every musician has a favorite. You inspired me."

Bethany stroked her hair. "I love your curls."

"What a random thing to say in a moment like this."

"It's not random. Your hair has always evoked a sensual reaction in me. When you'd pull it up for Friday night games? Goner. I'd stare at you all night. Sometimes I'd imagine you without the uniform."

"At the games?"

"At the damn games. I was gaga for you from day one. And then you'd pass me these steamy little looks when you thought no one was looking."

"I'd do it now, too. This time I don't care who's looking."

She realized Bethany had never been around the fully out and proud version of herself. Her inhibitions had definitely played a major role in what had torn them apart as kids. She wanted to make it ridiculously clear that it was no longer a factor. "I've dated women exclusively since I was almost twenty years old. Openly. Happily."

"You got serious with someone."

Reid nodded. "I was almost married. We were compatible. We had fun. She ticked the boxes. Even Mason was on board."

"Okay. Well, all of that sounds very promising. So why didn't it work?"

Reid traced Bethany's jaw, fully understanding why for maybe the first time. "Because no one makes me feel what you do. In the end, it wasn't fair to her to expect something she wasn't capable of delivering. It wasn't fair to me to settle for less than what I craved."

"I identify with those words more than you know. Wow."

She shook her head. "I'd do so much differently if I could go back."

Bethany nodded. "Me, too. But regret doesn't undo some of my issues that I still carry around like a backpack of rocks." The playful quality from earlier had evaporated from her delivery. In fact, the weight of the room had settled on them. "Well, that just came out of my mouth like a bolt of lightning."

Reid leaned back onto her elbow, frowning. "But maybe for a reason."

Bethany closed her eyes, as if counting to ten. "No. And I don't want to step on tonight because I'm hung up on something from over a decade ago."

"Why do I get the feeling this is more than just you slightly hung up?"

Bethany sighed. "I was mad at you, Reid, for a really long time. Sometimes old habits are hard to break."

Reid nodded, realizing sadly that picking up where they left off was, perhaps, a fairy tale. Time had gone by. Damage had been done, left to fester. She could pretend all she wanted that Bethany had fully forgiven her for the wedge she drove between them, but that didn't make it so. "Is what I did really so awful? We were kids trying to make our way through life without getting too beat-up. I made some bad calls, but I tried to make it up to you." She touched Bethany's cheek. "I tried to."

"I know. And I wish we'd both been a little stronger." She pushed herself up to a seated position and seemed to be looking for her clothes. An escape act. An end to the intimacy. "I wish I was now."

"Don't." Reid nearly didn't recognize the command of her voice. Bethany must have registered the change, too. She went still, looked back.

"We can't go in circles, okay? Tonight was wonderful. For a sliver of time, I forgot every problem I had and basked in…us. Let's not go backward."

Bethany seemed torn. On the one hand, the anguish in her eyes was apparent. On the other, she looked at Reid with the kind of longing that mattered.

"Come back here." The pause that hit stretched for miles. "Please?"

Bethany blinked, and her features relaxed. She let her clothes fall back to the floor and came back to bed. They stared at each other with quiet appreciation. This was a new space for them. While they weren't pretending the past didn't exist, they were choosing this moment in spite of it. A very important step. Bethany raised her arm and Reid slid beneath it.

"Let's just keep talking. Working through it. See what happens."

Reid kissed the underside of Bethany's jaw. "You got it." She received a protective squeeze that made her cling to the hope that maybe everything was going to be okay. There was no monster lurking in the closet, poised to rip this all away again. Maybe, just maybe.

❖

Veronica was always the first one to take lunch at the clinic, preferring to never feel the pangs of hunger if she didn't have to. As Bethany joined her in the break room, her stomach far into the land of rumble, she could see that Veronica had already polished off two yogurts and a bowl of quickly whipped together tuna salad from the can.

"We're like soldiers in battle. You're eating from a tin can right now."

"You never said how pretty she was." She pointed at Bethany with her wooden tab of a spoon.

"What?" She knew exactly who Veronica was referencing, but it was so much more fun to play naive. "Finish your fish and mayonnaise."

Veronica shook her head, and the luscious jet-black hair swayed. No one on Earth had hair like Veronica. Her conditioning regimen alone impressed. Who had the time? "Are you two back together?"

She sat, contemplated, and realizing it wasn't something she wanted to run from, she met Veronica's inquisitive gaze. "No. I don't think there's anything official between us. We're seeing each other. Exploring what might or might not still be there."

"And what have you found. Anything?"

God, yes. Too much. More than Bethany would have ever imagined. Reid was still *her Reid*, and life only seemed to have enhanced their connection. After their night together, she had no choice but to leap into very scary terrain. She could get hurt. She could have it all stolen back. And be left with half of herself all over again. On the other hand, it felt like stepping into the warmth after years in the bitter cold. Too hard to refuse.

And it wasn't like she could hide any of this from Veronica, who knew her as well as she knew her own very precise lunch schedule. "I don't know if you've ever found someone that feels like your other half."

Veronica held up a finger. "I have a thought on that. My brother—everyone just calls him Tam, you've met him at gatherings."

"Intense guy. Works in news, right? With Thea's woman-crush."

"That's the one. He has a theory that everyone has a variety of soul mates out there, sprinkled across the universe, and that it's up to us to find one of them in the masses. Ups our chances." She tented her hands. "He's too practical. Ignore him. I believe in one. Is yours Reid? That's the question."

"Yes. I know that part for sure. No one has ever compared to her. Still, is soul mate status enough? Do I have it in me to fully go there again? What if I'm meant to be alone and content? I was doing just fine before her grocery cart nearly took out mine."

Veronica stood and tossed her yogurt and tuna into the trash can, one carton at a time, sinking each basket to perfection. Damn her. "No, you weren't. I love you, but you were super boring. Even Thea said so, and she's the nice one."

"Don't throw me under the damn bus!" a voice yelled from down the hall. Of course she was listening in. *Of course.* Bethany smothered a smile. She adored these two in spite of their tough love.

"Listen, I give it straight. I've known you for years. Whether you're currently feeling mad or intruded upon or in love, whatever it is, there's a spark in your eyes that I've never seen before. Ever. I like it." She paused in the doorway and looked back. "Did I mention how staggeringly good-looking she is?"

"The most popular girl in school," Bethany said and covered her heart.

"I'd love to get to know her."

"Yeah?"

"Me, too!" Thea yelled. "Can she come over right now? I have two physicals and a limping sixteen-year-old this afternoon. Easy lifting. I'll even call and cancel all of them for one Reid encounter."

"I definitely identify with that sentiment," Bethany shouted back.

"But it's my understanding that she's got two American literature classes to teach this afternoon."

Thea appeared next to Veronica, shorter by a good four inches. "Fuck her for ruining my fun."

"Done," Bethany said to the response of two giant gasps. With her lunch in hand, she pushed past them, unable to bury the grin on her face at her own damn sassiness. "Dictation calls."

"You sure it's not a booty? Might check the call readout," Thea said after her.

"Is Dr. Cahill swaying her ass as she walks?" Veronica asked Thea.

"Damn straight she is. Proud little hussy. I'm jealous, too."

Bethany closed her office door, took a seat, and laughed. The lightness that carried her from one room to the next these days was a thing of wonder. So this was what life felt like when you weren't missing half of yourself. It also reminded her of sitting at the top of a staggeringly tall roller coaster, looking down. An exhilarating, yet terrifying blip of time. Whether she embraced the thrill or white-knuckled the seat in terror was up to her. As she sat there, hidden from the rest of the world, she threw both hands in the air and opened her palms. She was ready.

CHAPTER FIFTEEN

Chapman University buzzed with the recognizable anticipation of the Thanksgiving holiday. The students, wearing boots and sweaters, moved a little faster, excited to wrap up the academic week so they could leap into cars or planes and get to their families as soon as possible. Reid knew better than to plan anything substantial for those last two days of classes, realizing half her students would have taken off early, not caring about their attendance record. They'd discuss the reading and maybe cut out a little early, her gift to them.

She and Mason would celebrate their first Thanksgiving in the new house along with her mom and her husband, Mark. She'd just heard that Alice would make it just in time for dinner, too. The extra-exciting part was that Bethany would be joining them, a concept that seemed almost too good to be true. She tried to imagine them all in the same place, mixing it up over a pan of her favorite sausage dressing. Chilly weather. Wine. Football on the TV. All the people she loved. As she crossed the lawn from the English building to the parking lot, her chest ached with happiness. Yes, actually *ached.*

She was up by four a.m. on Thanksgiving Day, pulling the turkey from the bathtub, then moving it through the prep process, finally hauling it into the oven. Each side dish had its own haphazardly scribbled index card detailing the times it would need her attention, making her process more scattered than it needed to be. A little before eight that morning, Mason arrived in the kitchen with bleary eyes, his dark hair sticking up in eight different directions. The perfect complement to his Dr. Strange pajamas.

"Happy Thanksgiving, Mace! Parade's on soon."

He seemed unfazed. "I love you, but you sure can bang around in here."

She laughed and kissed his head. "It's a holiday. Cut me some slack and turn on the giant show for me."

Giant balloons, Al Roker, and a box of doughnuts later, the gang began to arrive. Her mother and Mark first. Of course she brought the most beautiful autumn bouquet and vase, designed by her for the centerpiece. Gorgeous. Her talent astounded. "Mom, you went out of your way."

"I did not. But I wanted that table to be worthy of you and the work you're putting in for all of us."

Mark hit the couch with Mason, and her mother placed the orange, yellow, and red arrangement on the long table Reid had already set. After seeming to do a quick assessment, she paused and pointed at the extra place setting. "Who's the extra spot for?"

Reid didn't delay. She was well-prepared for this question and had every intention of making Bethany's attendance a non-event. "You remember Bethany Cahill, right?" She set the butter in the shape of a swan on the table. Her mother had taught her that as a teenager. "She's joining us. You guys can catch up. Should be fun." So super-breezy.

Her mother froze. Because the conversation had stopped, Mark turned around from his spot on the couch and vowed to become a duck trainer.

Reid grinned. "Hey, I have a way with ducks. Don't count me out."

"I'm waiting for the story, Reid Katherine." Her mother's eyes were wide, her hair, now streaked with gray she'd embraced as grandma chic, practically vibrated. Reid was aware that she'd put her mom through the emotional wringer when her heart had been broken at eighteen. Her ability to comfort and soothe her child had been put to the test when Reid lost Bethany. When she'd cried in her bed, she'd watched her mom's eyes fill with secondary grief. She'd confessed to Reid later that she'd felt helpless watching from the doorway, and like a failure in her single parent role. She'd lost sleep and her appetite along with Reid. It made sense she'd be on high mom alert.

"There's no dramatic story here." Not entirely true. "We ran into each other and have been catching up."

"Is this the high school girlfriend?" Mark's facial expression now resembled her mother's, which meant at some point he'd been briefed on Reid's emotional past. Fabulous. The more the merrier.

Reid decided to field this one herself. "Yes, Bethany is that girl from high school, but when she's here could we downplay some of these facial expressions?" Her mother nodded, stared hard, and forgot to blink for the next eight seconds. "Not at all weird," Reid said, realizing this might just be a memorable afternoon. Nothing she could do about it but enjoy having the people who mattered to her all in the same room.

Just as the timer dinged on her baked yams, Bethany arrived. Reid held the door open and lost her manners. Instead of *Welcome! Happy Thanksgiving!* or *You made it!* Reid simply drank her in. Dark gray jeans and a long green sweater that came in at the waist and offered a small glimpse of shoulder. Good God, we were doing shoulder today? There should have been a warning memo. She had her hair pinned behind one ear and the rest down with an added lazy curl. "I've missed you." The words fled from Reid's lips without a filter.

"Me, too," Bethany said and looked behind Reid. "Full house?"

"Alice isn't here yet, but the others are. You know everyone but Mark. He likes snacks and football."

"Don't we all? Should I be nervous?" Her blue eyes seemed extra-luminous today.

"Nope. Leave that to me."

Bethany stepped inside and paused briefly in Reid's space, speaking quietly. "You look beautiful. Even if you do have flour on your face."

Reid pawed at her cheek with a laugh that help her chill the hell out. "The yeast rolls. They're such problem children."

"Everyone says so." Bethany followed her inside, and they were off. Her mom pulled Bethany in for a hug. Mom had apparently gathered herself and prepared.

"Bethany, I can't even believe it's you. You're all grown up. Goodness, you're pretty."

Mason launched into his thoughts about flying dinosaurs and why they were the most terrifying, and Mark offered Bethany the last doughnut hole. Not a bad start.

Her mom took a seat on the couch and smiled. "Bethany, if I remember correctly, you were dead set on medical school."

"Yes, that's true. And I went. Definitely a feet-to-the-coals experience that taught me a lot about myself, but I love my job. Zero regrets."

"She's a fancy doctor now," Reid called, checking the turkey and wondering what happened to that one index card that told her what time to butter the green beans. She was flying by the seat of her pants and not caring.

"Did you stick with surgery?"

Reid only had a visual of Bethany's profile, but she saw the change come over her immediately. Her posture sank, and she adjusted her hair that didn't need adjusting. Interesting. "That part didn't work out."

Mark turned to her. "Let me guess, you fell in love with another specialty and surgery flew right off the radar. They say it's not for everyone."

Reid paused her kitchen prep because she hadn't yet heard the story behind Bethany's slight career adjustment. "Not exactly, no. I injured my hand and sustained some nerve damage. It gives me some trouble now and then. Took me out of contention before I even really had a shot."

Mark frowned. He'd always been a nice guy. "Sorry to hear that."

"Me, too," Reid said, coming around the counter to fully participate. She'd noticed Bethany's hand shook sometimes but chalked it up to nervous energy. That must be one of the side effects she was referencing. "When did this happen?" she asked.

"College. By that time, you and I were already…"

Broken up, Reid's brain supplied. She nodded. Bethany looked incredibly uncomfortable. Her gaze fell to the floor and then to her hand and back again. Pieces were floating into focus and assembling for Reid. Well, some of them. Bethany had had a much harder time back then than she'd understood. This injury had likely been a major turning point in Bethany's life, and Reid hadn't been there to help her through any part of it. She'd not chosen a new path for herself after all—she'd had hers ripped away, which had to have devastated. The realization stunned her into inaction. All around her, the food prep stacked up. Yet she couldn't get her brain to fire.

"Should we check the turkey?" her mom asked quietly. "I can do it."

"No, no. I got it." She turned. Moments later, Bethany was next to her at the stove with a kind smile and her hand on Reid's wrist. Mark and her mom were absorbed in a football game, and Mace had his Nintendo fired up in his lap, giving them a private moment.

Reid blinked, emotion tumbling. "I didn't know. About surgery."

"How could you? But I'm okay now. Look at me." She flashed the kind of smile that made Reid want to snuggle up in her arms.

"I'm a sucker for your face. You know that?"

Bethany nodded. "I try to use my power for good. Now what can I do to be of assistance'?"

Reid, her storm quieted by a few quiet words from Bethany, picked up a masher. "Potatoes?"

Bethany grabbed it. "Get ready to be impressed. When I get to mashing, you aren't gonna know what hit you."

"Clothes on the floor?" Reid asked quietly.

Bethany nodded in sincerity.

She wasn't wrong. There were few things more sexy than Dr. Bethany Cahill in a kitchen, expertly moving around and making things happen. She remembered the spaghetti dinner she'd barged in on back in the day and resisted the urge to fan her cheeks. Reid got such a charge from the visual and more than a couple of times wished for some stolen time, just them. But instead, there was another wonderful element to the day: she got to see Bethany interact with the other humans she loved and adored.

"Will you check with Bethany and see if she needs any help with the fruit salad?" Reid called to Mason, who happily hopped up and joined them in the kitchen.

"How are you with a knife?" Bethany asked him.

"Conscientious and talented." He stared up at her for her verdict.

Bethany arched an eyebrow and handed over a paring knife. "Apples are yours." They went to work side-by-side over matching cutting boards, Bethany on oranges and bananas. The chatter was nonstop.

"People always seem to think that Thanos is the most powerful force in the universe. But if you think about it, what is he without the Infinity Stones?"

"You bring up a good point," Bethany said. "But the heroes do seem to have a tough time with him. Their powers don't hold up to his strength. Think about when Mantis is trying to get him to pass out."

That pulled him up short, and Reid smiled, pretending not to eavesdrop.

"Okay, so he's powerful." Mason touched his hair, his thoughtful signal. "I still think he gets too much credit."

"Valid," Bethany said, tossing her banana slices into the large glass bowl.

"I had no idea you were a DC superhero expert," Reid said.

Bethany stared at her hard. Affronted. "Marvel." She blinked in disbelief. "We were talking Marvel, Reid. You can't be serious. There is a distinct difference."

"Yeah, if you say so." She shrugged.

"I tell her a lot. She always gets it wrong," Mason said quietly and passed Bethany a knowing look. Oh, these two were going to be trouble together, and she loved every second of it.

"Dinner is served," she told the room a short time later, just as Alice dashed in the door.

"Did I make it?" She had her blond hair in a ponytail. She quickly ripped out the tie and gave her head a shake. "I had a last-minute client go long. On Thanksgiving of all days. People just want to be in shape for this big meal, I guess. Whoa." Yep, her little sister had just said that out loud, pausing in her tracks and tilting her head to the side as she studied Bethany. "Does Reid know you're here?"

"I think so," Bethany said, wide-eyed. To make sure, she turned to Reid, who nodded.

"Bethany is joining us for dinner. I meant to tell you. Time got away. Ready to eat?" She was talking really fast and knew it. Alice was aware of everything that had transpired between her and Bethany because a couple of years after the breakup Reid had let it pour out of her like a faucet over a few sisterly beers. It had been Christmas break and they were up late, and though Alice had known that Bethany had meant a lot to Reid, it wasn't until that night that she understood the depth of their connection, and thereby, Reid's hurt.

"So, is this a thing?" Alice's eyes went wide, and the hair she'd shaken out stayed in that just-came-out-of-a-ponytail shape, abandoned for a greater cause. She seemed half excited, half cautious. Both made sense.

"I think we're not making any big proclamations about that," Reid said as she washed her hands. No big deal. Inside, it was anything but.

She had the same question. To her right, she saw Mason grin. That was something, at least. "I made a fantastic turkey, though, and we all like food, so let's eat." It was her way of moving them out of the *What is this?* game. Now was not the time.

The meal and the company couldn't have been nicer. Surrounded by most of the people she loved in this world, Reid made sure to absorb every last second of warmth. Each smile, each kind word, each laugh. Mason did lots of checking in on Bethany, passing her glances to see what she thought was funny or interesting, which meant she'd scored major points already. Her intellectual side clearly had him impressed and intrigued.

"Mason, what do you want to be when you grow up?" Alice asked. "I mean, what's the plan this week? Six months ago, it was a monster truck engineer, so I'm following up." She offered a playful aunt wink.

"I don't know. Maybe I'll be a doctor. Or a scientist." Another quick glance to Bethany and then back to his plate.

"I think you'd be great at either," Reid said.

"Me, too," said her mom.

Bethany nodded along enthusiastically, and that seemed to make Mace quite happy. Reid squeezed her knee under the table because her heart couldn't let the moment pass. She was happy by a measure she wasn't accustomed to. She wanted to capture and hold on to this feeling forever.

When the dishes were done and the good-byes were said, Reid exhaled and leaned against the counter with a happy/tired sigh.

"It was really nice to see everyone," Bethany said. She'd slipped out of her low-heeled black booties a few minutes ago and looked comfortable and perfect in Reid's kitchen. Mason appeared with an Iron Man duffel bag.

"I'm gonna miss you," Reid said, cradling his little face. She could get drunk off staring at the kid. "Be good for Dad. Try to act interested in the things he plans for you guys. He means well." Mateo loved Mason to pieces, but his attempts to turn him into the popular kid he'd been himself were just never going to help their relationship.

"I will." He smiled. "He'll get all frustrated when I can't catch his passes in the flag football game."

"Laugh it off. Just a game." In all honesty, Reid was nervous because this game was a sore spot year after year. Mason didn't care about football, rarely at all, which caused Mateo to up the pressure because they were in front of his family. Next would come tears, sometimes from both.

"Tell that to him," Mason said. "You'd think it was the big championship one or something."

"I think you mean the Super Bowl. I'm gonna let your dad in." She passed Bethany an are-you-ready-for-this look and headed to the door.

❖

Bethany was transported back eleven years in the second Mateo walked through the door of Reid's home. The face of her romantic rival from so long ago was fuller now. His hair was much shorter in a crew-cut style and the perfect physique now came with a small tummy. He still looked great. She had to give him that. But he was a man now, the boy long gone.

"You remember Bethany from United," Reid said as he followed her into the kitchen.

He turned and she saw the recognition flicker. To his credit, he smiled. Genuinely. "Wow. Good to see you."

"You, too, Mateo. You have a really great kid."

Mason beamed and Mateo pulled him against his side. "This one? He's all right, I guess. Haven't sold him on the side of the road. Yet." He then ruffled Mace's hair, which pulled a laugh from him. Reid smiled, probably relieved to see them off to a good start.

Mateo grabbed the duffel bag. "I'll have him home by dinnertime Sunday."

"Great. Just make sure he sleeps and doesn't just read books or play games in his bed all night."

"We'll hit the clubs instead. Right, big man?"

Mason nodded along and smacked Mateo's hand when he offered a high five. "You know me."

Mateo looked between them. "So does this little reunion mean something? Are we rekindling?" Mateo had clearly been briefed. Reid flicked him a look and then passed a softer one to Bethany. Yep. It was all a very touchy subject, and Reid didn't know the half of it.

"Don't you worry about it," Reid told him in a playful voice, clearly attempting to keep things light and him out of their business. "Come here, sweet boy." She reached for Mason, who moved into her arms. "Have the best time and call me whenever you want. Even just to chat about nothing."

"I will. I love you," he said and kissed her cheek.

"He'll be fine," Mateo said and grabbed Mason in a silly headlock as they headed for the door. "My mom is already making him chocolate chip cookies with the nuts he loves."

"Score," Mason mumbled from deep in the vise.

Once they were alone, Bethany found she didn't have the words that were usually at the ready. She wasn't one to flounder these days, even in a stressful situation. Medical school had her trained for quick thinking under the worst of conditions, so why were her thoughts swimming and her emotions folding into themselves?

When Reid turned back to her, she froze. Bethany knew why. There were tears on Bethany's cheeks, and she hadn't been able to stop them. No matter how good she'd become at shoving all of that stuff down, here it was. Embarrassing, her trauma on display. Mateo, the past, the hurt, and all that she'd lost came bubbling to the surface, drowning her in potency. She'd never properly dealt with any of it. And now, she couldn't breathe. She couldn't speak.

"What is it?" Reid asked, moving to her instantly. She took Bethany by the shoulders and locked eyes. "What's going on? Say something."

Bethany tried to speak, but her racing heart seemed to take precedence over everything else, toppling her ability to communicate, respond. Reid led her to the couch and held her hand. Bethany closed her eyes and willed the feelings away. Didn't work. Her jaw was tight and her lungs searched for air.

All she could do was remember.

CHAPTER SIXTEEN

Then

The day of Ella's high school graduation party had gotten away from Bethany. Now a high school graduate, she felt more mature, like she'd joined a new club of adults. Tonight would be a great way to say good-bye to her school-aged self. It was supposed to be the most lavish party of the year, according to everyone who could type. Not necessarily a rager, but something more upscale which sounded like something the new, more sophisticated Bethany would enjoy. Apparently, Ella's parents had dropped a ton of cash to celebrate the new graduates.

Bethany was supposed to drive to Ella's house that night with Reid, which would have been perfect because they'd not gotten much time together lately. Graduation had been a whirlwind. Reid had had lots of family in town to celebrate. Bethany then spent the next couple of days completing her paperwork for the research program and packing her room up for the impending drive to Colorado. Things felt good between them, though. Reid had started to smile more and had been sending her heart emojis all day. They'd also discussed all the ways they wanted to kiss each other the next chance they had. But Bethany hit a last-minute complication when her dad was called to set just after their home air-conditioning went down. That meant she needed to stay back and let the repair team into the house, stepping all over her plans and stealing that little bit of alone time with Reid.

It also meant she was now arriving to the party an hour late and alone.

Here goes nothing. She was nervous as hell walking into the party solo but vowed not to show it. She put on her most friendly smile, hoping the jeans and green flowy top she'd picked out would have her blending in. She'd even applied a little bit of makeup and added some curl to her hair to bolster her annoying insecurities. And who was she kidding? She also wanted Reid to think she looked pretty tonight. They had less than two weeks together, and she wanted them to count. She longed to talk to Reid for hours, kiss her just as much, and make love until the sun came up. That wasn't too much to ask, was it?

The house was enormous, but she was getting used to that. All these kids came from a decent amount of money. Ella's parents were something out of a commercial, in the best possible sense.

"We're so glad you're here. Bethany, was it?" Ella's mom asked.

"Yes, ma'am."

"Just follow the trail in the backyard to the open area, and you should find them all," she said, a red and yellow pointy party hat strapped to her head. "We won't bother you kids. Just wanted to say hello as you came in. See each smiley face. Then we're gone. Poof."

The father with the matching pointy hat popped up from his chair in the living room. "Pretend you didn't see us!" he said with so much glee it was adorable.

"Thank you. I'll just…" She gestured to the back door, aware of distant chatter.

"Have the best time. Congratulations!" They'd said that last word in unison.

"Thank you," she said, laughing. They'd kept the smile on Bethany's face as she followed that path that was lined with tall hedges, something straight out of Wonderland. LA was such an interesting place. Twinkly lights lit her shrub-lined way, and when she turned that last corner, prepared to tell Ella how awesome her parents were, she paused because it was Reid's voice she heard speaking quietly on the other side of the hedge. Why was she whispering and to whom?

"You guys, why would you assume I'm gay? Just because she is? I don't think it's contagious."

She normally wouldn't eavesdrop, especially on someone she loved, but the words and their meaning anchored her right where she was standing. She'd surely misunderstood.

"It's creepy the way she stares at you then." Sunny. Bethany's arms fell to her side.

"Clearly in love with you," Jennifer said, followed by a laugh.

Then Reid's. Reid's laugh. Bethany's gaze fell to an individual leaf on the hedge. It had been torn and clung to the twig.

"That's gotta be hard," Jennifer said. "I feel bad for her. She's actually kinda cool."

"She totally is. And I don't know that Mateo and I will get back together, but I don't know that we won't. I'm just doing me right now. I like to keep my options open. But no, Bethany Cahill is not one of them, okay? So relax."

That was her cue. She took the corner and presented herself. Tears threatened and her throat felt tight, but she wasn't about to give in to either of those things in this moment. No way. She would stand tall, just like her dad had always told her to when the chips fell down. How could Reid take something so wonderful like the love they shared and stomp on it so horribly to her friends? This wasn't Reid preserving the feelings of the guy she broke up with. This was much worse. She was preserving herself. From Bethany. God.

"Hey," she said to the group just feet away. Reid went pale and quiet. The other girls' smiles dipped slightly. "I don't mean to interrupt the conversation. It was interesting information though. Helpful." She found a small smile. *Head high.* She pointed across the lavishly decorated lawn just as the sun was setting. "I'm going to chat with Ella."

She didn't see Reid follow her, but as always, she could feel her presence.

"Bethany. Whoa, whoa, whoa. Wait a sec."

She didn't wait a sec. She had no intention. She was hurt, floored, and angrier than she'd ever been. She'd not known what it was like to feel betrayed, but this must be it.

"Ella." She took the girl's hands in hers, probably surprising her with the formality. "The party is gorgeous, and your parents were so sweet and funny."

"Thank you," Ella said cheerfully. "Glad you made it. Grab a beer."

"I can't. Driving."

"Right. Very responsible of you." She paused, really taking Bethany in for the first time. "Wow. You look really pretty." Reid stood off to the side, arms crossed, panic across her face. She'd been caught.

"I hung up the tumbling attire for tonight."

Ella was still taking in her look, which meant she'd done something right, and now it was for nothing. Who cared if Ella thought she looked good? Her world had just imploded. Reid was clearly waiting for the exchange to conclude. Bethany could already imagine her explanation. Blaming it on the breakup. Needing time. None of it rang true anymore. She'd been patient for months for them to be a couple in the true sense of the word. Not only did Reid have no intention of making that happen, she was ashamed of Bethany and let those girls pity her in the middle of a party. What kind of person does that? Not someone who loves you. She didn't know which way was up, and damn it, her hands were shaking.

"Can we talk?" Reid asked, stepping into her space. She touched Bethany's forearm, which was the opposite of what could happen right now.

Bethany yanked it away, pulling a few stares. "No, I don't think we can." She heard others murmur a reaction.

"Check out Bethany and Reid," a guy to her right said in a low tone. "Did you just see that? What the fuck, man?"

She closed her eyes. *Steady.* This just kept getting worse. Humiliated and crushed, it was probably time to get out of there.

"I think I'm going to go," she told Ella, who was staring at them in shock.

"Yeah, okay. Whatever you need." And then she stepped forward to Bethany and quietly asked, "Are you okay? Would you like me to walk with you?" A show of kindness. She needed one.

"Could you?" she whispered, her throat thick and unable to produce much sound. Ella didn't hesitate and, to her credit, looped her arm through Bethany's and walked with her straight past Reid, who stared at the ground. Jennifer watched in curiosity. Sunny watched with a knowing quality. She knew more than she admitted. It was clear. Yep. A regular nightmare, all right.

"Everything okay?" Ella's mom asked, her forehead full of concerned creases.

"I'm not feeling well. Ella's helping me to my car."

"I can drive you home if you like," her father was quick to say.

"No. I'm fine to drive. Just probably need some distance from the crowd."

Ella got her safely to the car and leaned down through the open window. "Hey. Reid's a mess right now. But you know what I think? Her loss for not broadcasting you guys to the world."

Bethany blinked. Well, well. "Thanks for saying that." The small amount of friendship shown to her in this horrible moment helped more than Ella would ever know.

"No problem. Sure you don't want to stay? Tough it out? You might have fun. Who knows?"

"I don't think I can."

"I get it. Take care of yourself, okay?" Without school or cheer to connect them, she likely wouldn't see Ella or any of the others again before she left town. There was something shocking about that. All of it. She'd come to Los Angeles with nothing and would be leaving that way. This wasn't what she'd planned or imagined just yesterday. She felt empty. Hollow.

Once alone, she allowed the tears their entrance. She drove home through a wash of them, slamming on the radio, slamming it off when the sounds of The Skips blared, a reminder of the good times that now felt like a mirage. She saw Reid's face as she drove, felt her hand in hers as they walked through the park. Which of the words Reid had spoken to her were true and which ones were false? A blur. She heard them now, echoing in her ears, taunting her like the sucker she apparently was.

When she arrived home, she walked through her haze of emotion toward the front door, which was opened immediately from the inside by her dad, home from set. "Come here," he said without delay, his brows drawn low. He didn't pester her for details or demand to know who had upset his daughter. He simply slung an arm around her, pulled her close, and sat them both on the couch. "We'll stare at the tube and forget today. Just drop it off a cliff. You don't have to talk."

She nodded, clinging to the safety he provided. She focused on breathing, one deep inhale after the next. She would be okay if she could just keep the air moving. All she had to do was survive, even if it felt like her soul had been cut out. All the while her phone blew up with messages from Reid and a couple of calls. Bethany finally turned it off. In fact, three miserable days passed before she decided it was time to face Reid. Nothing felt the same. She understood that it never would.

Can I come over? the most recent text read.

Yes. We should talk. She tossed the phone onto the bed next to the stack of summer clothes she'd sorted for packing. She heard the buildings on campus were cold, so layers would be key. It had helped her stay afloat, concentrating on her future. Reid clearly didn't know what she wanted, who she wanted to be, and that meant Bethany had to cut the strings before she was drowned by the weight of it all. She'd move mountains for Reid, but it was time to face the fact that Reid wasn't prepared to move them for Bethany.

She sat on the porch, waiting for the blue car. When it pulled in, Bethany's heart hung heavy. Reid approached in cutoffs and a white T-shirt, hands halfway in her pockets. She didn't smile or move with much energy. She sat on the step across from Bethany, leaving space between them. Reid knew where they stood. Her eyes filled with tears before the words left her lips. "I'm sorry." She raised her hand and let it hang there before continuing. "I was floundering. After regionals, I felt like such a loser. And I thought if the world knew *everything* about me, they'd like me even less."

"The same way they feel about me? Think about that for a minute."

"Yes and no. I think a part of me missed being that girl they all looked up to."

"And that I would bring your social status down. Yeah."

"Trust me. I heard it. I was so selfish in how I behaved. I see that now. No excuses. I was clinging to an old identity that I don't even really want. It's bizarre."

"It is complicated, what you're going through. I'll give you that. I sincerely hope it gets better."

"You say that with such finality. I don't like it. How can I fix this? Tell me and I'll do it."

"I think you need time on your own for, I don't know, perspective. I do, too. We're not in the same place as each other, Reid. I want things you're by no means ready for, and I can't continue to pay for that." These were things she'd sorted out with the logical part of her brain. It didn't make it any easier to put the plan into action. Imagining life without Reid was near impossible. But it turned out she wasn't good for Reid in this moment, and Reid certainly wasn't good for Bethany or her already limping heart. It didn't mean she didn't love her more than she could describe. She had to harden her resolve, though. Wall off the emotions that wanted to override her decision.

"So you're walking away." Reid nodded her head. "I think that's a little extreme. Don't you?"

"I'm not walking away." *Stay strong.* "What am I walking away from? Were we ever even a couple? It feels a little like you were exploring a new side of yourself, and I was the vehicle for that. Maybe that's true. Maybe it's not. But I can't go off to school and guess for the next four years."

Reid looked shocked at her doubt, offended even. "I can't believe you just said that."

Bethany nodded. "Well, I can't believe you said some of the things you did either. Just how it is these days."

"Beth. That's awful. I'm trying to fix it."

"Don't. Reid." She pinched the bridge of her nose, which only mildly helped the crying headache she'd had for days. "It's never going to be the same. I hope you find your perfect, popular future."

"What if my future is supposed to be with you?"

"It's not. The forever factor? Laughable now. I'm the creeper who stares at you. Let's not forget." Okay, this was getting brutal. But Bethany felt like it was time she stood up for herself.

Reid was coming undone, and the old Bethany wanted to wrap her up. "I'm sorry I don't have all the answers the way you do. Some of us aren't as strong. I was hoping you'd cut me some slack, even if it doesn't seem like I deserve it right now."

"I've tried that. It didn't go well." Bethany stood, folded her arms.

"Okay, then. I'll go." She stood in a daze, seemingly shocked that this was how they ended, that they had at all. She walked slowly to her car, not looking back once. She spoke, though, her voice hoarse and wobbly, giving away her emotion. This had wrecked her. But it had wrecked Bethany, too. "I hope you love it in Colorado. Give that research program your all." There was no fanfare or dramatic good-bye. Not even a wave. Reid drove away in the blue car that changed her life on a ride home one day, and Bethany sat on her porch and cried. For herself. For Reid. For the loss of the future that she truly believed would be hers.

❖

The graduation party felt like a nightmare. Reid wasn't even sure why she'd gone.

She had arrived at Ella's party feeling strangely like an outsider, a role she wasn't used to playing. The longer she stayed, the worst it got. Ever since Mateo started dating Ruby Breshers from the dance team, Reid had become less central in her group of friends. The fact that she'd ruined their shot at regionals also left her with her own brand of scarlet letter. Her instinct was to turn to where she was most comfortable, Bethany, and shut out the rest of the world. It wasn't like anything compared anyway. That worked nicely until large, inclusive gatherings like Ella's popped up, and then she was faced with her worst fear. Rejection.

She was supposed to have arrived with Bethany, and that would have helped keep her strong. On her own, she'd smiled and feigned a confidence she didn't feel. Playing a part she knew well. In the midst of a chat with her friends, Sunny studied her curiously.

"What?" Reid had asked, self-conscious. "Crumb on my face?"

"We're still worried about you is all," Sunny said with a soft hand to her arm. "You're not yourself. Everyone agrees."

"What are you talking about? I'm still me."

"You're with her all the time," Sunny said, clearly over it. Annoyance dripped from her tone.

"Not that we don't like Bethany," Jennifer rushed to interject. "She's a beast in the air. I've never seen someone with her skills. I'm just a little shocked to think she's who you might end up with. No offense."

"Because really?" Sunny slowly slid a hand onto her hip. "You used to be Reid Thatcher."

"I still am." That's when Reid panicked. "Let me clear this up." It had been the moment she knew was on its way, when her friends would ask her straight out about her sexuality. She'd been ready to lay it all out there, had thought through her words multiple times. Regardless, she'd caved and scrambled for the only explanation she could manufacture, that they were wrong, and she was still exactly the same as the girl they'd grown up with. She wasn't weird or different. Yet her behavior made no sense. This was actually an awesome new part of her life that she was genuinely excited about. Why was she publicly backing away from the truth? She was a kid who'd climbed the ladder of the high dive and chickened out when she came face-to-face with the jump. She'd disavowed Bethany and her true feelings. The second the words left her lips, she regretted them. But there'd been no time for that. Bethany had appeared with the crestfallen look that had haunted her dreams for the past week. Reid's eyes weren't capable of crying more tears, yet somehow, she found a way. She was nauseous, miserable, and her heart ached.

"She's upset right now," her mom said, cradling Reid on her disheveled bed. She hadn't had the energy to make it. "She was hurt, but she'll come around."

Reid sat up and wiped her face, a move she'd perfected over the many days of melting down. "The thing is, I could have tried to get her to forgive me or for another chance. But I couldn't do that because she deserves so much more than me, Mom. I'm weak and selfish and I had all of this coming to me."

"Lessons are tricky things. Sometimes to learn them you have to pay a price. I'm not so sure this is permanent."

Reid immediately rejected the thought because she couldn't grant herself the gift of hope. "She should go to college and find someone amazing and fall in love." The tears hit again. "Oh God. She probably will, too, while I'm not sure I'll survive without her." She buried her face in the wet pillow and started all over again. Her mother's warm hand landed on her back.

"First heartbreaks are rough. I promise you, you'll get through this."

"I don't want to," Reid whispered. "I don't ever want to forget this."

As a cathartic measure for herself, and in part because she didn't know what Bethany might be going through because of Reid's actions, she sat down and wrote an email.

Beth,

By now you're likely settled in at U of Colorado. I bet it's a lot different than here. I wish we had talked again before you left. I understand why we didn't. I miss you. I love you. I didn't mean any of those awful words. This was a wake-up call for me, and as I transition into this new stage of my life, I plan to devote a lot of time to working on myself and becoming comfortable with who I am. You've shown me just how great it can be. If you find that you ever want to talk to me again, please reach out. I promise it will be different. If you don't, well, I want nothing but success and happiness for you.

Always,
Reid

Though she waited, checked her email daily, and watched social media in case Bethany reactivated her accounts, none of those things happened. Each passing day made it clearer. Bethany was gone, and so was Reid's happiness.

❖

The damned email. Bethany had almost been able to breathe at school. Barely. The hours demanded of her during that first semester were long, and the work was grueling. She needed a 4.0 for med school and planned to get it. But the studying had kept her mind off Reid, and helped her not think about how much she missed her. Then the letter arrived in her inbox. It was short in nature but sincere, and with distance between her and the night of the graduation party, she could somewhat understand the pressure Reid must have felt from her friends. She didn't excuse the behavior, the words, or their effect, but she was beginning to find forgiveness. The letter brought her longing straight to the forefront again. The more she let herself think about Reid, the more she luxuriated in the thoughts. The fullness of her lips, the way her smile radiated when she lit up, her skin and its smooth surface, the addictive sound of her laugh. She missed the way her hair smelled and the sly teasing she slipped in, just to give Bethany a hard time.

She'd be at school now. Midway through her first semester, as well. She tried to focus on anything but Reid, but that tug simply wouldn't leave her. That had to be for a reason, right? They'd hit an awful bump, but maybe their story wasn't quite over? She sat with the question, turning it over and over.

Two weeks later and Bethany knew that what they had was worth fixing. She tried to pick up the phone a couple of times and call. She wrote about a hundred text messages and then deleted them. A really long email that didn't seem to fully capture all she needed to say. She never sent it.

Finally, one Friday, Bethany finished up midday, channeled her father's love of road trips, and drove the seven hours to Santa Fe, hyped up on love and adrenaline. Ready to just let go and find a way to make things good again with the woman she loved and hoped to marry one day. They needed work, yes, but all good things did. She smiled for most of the drive, thinking about what city they might wind up in after Reid graduated and Bethany worked her way through medical school. They'd go out to dinner with friends and meet up for dates after work, falling into bed together at the end of a long day. Maybe they'd even get a dog.

After a restless night in a Holiday Inn near campus, Bethany located Reid's dorm after lunch and hoped she'd be easy to find. The sunny campus was honestly quite beautiful, and the energetic students enjoying the weekend only helped amp up her excitement for this whole adventure. It felt very much like her life was about to right itself, and everything would be okay again. The sky would be blue. The grass would be green, and she could miss Reid desperately while talking on the phone about their days together, each night.

Mateo. It didn't make sense or match up.

She blinked as she walked across the lawn in the direction of Hokona Hall, Reid's dorm. He didn't go here. He'd signed to play football at Fresno State. She stopped walking, not sure what to do. Confused, she decided to hit pause. She took a seat on a nearby stone bench and decided this was not the moment to burst onto the scene. She'd been right because as Mateo hit the bottom step of the exterior stairs, Reid emerged from the building in jeans, a lavender shirt, and black boots. He opened his arms, and she fell into them. Bethany forgot to breathe. They talked a moment and were off, her arm linked through his. Innocent enough, right?

That was until he'd kissed the side of her temple, and she'd responded by leaning her head on his shoulder as they walked. A kiss on the lips. It wasn't friendly. This was one of those intimate exchanges between couples that other people felt guilty for watching. The barrage of emotion inched in like the tide to completely drown her. She never would have made the trip if she thought there was the tiniest chance that Reid was rekindling anything with Mateo, of all people. This was the worst possible outcome ever. Her limbs were numb and her brain had downshifted, no longer helping her in any capacity.

Hindered, she sat on the bench another two hours, trying to sort through her foolishness and shock. Maybe she'd call Reid when she got back to Boulder, but she wasn't feeling especially confident or wanted in this moment. So much for big declarations and the joy of a long-awaited reunion. Maybe it was time to face the fact that her first love would be just that, a story she told one day. The thought gutted her. She loved Reid. Maybe she always would.

Dejected and emotionally drained, she limped her way back to her car, dragging her heart behind her. Part of it was her own damn fault for not finding a way to forgive Reid sooner. She carried the weight of regret with her daily. She was the one who did the breaking up. Reid had still wanted to try. And look where the whole thing had landed her, in a foreign city feeling like a fool. The other part of her blamed Reid for sending that email and making Bethany believe that they could come through this.

She cried her way onto the highway and through traffic, wondering distantly about lunch, knowing she wouldn't have the ability to eat it. Crestfallen. Embarrassed. Barely able to see the road through the tears that choked her.

Chapter Seventeen

Now

The room was silent and still as Reid took in the information she still couldn't quite believe. The sound of the kitchen fluorescents took over, humming their underscore.

"I'm sorry." Reid shook her head. "I'm still sorting through this."

"It's okay," Bethany said. "I realized recently that I've had years to process our full history, but you're just being handed new pieces."

"Right. So if you'll indulge me a minute."

"Yes. I'm trying. The topic isn't my favorite." Bethany scratched her cheek, a sign she was uncomfortable.

"There are parts I don't understand." Reid's head was a jumble. She stood and walked the length of the room and turned back. Bethany was right about the pieces being new. They were in her hands now, but she'd yet to figure out how to assemble them. "If you came to Santa Fe, why didn't you say something? Jump up and down. Send a text message? Change the course of our lives." She wanted to shout all of those questions, but Bethany didn't seem to be in the state of mind to handle that. In fact, she hadn't stopped subtly shaking since telling Reid the story of her visit. That had Reid worried.

"The me of today would have done that. The brokenhearted kid version lost all direction. Once I saw you with Mateo, it was like a door closed. The looks on your faces told me a lot. You guys were back, and I should finally let go whether I wanted to or not. The universe was making things pretty clear."

Reid rolled her lips in. Dammit. "We did give it another try.

Mateo and me. I was floundering in school, missing my family, and thinking constantly about you. Only you'd never answered my email or reinstated any of your accounts, so when he called and was so sweet, it was like this lifeline to an easier time. He came to visit. I tried it back on. It didn't take. He felt like a bull in a china shop after you."

"Oh." A pause. "So…Mason, I assume."

She nodded. "I wasn't on anything and we weren't safe. We were intimate twice in total, and it was all I needed to know."

"I wondered."

"Mateo went back to his life, and I came out officially just in time to find out I was pregnant. It was a big month." She raised her shoulder, remembering that time in her life as so formative to who she had become. Juggling life as a single mom at twenty while still pursuing her degree one course at a time had been difficult at best. She'd moved home and relied on her mom and Alice for help. Even her dad had pitched in on babysitting duties. It made her stronger, though, toughened her up like nothing else could have. "Beth, if I had seen you that day, things would have gone so differently. Please know that." She squinted as if it helped her to see into the past.

Bethany's eyes shone with emotion. "We weren't meant to be. Mason was."

That was a positive thing to say. Because Reid wouldn't trade her son for anything. "Maybe we were. Just not back *then*."

Bethany offered a smile, studied the wall. "It's an interesting idea." Her words were nice enough, but Bethany's mood hadn't shifted from the wash of melancholy. Reid rolled her shoulders, uneasy and not sure why. She decided to get them out of it in any way she could. Levity, maybe.

"So, when you left Santa Fe, did you curse my name forever? Throw darts at my photo? I wouldn't blame you. It makes a little more sense why you never did reach out." Reid shook her head, still trying to absorb this new information. Bethany had wanted them to be together enough to hop in the car and drive hundreds of miles.

"Not exactly. No."

"Okay. What was next for you?"

"That's the thing. I probably shouldn't have gotten on the road that day. My emotions overflowed, and I wasn't focused." Reid stayed quiet. There was something looming on the horizon that made her feel sick. "I remember the screeching of brakes. Mine. And then the flashing lights."

"Oh no." Reid hadn't moved. She couldn't.

"My dad was there when I woke up. Seventeen days in the hospital and lots of rehab. I took the rest of the year off from school and started fresh the next fall."

Reid hurt all over. Her heart ached. This didn't seem right. But it was. "You mentioned your hand. It was badly hurt."

Bethany met her gaze. "It wasn't your fault. Not at all."

"Are you sure about that?" Reid's hand moved slowly to her mouth. "Because I'm not."

"Trust me. I'm positive. But for a long time, it felt like I couldn't disassociate you from the accident, from what I lost that day. The two were tied together, and they shouldn't have been."

Reid closed her eyes. "You never became a surgeon."

"By the time I got to med school, I'd made so much progress. But I knew it wouldn't be enough. A shaky dominant hand doesn't position you well for competitive surgical programs, and I quickly had to face the facts."

The ceiling had crashed in. Reid didn't have the appropriate words. She imagined Bethany living with such a harsh reality and hated that she'd played any kind of role. "No wonder you hated me. I hate me."

"That's just it. I talked a big game, but I didn't hate you, Reid. I could never. You were my everything." She shook her head. "And in my very dark moments, I'd lose myself in thoughts of us. So in many ways, you were the lifeline that helped me through it."

They hadn't touched at any point in the conversation. They were separated by quite a few feet, yet that was all Reid wanted. To hold Bethany, to touch her, to take it all away. But she was afraid. Instead, they stared at each other, absorbing the new understanding between them. Everything reflected the importance of all that had transpired. Yet she was still Reid, and this was her Bethany.

"I love you." Those were the words she chose. They were the ones that floated to the surface above all else. Hearing them out loud centered Reid and made the world slow down. It was just them now.

"I love you, too." Bethany's eyes were soft. Reid knew that stare. It was the same one Bethany used when she'd hold her after they'd made love, her bedroom quilt pulled up to their bare shoulders. They'd kept each other warm with body heat and gentle touches. Those soft eyes. She'd missed them.

But there were still the real-world ramifications of their situation. "I don't know what to do about all of this, though."

"I have an idea," Bethany said.

"I'm listening."

"Why don't we each take a little time, some hours to ourselves, and think about what it is that we truly want. This was all sprung on you, and maybe it's too much. Maybe it isn't. But I don't want either of us to feel pressured to wade into deep waters we're not comfortable in."

It was fair.

Reid's head was jumbled and beginning to throb. She'd been up since four a.m. prepping the turkey and stuffing. This was not exactly how she imagined the evening ending, but maybe it was for the best. They didn't have to rush and, if anything, should take their time as they examined their past and potential future together. "Okay. We can do that. What's your plan?"

Bethany sighed, reaching through her thoughts. "There's supposed to be a good band playing out at the lake next Saturday. Meet me at the boat ramp. Four o'clock. What do you think?"

"The plan has potential." It also made Reid incredibly nervous.

"We can talk, listen to some music. A no-pressure night. But we have to promise each other something."

"I'm listening."

"If either one of us wants to go her separate way, we say okay, hug it out, and get out of there. No hard feelings."

"I can agree to that." A pause. "It's not The Skips, is it?" Reid asked.

That pulled a much-needed laugh, shattering the built-up tension. "I wonder whatever happened to them."

Reid didn't hesitate. "Insurance salesmen. Surely. Too many kids and thirty extra pounds." Another laugh. It's all they could do. "Friday, then," she said with a decisive nod. "Seven o'clock."

Bethany stood, and Reid exhaled slowly. This was so much bigger than her heart had ever planned, and she was feeling more overwhelmed with each moment that passed. She wasn't even sure of quite literally her next step. Did she follow Bethany to the door? Thank her for coming to dinner? Open her arms for a chaste hug? She didn't feel close to the same person she had been an hour ago. How could she know how to behave?

Bethany, always able to read her mood with startling accuracy, shrugged, tossed a gesture to the now empty table. "I feel like I came over for dinner and upended your world. I'm sorry about that."

Reid made a circular gesture near her head. "I'm just letting everything settle. I promise, at some point in the future, I'll have more appropriate words. For now, I'm sorry about the accident and what happened to you." Her voice shrank to a whisper without permission. The lump that rose in her throat ached. "I can't quite believe it."

Bethany didn't speak for a moment. It allowed Reid to catch how important it was for her to hear those words. She seemed to be turning them over, internalizing their effect. Therapy. That's what all of this was. But what if they were beyond repair? Her guilt. Bethany's hurt and regret. She imagined a tower so tall, built on their recriminations, that it toppled them. Before it did just that, she was instantly in Bethany's arms, clinging to her, needing her close for one more moment. Even if this was their last. She couldn't let her walk away without it and tried to memorize every detail.

"Maybe I'll see you next Saturday?" Bethany asked.

"Yeah, maybe."

Bethany offered her hand a squeeze and was though the red door. Reid walked back to the kitchen, lost in her thoughts, swirling, drowning between their sharp overlap. If her soul could bleed, it would. She leaned against the counter, gripping the lip behind her for support. Finally, she slid to the floor, hugging her knees and giving in to the weight of emotion. Fresh, hot tears ran unencumbered. It wasn't fair that others paid the price for actions she'd taken, knowingly or not. She'd shoulder the guilt always. She wasn't sure there'd be room for anything else.

❖

The Blue Moon Diner hadn't changed much in eleven years. If anything, it had managed to get bluer. Bethany would know. She'd been meeting her dad there the first Monday of every month since moving back to California. Even his new and wonderful marriage hadn't gotten in the way of their one-on-one dinners. That was because she had the best new stepmom in his wife, Kay. She thanked God for someone so wonderful to watch over her dad and make him laugh.

"Pretty sure this onion ring was crafted in the image of George Michael," he said, holding one up.

Bethany studied it and couldn't disagree, remembering his vintage albums in the living room. "Those bad boys never disappoint. But they don't seem to care about the ring moniker at all. Admirable." She grinned. As always, it was good to see him. He'd started his own lighting company five years ago and had seen a decent level of success in the TV and film industry, though these days he spent half his time behind a desk making it all happen. It was a good mixture of hands-on work and bossing other people around. He'd done well. Even if his beard sported a lot more gray these days.

"How's Thea? Did she ever get herself that dog she wanted?" His eyes crinkled at the sides when he mentioned her friend. They'd developed a quick rapport, which included Thea sending him socks she knitted with hamburgers on them.

She laughed. "That had to be six years ago, Dad."

"Well, dogs live a long time."

"Good point. Yes, Hercules is seven pounds of white fluff and visits the office frequently." She tapped the table. "I actually want to discuss another friend with you, if that's okay."

"Is Veronica getting bossy again?" He dabbed his mouth free of ketchup. "She's a ballbuster. I don't mess with her at parties." The female server passing their table raised an eyebrow. Bethany offered an apologetic smile.

"No. It's actually Reid Thatcher from high school. Remember her? She's the friend I spent Thanksgiving with." She let that hang in the air for a moment, focusing on her barely touched burger and finally taking a bite. Her appetite had been on hiatus since Thanksgiving, four days ago. "We've been seeing each other again. Kind of."

His eyes went big and he rubbed his beard, a sign of stress. "Wow. Haven't heard that name in a while. How's that going?"

"Really well." She sat there a moment. "I think. Also, we had kind of a difficult day. I told her about the accident and that I'd come to see her. All of it."

"Oh, this dinner just took a heavy turn."

She rushed to fix it. "No. I don't think it has to."

"Then you've never dealt with you before in regard to those particular topics."

"I loved her," she said quietly. "I think I still do. Nothing in my life has ever compared."

"Go on."

"I've never fit with someone like that before. I don't think it was a characteristic of first love either."

He was quiet for a moment, his eyes never leaving her as he worked it out. "I think it comes down to one damn thing, but it's an important damn thing."

"I'm listening."

"Well, I've been here through all of it. Seen all the things you've overcome and the things you didn't."

"That's fair."

"You carried a lot of grief in your heart for a very long time. It was awful." He tossed his napkin. "And Reid was tied to it like a trailer to a flatbed. Until you can lose the grief or cut the trailer free, you're not going to be able to move forward into something worthy."

Bethany understood his meaning. If she wanted to truly love Reid in the purest sense, she had to approach it with a clean slate. "So the question becomes, have I made peace with all that happened? Can I love her for who she is today, and let go of any resentment from the past?"

"Well. Can ya?"

"I think so. I want to. Since she's been back, I'm excited about waking up each day. My brain is all busy thinking about her. Making plans."

He grinned. "Really? Because I think that says a lot. I liked Reid. She was just a kid, Beth. We all have sorting out to do at that age."

She nodded. "I know. And she's still amazing. Her little boy is, too. Another reason to be sure I'm sure. I can't risk his feelings."

"A big one. Kids aren't to be messed around with."

"Is that why you never brought many women home?"

"That's exactly why. You'd already lost one mother. I wasn't about to let you get attached to another unless it was right."

"I'm glad you found Kay." Her stepmother, a massage therapist and all-around nurturer, kept her father grounded and loved everything about his relationship with Bethany. She was a keeper.

"Sometimes you just have to be patient until the right one rolls in."

"Or rolls back in," she said wistfully. Her stomach tightened. She stood on a precipice and knew it. But if she was going over the side, she very much wanted Reid with her. "I think I might just have to go for it."

"In that case, we'll need more onion rings. Celebratory ones."

"I can't argue with that."

Reid was struggling. Sitting alone in her darkened living room with her son tucked away in bed, home from the holiday weekend with his dad, she wasn't sure how to forgive herself. The fire flickered. Her heart hung heavy. The idea of Bethany hurt and struggling kept flashing in her brain like a movie she couldn't turn off.

Bethany's forgiveness was everything. But could she forgive herself?

She stood from the leather chair in the corner of her living room and walked to the kitchen, the movement helping her loosen her thoughts. As she walked, she heard the voices from the past floating back to her. Two teenagers lying in each other's arms in the dark. Just like her dark now.

"What am I going to do when you're in one state and I'm in the other?"

"Talk all the time. Wait for each other. Visit like crazy."

"Don't forget about me, okay?" Reid asked.

Bethany traced the infinity sign onto her shoulder. "The forever factor. Remember? That's us."

She dropped her palms flat on the warm surface of the counter, aware of the goose bumps that popped up across her skin. It didn't *matter* what hurt they'd caused each other in the past. They loved each other *today*. That much was clear. She loved Bethany. She couldn't imagine going back to life without her, which meant they had to be strong, and concentrate on what toppled everything else. Each other.

She just had one person to check in with first.

"I want to talk to you about Bethany," Reid said on Saturday, flicking her right turn signal.

"What about her?" Mason asked from the passenger's seat. They were on their way to her mother's place for a Grandma/Mason day. The holidays were a chance for everyone to spend a little extra quality time together, and Mason was at the top of that request list for most of her family members. Sought after, that kid. Beloved.

"How would you feel if we saw her more?"

"Definite yes. She knows all sorts of things. Remember when I told you that there were over seven hundred species of dinosaurs?"

"I do."

"She's the one who told me."

"Whoa." Reid nodded, showing off how impressed she was. "She's pretty smart. Does that mean you like her?"

"Yeah. A lot." A pause. "Are you asking because of the dating thing?"

"Hmmm." Reid pulled the car to a stop at a red light. They were two blocks from her mom's, who had a flower pressing project all designed for Mason that afternoon with plans to keep him overnight. "What do you mean by that?"

"Well, you're dating each other, right?" He was always such an observant kid, but this one surprised Reid.

"Yes. We are."

"Good. You could get married, too."

Reid laughed through her newly tight throat. Relief flooded. "You think that would be an okay idea? I mean, someday?"

"I'd be down. She could live with us. Do you think Mimi will let me use her clay? I'm working on a new design for a sports car."

Reid swallowed back the emotion. "I think she would. She loves it when you invent things. It's her favorite."

"Cool. Race ya inside." Once she killed the engine, Mason was out like a shot. Reid grabbed his bag and followed him in, knowing in just hours, she'd be at the lake. Time to figure out just what she planned to say. And what she planned to wear. And what she was going to do if Bethany decided to break her heart. Or worse, didn't show up at all.

CHAPTER EIGHTEEN

Lake Mission Viejo sparkled and swayed. Always had. Today was no different. Bethany had visited the outdoor oasis too many times to count, and somehow, it was never enough. Tonight, the place was on fire. Music from a local cover band blared from the large stage set up with a view of the water behind it. The free concert had attracted hundreds to the lake. Blankets, picnic baskets, and food booths were in no short supply.

She and Reid had agreed to meet away from the throngs, along the water between boat slips fifteen and sixteen. Bethany was early on purpose, needing time to settle in to what she was about to do. She pulled her green army jacket over her chest, absorbing the chill off the beautiful blue water as she listened to the distant sounds of the band playing a song she recognized but couldn't name.

"I always liked it when you danced."

She turned around. Reid made her way up the walk. Jeans, a yellow sweater, and white canvas sneakers. The most beautiful woman on the lake. She was also carrying two cups of cocoa from the stand Bethany had passed on the way in.

Bethany shrugged. "You weren't supposed to see that."

"But I'm happy I did. You look great." But there was a measured apprehension in her eyes. What did that mean? "For you," Reid said, handing over a cup. "Want to sit?"

Had it been a warmer day, they might have dangled their feet at the water's edge. Sitting along the dock would have to do instead. Her heart beat way too fast. Nerves. She clenched her palms, suddenly aware of all she had to lose. Her right hand showed off its tremor. She steadied it with her left.

"You first," Reid said, staring off at the water. She sipped her cocoa.

"You just get to it."

She turned and faced Bethany. "Seems like there's a lot looming. Let's just knock it out. Tell me where your head's at, and then I'll tell you about mine."

Bethany nodded. Reid's gaze landed somewhere on Bethany's forehead, and then she realized Reid was watching the way the wind caught her hair. She placed a hand there to tame it. As if on cue, the wind calmed and the air went still.

"I guess that's why we're here." The band finished a song, and the crowd went wild. Bethany paused to let the noise die down. She nodded and few times and then went for it. A leap from the high dive. "I love you."

Reid's eyes widened almost imperceptibly. She offered a slight nod before her head dropped and her gaze landed on her hands, which she had cradled in her lap. She'd broken their connection. Telling. While it nearly took the wind out of her sails, Bethany had to say what was in her heart. If this was the last time she'd see Reid, she needed her to know a few things.

"Even when I was convinced there was zero chance of an us, I still loved you with my whole heart. I do now more than ever. Seeing the woman you've become, the mother that you are to that amazing little boy, only makes me love you more. I want you, Reid. I want us. So much so that I can barely cobble together the right words, and my stupid hand keeps shaking, so forgive me."

Reid was crying. Not a lone tear cascading down her face before she said something equally emotional to Bethany as the sun glistened in her beautiful green eyes. No, full-on, shoulders-shaking crying.

"It's okay," Bethany told her. "Whatever it is. It's okay."

Reid still hadn't said a word. When she raised her face, her cheeks were swollen and wet. Her eyes red-rimmed. She raised a palm in explanation, but no words came, which made her drop it in defeat, opting instead for more crying, this time with noise. Bethany wasn't sure what to do, so she put her arm around Reid and let her cry for as long as she needed. All the while her own throat constricted with dread and her spirits fell. The sun didn't seem as bright, the water's beauty less defined. The world was returning to its existence before Reid, and she understood why, where this was going.

"I'm really sorry," Reid finally said, sitting up straight and separating herself from Bethany. She brushed the tears from her cheeks, leaving streaks. "This wasn't how I wanted to handle this."

"Is there really an ideal way?"

"To start a new life together? Yeah, I would think so."

Bethany paused. "What are you talking about? Aren't you about to launch into a breakup speech?"

"No. I'm a blubbering mess overcome with relief that you didn't."

"You're happy right now?" This was a curveball. She felt the sides of her mouth tug.

"This is my happy face," Reid said, pointing as more tears streamed down her face. "But now I can't remember my speech."

Bethany full-on laughed. "I don't know whether to hug you or shake you, but you're probably the most adorable person I've ever met."

"Well, that's something," Reid said doing the windshield-wiper hands again. "Oh! I remember!" They shared a laugh, and Reid took Bethany's right hand in hers, stilling it from its tremor. She then gathered the left one, too, and exhaled slowly, giving the mood a chance to settle. "My life hasn't been a bad one. I've laughed, enjoyed the people that I love, and enjoyed the direction of my career. But something was always missing." She kissed the back of Bethany's right hand. "I know without a doubt that it was you." Oh, that hit just right. Bethany took a moment to savor Reid's words. "I'm so sorry we didn't have a back then. I will spend the rest of my life making our life a happy one. But I don't want to see another sun come up without knowing fully and completely that you're mine."

Bethany's smile felt a little wobbly after hearing all of that. Her chest ached but for an entirely good reason this time. This was a moment she'd never in a million years imagined, which was why she'd run from it for years. "That's the thing. You don't have to." But her voice was at half strength, and the music had picked up volume. Reid squeezed her hand and leaned in, resting her forehead on Bethany's, connecting them. After a moment, she caught Reid's lips with hers, and that very second, the crowd erupted in cheers and applause, most certainly in their honor.

"I think the verdict is in. The forever factor is real," Bethany whispered in her ear.

"Certainly more useful than calculus." Reid smiled against her mouth and went back in for another kiss as the California sun said its good nights on the way down.

❖

It had taken a while to get her key in the door. That was on them. They'd not stopped kissing since exiting their respective cars in Reid's driveway. It was after ten, and after dancing together at the concert, strolling hand-in-hand along the water, stealing glances and touches along the way, the sexual tension had grown to the point where they were no longer able to stay publicly appropriate.

"My place?" Reid asked with her best sexy eyebrow arch.

"And fast," Bethany said, nodding most seriously. Oh, she was ready to go, and Reid loved it.

She'd finally gotten the damn door unlocked and opened with Bethany's mouth doing amazing things to the spot where her collarbone met her neck. Her underwear was wet, and her knees shook. She wasn't quite sure where the light switch was because her brain shorted out three minutes ago when all this started.

Bethany walked her into the house backward, her hands on Reid's hips. It was her show for now, and Reid liked that a lot. They passed the formal dining room with the table and chairs she'd inherited from her grandparents. Bethany turned her around, and she grasped one of the chairs from behind, holding it for support. Bethany's hands snaked beneath Reid's sweater, cupping her breasts and pulling her body against Bethany's. She moaned with her mouth closed, trying to steady herself. Her jeans were unbuttoned from behind and slid down her legs. Sweet heaven, what was happening and how was it so amazing? Her panties were around her ankles and Bethany's mouth was on the back of her neck. She ached to be touched. Was willing to beg if need be. Bethany didn't disappoint. She slipped a hand between her legs from behind and caressed her softly. Reid's eyes slammed shut, and she adjusted her legs for better access. "Mm-hmm," she murmured. "Please. More."

Bethany stroked her harder, setting the pace. She followed, holding on to the chair posts. Bethany's fingertips circled and squeezed gently. She turned Reid around, dropped to her knees, and went to work. "God, your tongue," Reid said, bracing. It was only moments before pleasure ripped like a star across the sky.

They weren't done. The bedroom was next. Tangled sheets. Unhindered passion that came with the understanding that this would be one of many times to come.

When they came together again that night, it was an echo of that forever promise. There were moments that scorched, where every touch was hot, sensual, and untethered, but there were soft moments, too, demonstrations of love and tenderness where they stopped and stared and smiled and marveled.

"It's going to be a good life, isn't it?" Reid asked as the first sliver of the California sun peeked out over the trees.

"It's going to be that and more. I have a feeling." She grinned against Reid's shoulder. "But we're going to have to be careful moving forward."

"What does that mean?"

"I'm not going to be able to take you up against the dining room chair when your son's home. Bad form."

"I guess we'll have to make good use of our time when we have it," Reid said, sliding on top. "Because I don't plan to let go of those saucy little moments. Are you kidding? You better always take me up against chairs." She looked skyward. "That might be the most poetic thing I've ever said. Should go on a magnet."

"I can't argue. You have a way with words."

"Where are we going to live?"

"I don't care," Bethany said. "I just want to be where you are. I can wait for the right time. We have tons of it."

"I want Mason to really get to know you first and see how a mature relationship progresses."

"Me, too. But once he's ready, we're shacking up. He and I will talk dinosaurs while you plan lectures on the great American novelists of the last century."

"Then he'll go peacefully to bed, and we'll have wine. And orgasms."

"Done."

"Planned."

They laughed and Reid placed a kiss on her lips. Bethany exhaled. "I promised you forever once upon a time, and look at us now."

"We made it."

EPILOGUE

One year later

"Get out of here already," Mason said as Reid kissed his adorable face about eight times while he squirmed. "Aunt Alice is about to teach me how to cheat at Mario Kart."

Bethany laughed, accepting a quick hug from Mace as he scampered back to the couch where his aunt waited with a grin. She turned to Reid. "I think we're being kicked out."

"You are," Alice said, shooing them away. "Go on your date, already. We've got things to do here. Mason and the house will be just fine."

Reid gasped and remained in place an extra beat. She wore jeans with the cutest tan boots she'd scooped up at a little boutique near campus. She looked killer in them. The long-sleeved red scoop neck made everything about her pop. "I don't know whether to be offended or thrilled."

Bethany laughed. "I'm both. Let's get out of here before they change their minds." She took Reid's hand as they left the house and walked to her car, their everyday custom. Life with Reid and Mason was both peaceful and fun. The house they'd recently purchased together was always full of laughter and activity. A great big room for Mason just down the hall from theirs. A big back deck for evening hangouts or barbecues and a yard for the dog they were talking about adding to the pack. Bethany had cut back on her late nights at work even if that meant taking on fewer patients. Her partners were all in favor. She had people waiting at home for her now and couldn't wait to return to them each evening for dinner around the table. Even Mateo had accepted her into the fold.

"Thanks for being cool to my kid," he'd said one Friday when he'd picked up Mason for the weekend. "He says really nice things about you. And his mom? Well, she smiles more than I've ever seen. I don't know." He shrugged. "It's nice to see."

"Thanks, Mateo. I feel like I'm the lucky one in this scenario."

"Oh, I feel you on that, too." He'd given her shoulder a little knock to let her know they were cool just as Reid and Mason appeared with his overnight bag.

Things had definitely fallen into place nicely.

As they hopped in the car for their date, Reid turned to her. "We never decided on a place to eat."

"I have an idea." She started the car and they were off. They listened to music as they maneuvered LA traffic, a playlist of songs Bethany had put together on purpose, full of tracks that held special meaning for them.

They drove happily to the sounds. "Did you hear what happened at Sunny's gym?" Reid asked. "They're pushing her out."

"Get out." Bethany's eyebrows rose. "I don't understand."

"Apparently, she doesn't own the place, just runs it, and the parents are sick and tired of her leadership style and started a petition to have her fired. It worked. They didn't care for how she spoke to their kids."

"I didn't see that coming. This is too good to be true."

"Yet, it is."

"Amazing. Bad guys never get their due." Bethany couldn't help but grin. "I can't imagine she'll have an easy time getting a similar gig after that. The community is too small."

"Time for a reinvention," Reid said. "She desperately needs one."

"Maybe this will be a wake-up call, and she'll finally turn things around. Fight for the good guys for a change."

They shared a laugh over that one. Not likely. Reid turned up the music. "Do you remember this song?"

Bethany smiled. "I do." They used to lie on her bed and listen to the slow, angsty ballad on repeat while they clung to each other, stared at the ceiling, and talked about everything ahead. And here they were. Ahead. In the midst of it now.

Reid looked over at her, clearly realizing where they were headed. "The park? You're taking me to the park, aren't you?"

"Is that okay?"

"Wow." Reid shook her head. "We're really on a tour of memory lane tonight. I haven't been to this place in so long. Are you feeling sentimental?"

"Maybe. I'm just thinking a lot about you. Us."

"You are sentimental. Look at your cute face."

Bethany felt her cheeks heat. "Just that kind of night, and I want to enjoy it with you, the prettiest woman I've ever seen in my life."

Reid leaned across into Bethany's seat and kissed her. "I love you."

"I love you, too. Let's go."

Evening was quickly inching toward night, so she knew she didn't have a lot of time. She grabbed the leather picnic satchel from the back seat of the car and smiled at Reid. "What? I brought a little refreshment and some fancy glasses. Gotta plan ahead."

"You brought wine. I was already in love with you, but there you go turning up the volume again." Reid's crisp green eyes shimmered. She was impressed, which was exactly what Bethany was going for.

"Follow me." She led Reid through the park to the spot she used to revisit in her mind all the time. It hadn't changed a whole lot, which helped. Same giant oak with the big branches offering a canopy, same sounds of insects living their lives among its branches.

When Reid saw where they'd landed, she placed a hand over her heart, struck. "This is the spot where I first kissed you. On that Saturday we had off."

"I thought we owed it a visit. The start of it all." She popped the cork on the sav blanc she'd picked for the occasion. The good stuff, too. She poured Reid a glass and then spread out a blue and white checkered blanket. "And since I don't have any calculus for us to work, I thought a park visit might be a fitting replacement."

Reid took a seat next to Bethany. "I love being out here." She looked around as if soaking up every little detail. "It will always be you I think about when it comes to this place."

"Us," Bethany said, touching their glasses. "That's actually what I want to talk to you about."

"Okay." Reid blinked at her, clearly curious.

"I'm ready to get started. The past year has been the best of my entire life, and I don't see anything changing. This is it for me. You are. Mason."

Reid squeezed her hand. "For me, too. I'm the luckiest. I'm reminded every day."

"So hear me out."

"Look at you. Okay. I'm listening."

"I've never been great with words or the spotlight, but I need to hop onto an imaginary stage for a minute." She reached for her bag and returned with a blue box that contained the ring she'd been designing with a jeweler for months now, making sure it was absolutely perfect. Absolutely *Reid*. And it was. She opened the box and watched Reid's face transform.

"Beth," she whispered. "What did you do?" She was beaming.

"I want to marry you." She held up a hand. "I know we said *down the line*, but I don't think I can wait longer than it will take to plan the most beautiful event in history. But most importantly, I'm interested in all that comes after. The life. The memories. You and me and Mason."

"And whoever else might come along?" Reid asked, her eyes brimming.

"Yes!" Bethany laughed through her own tears. "Please. That. I want it all with you. Every life experience."

She didn't go down on one knee, she went down on two, kneeling before Reid, offering her the respect and reverence she deserved. "Reid Katherine Thatcher. Every moment you're in my presence topples the rest. Our past was full of ups and downs, but it made us the super couple we are today. We don't mess around with life."

"That's for sure." Reid covered her mouth and gestured for Bethany to proceed.

"We don't take a single second for granted, and I love that about us. I never want to experience life without you again." She took a deep breath. "I promise you forever and mean it with my whole heart. Will you promise it back? Will you marry me?"

Reid pulled Bethany to a standing position so they were face-to-face. "We will walk together through life. I promise you that, here and now. I would like nothing more than to be your wife. To kiss you every damned day and remind you how much I love you. So the answer to your very important question is yes. I'd marry you tomorrow if that's what you want."

"I'm engaged!" Bethany said loudly, which pulled a laugh and earned her a very saucy kiss, which she happily returned. With their shoes tossed to the side, they spent the next hour sipping their wine, Reid's head in Bethany's lap, and coming up with details for their wedding, which they decided should be no small affair.

"After all we've gone through to get here, we've earned it. We deserve the celebration of a lifetime."

"And we're going to have it."

Reid scrunched her shoulders. "Mason in a tux. I love it."

"I asked his permission, you know."

Reid popped up and turned. In a small voice she said, "You did?"

Bethany nodded. "He says he can't wait to see you as a bride. I happen to share the excitement."

Reid's eyes went wide. "I just realized I'm going to be the wife of a doctor. A doctor's wife."

"You're *just* realizing that?" Bethany settled onto her back and watched Reid think it all through like the adorable woman she was.

"I'll need a new wardrobe. Shoes worthy of the title." She climbed on top of Bethany, just like she had all those years ago in the same spot. This time there was no hesitation. "There are probably important functions to attend. Hands to shake."

"So many." Bethany nodded, adjusting a strand of Reid's hair from her forehead. "And then there's the after-party at our place."

Reid's eyes went dark and sexy. "Will there be one tonight?"

"I was seriously hoping so."

Reid kissed her good and thorough, their tongues tangling. "You have a date. For tonight. And forever."

About the Author

Melissa Brayden (www.melissabrayden.com) is a multi-award-winning romance author, embracing the full-time writer's life in San Antonio, Texas, and enjoying every minute of it.

Melissa is married and working really hard at remembering to do the dishes. For personal enjoyment, she spends time with her Jack Russell terriers and checks out the NYC theater scene as often as possible. She considers herself a reluctant patron of spin class, but would much rather be sipping merlot and staring off into space. Bring her coffee, wine, or doughnuts and you'll have a friend for life.